FIND WONDER IN ALL THINGS

PERSUASION REVISITED

KAREN M COX

Adalia Street Press

FIND WONDER IN ALL THINGS

(Second Edition)

Copyright © 2020 by Karen M Cox

Adalia Street Press

978-1-7340998-0-5

978-1-7340998-1-2

First edition published 2012 by Meryton Press

For my husband

Against his nature, he showed me patience,
so against my inclination, I took a leap of faith...

ALSO BY KAREN M COX

Undeceived

Son of a Preacher Man

I Could Write a Book

The Journey Home

1932

ANTHOLOGIES

Elizabeth: Obstinate, Headstrong Girl: "Resistive Currents"

Rational Creatures : "A Nominal Mistress"

Dangerous to Know: Jane Austen's Rakes and Gentleman Rogues : "An Honest Man"

The Darcy Monologues : "I, Darcy"

Sunkissed: *Effusions of Summer:* "Northanger Revisited 2015"

CONTENTS

PART I

CHAPTER 1

MAY 25, 1991

*H*ey, you ever talk to Virginia Elliot anymore?" James Marshall stole a glance at his friend Stuart, who was drumming his fingers on the steering wheel and singing along to the radio.

"Nah, not for a couple years now."

James leaned back against the head rest and watched the scenery rush past. Speeding down the interstate toward the lake sent James back to the last summer he stayed on the Pendletons' houseboat. That was six years ago, when he was fourteen, and he was sure a lot of things had changed. Stuart and Virginia had kept up their summer romances for a few years, breaking up when Stu returned to Ohio at the end of vacation. They wrote sometimes, James knew, but his friend hadn't mentioned her in quite a while.

"I didn't go to the lake last summer," Stuart said. "And the year before that, she had that redneck boyfriend, remember?"

"Nah, I don't remember stuff like that."

"I know I told you about it. The guy was a total jerk. He pulled me behind the marina shop once and said he'd feed me to the fish if I so much as looked at Virginia."

"I'm surprised she put up with that." It certainly didn't jive with the independent Virginia Elliot they knew when they were younger.

"I don't think she knew. Laurel said the guy was bad news, but Virginia wouldn't see it." Stuart looked sad—or embarrassed maybe—it was hard to tell. "I didn't need that," he said.

"No one needs that."

"Damn straight."

Stuart flipped up and down the dial for another radio station with a decent signal that reached into the mountains. Finally, he gave up and punched off the music altogether.

"Hope you brought your own music. There's no reception down here."

"I brought a few cassettes."

"Hey, it's the nineties, and compact discs are the way of the future, man."

"Yeah, I know, but I'm saving up for a car."

"Gotta have wheels, I guess. When you're ready to buy, let my dad know. He might be able to get you a deal. He's done ads for a bunch of the dealerships around Cincinnati."

"I will. Thanks." James took another swig of soda. "It feels weird to be coming back here." The lush green of the bluegrass was giving way to the foothills of the Appalachians, which meant they would be arriving soon. He stared out the window, remembering when they were kids during the summer of 1984...

JAMES BENT over the tackle box, picking through the various lures from Mr. Pendleton's collection, a bucket of bait on the dock beside him. He was so engrossed in his task that he nearly jumped out of his skin when he heard the harsh hiss from behind.

"Quick! Over here!" Stuart urged him in a stage whisper as he raced to the stern of the Pendletons' houseboat.

"Wha—?"

"We're hiding from Laurel and Dylan and Crosby. You wanna take the runabout up to the tunnel, don't you? If the little brats find us, then Mr. Elliot will make Virginia mind them—and then she can't go with us. Hurry!" He waved his hand in a frantic gesture, urging his friend to follow.

James hopped up on the weather-beaten boards of the dock and took off after his buddy. "Where are we going? It's a dock. There aren't too many places to hide."

"Virginia said to wait behind the ice machine, up by the gas pumps."

The boys ran up the dock, their traitorous footsteps thundering in their ears till they reached the marina shop and the sanctuary of the gas pumps behind it. Stuart grabbed the metal pipe rail and sailed over it, landing in a crouch, ready to spring. James followed, but he was too skinny and little to leap over like Stu. He ducked under, and the two middle-schoolers huddled close together, peering around the corner of the ice machine to watch for enemy six-year-olds and the eleven-year-old tagalong.

"You don't have to hide, you know." A voice from behind made James's heart skip a beat.

He and Stu whirled around to see a girl sitting cross-legged between the gas pumps. Munching cookies from a bag, she eyed them as they gaped back at her.

"Laurel, how did you—?"

"You don't have to hide," she continued as she brushed crumbs from her lap and wadded up the bag, "because Daddy took the boys fishing this morning. They won't be back till lunchtime." She stood up and swept her long red braids behind her. "So, all four of us can go to the tunnel."

"You're not going," Stuart declared. "You're too little."

"I'm not too little. I'm eleven, and I can run as fast as you."

James took a dubious look at the little round frame and short legs. "I don't know...Stuart runs pretty fast, Laurel—faster than me even."

She turned. Big blue eyes that seemed to take up half her lightly freckled face pleaded with him. "I'll keep up, I promise. I won't be any bother."

James wavered. "Well, I guess it wouldn't hurt—not really."

Stuart shook his head. "I don't want to be babysitting all day while we look for artifacts."

Laurel looked at him with contempt. "There aren't any real 'artifacts.' Most of the stuff is just old junk you tourists dump off your boats."

"Then why do you even want to go?"

Laurel opened her mouth to answer, but a soft voice drifted from behind them. "I said she could go, Stu. She was going to be all by herself today."

The boys turned around, and another girl stepped around the corner of the ice machine. Her hair was red too but more of strawberry blonde, a gentle color to match her gentle demeanor. She walked over, put her arm around her younger sister's shoulders, and faced the two boys, self-assured and serene.

James watched in amusement as his friend stammered and finally acquiesced. That summer he had noticed a difference in Stuart where Virginia Elliot was concerned. The previous year, he and Stu spent long days on the runabout, exploring around the lake, talking about Reds baseball, and fishing. But this year, Virginia had been a constant in most of their plans. Granted, she wasn't a "girly girl"—growing up on the lake had ensured that she could fish, water ski, and hike as well as any boy—so James had to admit it wasn't a huge pain to have her around. She didn't care much for baseball though, and there were some things the boys couldn't discuss when she was there — like her, for instance—and now, she was Stu's favorite topic.

Stuart looked sheepish, but James just shrugged. "I don't care if the kid comes with us."

Laurel beamed at him.

"Come on then." Stuart's voice was gruff, endeavoring to sound nonchalant. "I want to get going before it gets too hot."

The four made their way down to the slip where the Pendletons kept Stuart's johnboat. He dug the life jackets from under the seats and passed them out. He inspected one, checking it over and sniffing it for mildew before handing it to Virginia with a wide grin. James fished out one for himself and tossed the last one to Laurel.

"This one stinks"—Laurel wrinkled her nose—"and it's got moldy spots on it."

"Sorry, kiddo," Stu answered. "That's the only child-sized life jacket I've got."

She sighed and put her arms through the armholes, struggling to fasten it around her plump middle.

"Here." James reached over to loosen the belt. "You're bigger around than that."

Virginia stepped over and took the vest out of his hands. "I'll do it. It's got nothing to do with the middle. You have to put the bottom strap between her legs 'cause it's a child's jacket." She tossed a scathing look at James over her shoulder. "That's all."

He held up his hands in surrender and backed up a step. "Sorry— didn't mean to offend."

"Never mind all that." Stu was impatient to get started. "Let's go."

James grunted. *Girls are so weird.*

The girls settled in the bottom of the boat, almost in the center. Virginia's arms and legs surrounded Laurel in a loose but protective cage. James untied the ropes while Stu submerged the prop and started the engine.

"Hop in," he told James.

James stepped over the girls and sat in the bow. Stu pushed off, made his way aft, and they drifted away from the dock, idling toward the boundary of the no-wake zone. Once in the middle of the lake, Stuart engaged the motor, and they were off toward their morning's adventure.

James faced into the wind, closing his eyes and letting the warm sunshine wash over him as the cool spray sprinkled his face and hair. A bump in the ride lifted him off the seat and reminded him he had a duty to perform. He opened his eyes, shielding them from the sun with his hand and looking for logs or other debris just beneath the surface of the lake.

Stuart steered the boat this way and that, slicing through the blue-green water. It had been a dry summer, and the water level was low, encircling the lake with bare, muddy walls. Tangled trees and brush-covered rocks jutted above those walls like tall buildings looming over city streets.

They rode about a half mile and then around a bend, so Elliot's Marina was now out of sight. The lake was relatively deserted on that weekday morning, and they met only a few die-hard fishermen along the way. James held up a hand in greeting as they passed each other, and the men waved back. Most everyone on the lake knew the Elliot girls on sight because of their father's three-season marina—and their Eastern Kentucky red hair.

Stuart slowed the motor as they approached their destination: an old railroad tunnel carved through the hill many years ago. The boys leapt out right before they hit bottom, silt squishing around their boat shoes. After they had the boat secured, the girls climbed out, and the four of them stood looking at the tunnel.

After long years of exposure to wind and water, the weathered stone made a perfectly round opening in the hill. The lake—now the life's blood of the community—had been man-made in the 1950's as a source of energy, drowning both the railway tunnel floor and the little town that was once nestled in the valley between the two hills.

"I'll go first," Virginia volunteered. "Laurel, you stay right behind me."

"I'll bring up the rear," Stuart said. He straightened his shoulders and put a little swagger in his voice. "Just to make sure everyone makes it okay."

Virginia smiled at him, and James rolled his eyes. Stu had developed this lame tendency to play the hero. Did he *have* to point out that he was the tallest and strongest of the four? Wasn't it pretty obvious to everyone?

The older girl began her ascent up the bank. It was only a couple of feet, but still, it was steep enough to require using all four limbs. Virginia grabbed hold of rocks and tree roots, patiently giving directions to her sister just behind her. After a minute or two, they were all standing by the tunnel's entrance, peering into the darkness.

"Can you really find people's dishes and furniture and stuff?" James wasn't convinced that this little trip wasn't a fool's errand.

"Yes." Laurel nodded emphatically. "We've found all kinds of things —clocks and silverware—and once we found the steering wheel of an old car. What kind did Daddy say it was, Ginny?"

"Model T," Virginia replied. "But it probably came from the dump. People didn't leave their cars in town when the Corps of Engineers flooded it. They packed everything up and moved the whole town up to the plateau."

"There was a graveyard though," Laurel went on, "and some people say they've found old coffins in the lake. Stuff gets caught in this tunnel when the floor is under water."

James looked at her. "Coffins? Really?"

"Oh, Laurel. That's just tall tales those men tell when they come up to the cabin to buy…supplies." Virginia cast a quick glance at the boys and turned back around.

"Virginia, we all know your dad sells beer on the sly." James had heard how Mr. Elliot ran a small bootlegging operation out of his cabin up the hill from the marina. Most counties in that area of the state were dry—had been for as long as anyone could remember—but it didn't stop people from drinking when they vacationed on the lake, and bootlegging was a profitable practice.

Virginia and Laurel exchanged looks but didn't reply. The local law enforcement looked the other way regarding their dad's little operation, but outright admitting that he sold contraband was still not a good idea.

Stu gallantly changed the subject. "What I'd like to find are some Indian arrowheads. Have you ever found any of those, Virginia?"

She shook her head. "I haven't, but some kids say they found arrowheads around here when they were hiking."

Stuart retrieved a flashlight from his cargo shorts' pocket and shone it into the tunnel to light their way. The other two big kids took his lead and brought out their own lights.

"We can't go in too far," Virginia called, her voice echoing in the tunnel.

"It's blocked up with rocks and stuff." In the quiet that settled over them, James could hear the drip, drip of water, like the ticking of the "tell-tale heart" he read about in seventh grade English class. He put his hand against the wall, feeling the cool, rough concrete under his fingers. The bottom of the tunnel was still muddy from ground water and rain, and in some places, it was slick with moss. He crept forward, taking care not to slip.

Suddenly, James heard a blood-curdling scream in front of him. He heard Virginia call in a panicked voice, "Laurel? What is it?"

"It's bones—lots of bones! They must have fallen out of a coffin!"

"What? Oooh, cool—I wanna see." Stuart backtracked with his flashlight trained on the ground. James hurried to catch up. Laurel stood, pointing, and he shone his light down where she indicated. Indeed, there were bones there—a pile of skinny bones, about six to ten inches in length.

"These can't be human," James scoffed. "They're too little. It's just some animal, Laurel." He huffed, half in annoyance, half in relief. "Kids!" The idea of finding human bones didn't appeal to him the same way it did Stu.

"You've been listening to too many old fishermen's stories."

She lifted her chin in defiance. "Well, how was I supposed to know? I've never seen a real human skeleton before."

"There's something over here." Stu's light disappeared in front of him, although the glow still showed his silhouette near the wall of the tunnel.

James heard him kicking debris around. There was a clatter of metal against stone and the rustle of movement. The light fell almost to the ground. The others came up to stand around him and help look.

"It's nothing—just some beer cans, some torn plastic something or other." His disappointment was obvious.

Virginia laid a hand on his shoulder. "We'll keep looking."

Another twenty minutes of searching, however, revealed only more tin cans, a bottle or two, some rusted fishing lures, and a bucket.

"I'm going back outside," James announced. He was tired of the damp darkness, and there was nothing interesting about this tunnel anyway—well, except for the fact that trains used to go through it, and now it was under water for part of the year.

"I'm coming too," Laurel piped up.

"We'll be out in a minute," Virginia called. "James, will you watch after Laurel?"

The younger sister snorted and muttered under her breath, "I'm not a baby."

James could relate; he had said the same thing many times. That's what you said when you were the baby.

"My big sister is the same way," he told Laurel.

"You have a sister too?"

"Yeah, she's seventeen."

"How come she never comes with you down here?"

"I come with Stu's family. There's no one her age in their family for her to hang out with. She's *too cool* now to hang out with middle-schoolers."

"Oh."

They walked on in silence, picking their way over the rocks and debris on the tunnel floor. The sunlight from the entrance cast a welcome light on their surroundings.

"What about your mom and dad?"

"Dad can't get off work, so they can't come—and…"

"Yes?"

"And my parents can't afford a boat like the Pendletons'. My dad is a CPA."

"What's a CPA?"

"An accountant—he writes up people's taxes and sends them to the government." He went on after she didn't reply. "Stu's dad is president of a company that makes advertisements."

Laurel's face was a complete blank.

"You know, advertisements, commercials, billboards—that kind of thing."

She nodded, but he still wasn't sure she grasped the concept. He found that he rather liked the role of "older kid," even if he was just a little older. He enjoyed explaining all about the world to an eager, little girl with big blue eyes. He and Stu were the same age, but Stu had been so many more places and done so many things that he was the one explaining the world to James most of the time.

He turned back around and made his way to the mouth of the tunnel, switched off his light, and stared out over the green water and the darker green hills surrounding it. A humid haze blurred and muted the outlines of the trees, and a thick heaviness filled the morning air. The sound of cicadas rose and fell in a lazy rhythm.

"You wanna wait here or climb down?" he asked.

"Wait here, I guess. They won't find anything in there. Virginia said she told Stuart as much, but he still wanted to come, so she came with him."

"Hmmph."

"She likes Stuart a lot, so she'll go along, even if she knows it's stupid."

James said nothing.

"I left with you because I think she wants him to kiss her."

James turned around to look at Laurel, taken aback. He glanced back at the tunnel. "Nuh-uh."

"What's the matter? Doesn't he want to kiss her?"

"I don't know," James replied, annoyed. "He probably does."

"She says now that she's thirteen, it's time for somebody to kiss her, and he's a good choice."

James had no idea how to respond to that, so he stayed silent.

"Boys like Virginia. I think it's because she's beautiful, but Daddy says it's because her soul draws people in, makes them feel comfortable."

James decided that girls thought about the strangest things.

"Do you like Virginia?"

He shrugged and looked off in the distance. "She's okay—for a girl."

There was another long silence, which Laurel finally broke.

"A bunch of us are gonna play Kick the Can up by the cottages later. You wanna play with us?"

"Maybe."

"I can't play tomorrow because Daddy's taking me and the boys to the Appalachian Craft Fair."

"Really?"

"I told him I want to be an artist, so we're going to look at different kinds of arts and crafts. But the boys don't care about that stuff. They just want to eat funnel cake."

"Hmm."

"What do you like to do?" she inquired politely.

A corner of his mouth lifted in a lopsided smile. "I like to eat funnel cake."

Laurel rolled her eyes. "No, that's not what I mean."

"I know. Let's see—I like to play dodge ball, and I'm a good runner, so I'm going to try out for the track team when school starts. And I like to read comic books and play cards. And I wanna learn to play the guitar."

"Ooh, playing the guitar—that sounds fun."

There was another lull in the conversation. Laurel swung her feet over the ledge of the tunnel's entrance. She turned at the sound of footsteps behind her. James turned too, and his eyes were immediately drawn to Stuart and Virginia's clasped hands. From the glazed look on Stu's face and the smug smile on Virginia's, it appeared that Laurel had the whole situation pegged exactly right. It looked like Stu had just been kissed but good. James shook his head. He liked girls as much as the next thirteen-year-old boy, which meant sometimes he couldn't help but think about them and sometimes he'd rather not. But that look on Stu's face was a little unsettling. He wasn't sure he was ready for that.

"You guys all set?"

"Did you find anything?" James asked.

"Umm . . . no. Nothing. I guess it was a waste of time after all."

Virginia just shrugged. "Not a complete waste."

Stu cleared his throat. "Right. Well, let's shove off then." He kept hold of Virginia's hand as they began the trek down to the boat.

Virginia reached behind her and gestured for Laurel. "Here." Laurel took her sister's hand and then reached for James, but he just gave her grimy little paw a wary look. "No thanks. I need both my hands to keep me from slipping."

She frowned.

Stu and James pushed the johnboat out in the water before hopping in and starting the motor. Stu brought it around while the others finished putting on lifejackets. He stopped to fasten his, and they took off for the dock as fast as the little boat could move.

As they emerged from the cove, the hot sun beat down, and James felt the top of his head begin to sweat. Damp waves of brown hair were soon blown stiff from the constant wind in his face. A Coke or a glass of lemonade sounded good right then. He hoped Mrs. Pendleton had brought drinks back from the store in town when she'd gone to get some more of that suntanning oil she used. He wondered whether she would bring them back something for lunch, too. Then he wondered how they would spend the rest of the day. During the hot afternoon hours, they'd probably stay in the Pendletons' houseboat and play poker. Later, they could play Kick the Can with the little kids up at the cottages or take a hike around the campground. Mrs. Pendleton had said they were eating dinner at the marina restaurant that night, and then there'd be more walking around the dock and maybe some fishing as the sun set. The next day, it would all start again. It seemed as if days on the lake lasted forever and ran one into the other, as the long, lazy days of summer should.

"So, long story short—yeah, it's a little weird coming back here," Stu said, bringing James back to the present. "I'd like to see Virginia, though—catch up and whatever. Do you think she'll be home from college for the summer?"

"How should I know?" James shrugged and took another drink. He had the sense that he should have savored those moments as a kid on the lake. His dad often reminded him, "The best times are when you're young and have no responsibilities." School and Ohio, his parents, and all the rest of life seemed so far away back then when his only realities were the boats and the water and the hot, summer days without end.

"Well…" Stuart's voice drifted off for a few seconds, and then he changed the subject. "It was killer that her dad had that busboy gig open up at the restaurant. You'll get to stay down here all summer."

"Yeah, unlucky for the other guy, but great for me. I couldn't find anything better around home this year. It was great of your dad to put in a good word for me."

"What happened to the other guy?"

"Had a motorcycle accident—broke his leg in two places."

"That sucks. If I didn't have to go to Europe with the parental units, I could have taken the job myself."

"I need the money more than you, buddy. And I needed to get out of that house."

Stuart cringed in sympathy. "Is it bad?"

"Oh, yeah, it's bad. Even worse since my sister got married last summer. They hardly speak to each other, but when they do"—he shook his head—"fighting, silent treatment, fighting, silent treatment, and they're mad at me the whole time I'm home. I'll do anything to get out of that hellhole."

"Even wash dishes and clear tables?"

"Even that."

CHAPTER 2

*J*ames walked into the marina restaurant and plunked his duffle on the floor beside him. He wanted to talk to Mr. Elliot before going to the Pendletons' houseboat, which would be his home for the next two and a half months.

He looked around the restaurant; it hadn't changed one iota since he was last there. The same Formica-topped tables, their fake wood-grain chipped off in places, were scattered about the dining room. Arranged around the tables were the same vinyl-upholstered chairs his legs used to stick to on hot summer nights. He smiled when he saw the old, revolving pie case still standing next to the cash register, proudly displaying every type of soggy-crusted cream pie known to man. The air was filled with the familiar smells of fried fish and Thousand Island dressing. Turning toward the wall of windows that overlooked the lake, he saw a leggy redhead leaning over a table and scouring away with her dishrag. The circular motion of her arm initiated a nice circular motion of her backside. He noticed this in a purely aesthetic way, of course. He was all set to call out, "Hey Virginia!" when she turned around, and he stopped short. It wasn't Virginia.

The dark blue eyes speared him from across the room, and his breath caught. *It can't be, just can't be—can it?*

"Laurel?"

She stopped, dropped her arms to her side, and stared. Suddenly, her face bloomed into a riotous mix of recognition and joy.

"James? How are you?" She held out her arms and walked toward him, wrapping him in a warm, but not too intimate, embrace—the way one should embrace a friend from long ago. He encircled her in his arms.

"Wow. I almost didn't recognize you! I thought you were Virginia at first."

She laughed as she stepped back to get a good look at him. "I was twelve years old the last time you were here."

A million thoughts raced through his head: smooth, sweet-talking things like, *You sure grew up right,* and numbskull things like, *When did you grow legs up to your neck?* He settled for another, "Wow!" and a particularly lame, "You've changed a lot in six years."

She shook her head in amusement. "It's so good to see you! Daddy says you'll be working here this summer?"

"Um, yeah—I was just checking in with him before I went over to the boat to unpack."

"So, I guess you are staying with Stu?"

"He'll be here for a couple of weeks. The Pendletons are heading for Europe at the end of June. They'll be gone for the rest of the summer, so I'm 'boat-sitting' for them."

"Oh, I'll have to tell Ginny." She winked at him, and he felt his heart stop and blood burn up his neck to his cheeks.

She was almost staring at him, and suddenly she shook her head a little, as if waking from a daydream. "I'm working here too, waiting tables—trying to save some money for college."

"Me too."

"Where are you again?"

"University of Dayton."

"Ah."

"And you? Where are you off to?"

"Benton College."

"Where?"

"It's a liberal arts college just a bit north of here."

"Oh." He paused, expecting her to explain some more, but when no other information was forthcoming, he gave a self-deprecating little laugh. "Never heard of it."

"You missed the signs on the interstate, huh?"

"Guess so."

She tilted her head and gave him a radiant smile. *Christ, has she always had a smile like that?* He felt warm all the way down to his toes but squashed the feeling down deep. *What's wrong with you, Marshall? This is Virginia's kid-sister—not some college co-ed.*

"It's just so good to see you. I can't get over it. You bring back memories of good times." She turned toward the door that connected the restaurant to the marina shop. "I'll tell Daddy you're here," she called over her shoulder.

He couldn't help himself—he watched her rear-end in those white sailor shorts as she went. Mr. Elliot happened to appear in the kitchen doorway just in time to catch him staring.

"Hello, James." His mustache twitched in amusement, and James realized her father had seen the whole ogling move. How embarrassing—not to mention job-endangering!

"Oh, there you are. Look, Daddy. It's James Marshall. You remember, right?"

"Sir." James sprang forward and held out his hand.

"It's pleasant to see you again." Mr. Elliot had a strange, almost formal way of speaking. Somehow, though, with his wire-rimmed glasses, his balding head and his scraggly ZZ Top wanna-be beard, the odd phrasing fit him.

"Thank you for the job, sir. I'll do my best."

"I'm sure you will." He indicated the duffle on the floor behind James. "Why don't you go on over and put your things away." Mr. Elliot checked the clock on the dining room wall. "I'm going to put you on the two-to-ten shift, which gives you a little more than three hours to rest up and get settled. Hate to put you to work your first day down here, but what can I say? We're short-handed."

"No problem. I'm ready when you are." He looked at Laurel, forcing his features into a nonchalant expression. "You work tonight?"

"No. I've got the lunch shift today, nine-to-two. But I'm sure we'll see each other around. I'll have to go hunt Stu down after work and see how he's been. I haven't seen him in a couple of years, but he won't be the shock you were—all grown up and everything." She approached the kitchen. "See you this afternoon, James."

"Bye, Laurel."

She lifted her hand as she disappeared behind the swinging kitchen door.

"That's my girl." Mr. Elliot beamed with pride. "Did she tell you she got a free ride to college?"

"No, sir."

"Yes, well, it's not exactly free. All the students accepted at Benton work at the college to pay their way, but we're awfully proud of her in any case. We'd have been hard put to pay tuition for her and for Virginia. Laurel's going to study art, either art studio or art history."

James considered what his own father would have to say about art as a major. But then, he supposed sons were usually expected to choose majors that leant themselves toward a steady paycheck. James's own major was business, and while he was definitely enjoying college life, he couldn't have picked a more boring major. He wondered whether Mr. Elliot would be as pleased if Dylan and Crosby decided to major in art. *Yeah*, James decided, *he probably would.* The man was downright impractical.

"What's Virginia studying again?"

"Pre-dentistry. Can you imagine? The girl wants to be a dentist. Sounds like hell on earth to me, but it's what she wants, so we're happy for her too."

James didn't quite know how to respond to that. "Um, well—I'll just go put this stuff away then, and I'll see you at two. What should I wear?"

"Jeans and a t-shirt will be acceptable. Nothing too fancy. It'll just get stained."

"Right. See you then." He headed out the restaurant door.

· · ·

ABOUT NINE O'CLOCK THAT EVENING, James was up to his eyeballs in dirty dishes when the door to the restaurant banged open, and he heard the laughing voices of Stuart and Laurel. He peered out of the kitchen and watched Stu amble over to a table James had just finished wiping off.

"Hey Stu, that one's already clean and the condiments stocked for the night. Let's sit on the deck and not mess up anything right before closing time." She headed toward the screen door leading out back.

"Spoken like a real waitress," Stu joked.

"Yeah, well, we can't all be spoiled brats like you," she said with a grin.

James was grateful. His back ached between his shoulder blades from carrying plastic bus tubs of dirty dishes to and fro, and he certainly didn't need Stuart to give him any extra work. He wasn't a wuss; he was in good shape for track and long-distance running, but he was starting to realize that there wasn't a lot of upper body strength needed for intramural cross country.

He wished that last couple would finish their coffee and chocolate pie so he could get out of there.

Back in the kitchen, he sprayed down the second-to-last load of dirty dishes for the night. Laurel appeared through the swinging door and fished out two glasses, stepping over to the soda fountain and drawing off two Cokes.

"Hey, Jim Dandy, how'd it go tonight?" Her cheerful expression irked him.

"Fine."

"It gets easier in a few days. Pretty soon, your shoulders won't be so sore."

"Hmmph."

Her lips pursed in amusement, she turned around, bumping the door open with her hip.

James continued cleaning and stocking under the directions barked out by Phil, the shift manager. He peeked out into the dining room. No Laurel, no Stu, and—this was a bonus—no coffee-drinking couple either. Darlene, the waitress, was counting out the cash register, and Mr. Elliot had appeared out of nowhere to divide the tips at one of the tables near the back. Laurel came back in and kissed her dad on the cheek. He received her token of affection with a smile and without looking up from his task.

"Daddy, Stuart and I are going up to The Loft for a bit, okay?"

"Home by midnight, Punkin. Your mother will have a fit if you're out too late."

She rolled her eyes.

"You're still under our roof, you know, even if you are almost off to college."

"Yes, Dad." She took a sip of her Coke and turned to see James carrying his bus tub to the last messy table. She met him there.

"Want some help with these?"

He shrugged.

"What's the matter?" she asked, as she stacked plates and cups.

"Nothing. Just tired, I guess."

"Oh." She picked up a fork. "Stu and I are going up to The Loft for a bit."

"Yeah, I heard. What's The Loft?"

"Just a local place to hang out—pool tables, a jukebox. There's live music sometimes too. Wanna come?"

He was slightly annoyed. "In case you haven't noticed, I'm working here."

"I meant when you're done. You should be finished by about ten thirty or so. Come on—say you'll come. We can catch up and rehash the splendid days of our youth," she said in an earnest tone, nodding as she took another sip from her straw.

He caved in an instant. "Well, okay. Where is it?"

She led him by the arm to the window. "Just up the ramp and then take that first left. It's a gravel road—not too far though—maybe a quarter mile. The locals take turns playing music sometimes. A few of them are pretty good." Her smile was inviting, and he was just about to return it when the screen door to the deck slammed shut, making them both jump.

"Hey, ready to go?" Stuart walked up and set his glass in James's bus tub.

"Sure," Laurel replied. "I think I talked James into stopping by after work."

"Great." He turned and headed for the door. "See you there."

They departed, and James was left feeling a little envious. He would like to escort pretty girls around the marina and up to the local music joint too, but he had to work for a living. Then he felt guilty. The Pendletons had given him a place to stay for the summer, rent free, and Stuart had given up his only down time at home to drive him there. It wasn't Stu's fault that James had to work summers. It was just the way it was.

For the next hour and a half, he heard the music from the top of the hill as he wiped counters and mopped floors. The tunes were right up his alley, too—a mixture of rock and country that floated on the night breeze over the water and into the screened windows of the restaurant kitchen.

A little after ten o'clock, Mr. Elliot came into the pantry where James was wiping down shelves and handed him a wad of bills.

"Tips," he explained. "Don't spend it all in one place or on one girl." He winked. "You need a ride up to town tomorrow to open a bank account?"

"Um, no thank you, sir. Stu said he'd take me in the morning."

"Ah." Mr. Elliot nodded. "Well, I think we're pretty much done here. Why don't you head on out and join your friends?"

"Sure. Thanks."

"And keep an eye on my daughter," he called after James good-naturedly. James held up a hand in acknowledgment as he stepped out the front door of the restaurant and into the warm, summer night.

CHAPTER 3

The stars winked in the dark Southern sky as James locked the boat and headed toward the marina's highway entrance. The faint glow from the town's lights several miles away obscured the stars on the horizon, but here the sky was clear, and the night was quiet, except for the music. The wooden dock creaked beneath his feet, swaying gently from side to side as he walked along. The lake lapped at the buoys in an easy rhythm, a black, living thing underneath him—eerie, and yet soothing in its vast darkness. Adjusting his stride, he traversed from the dock to the pavement, and then to the steep drive that led to the highway above. Following the road, he picked his way along the shoulder of the highway until he reached the gravel drive Laurel described. A battered mailbox proclaimed in shiny but peeling letters that he'd arrived at The Loft. Another steep climb and he was there. He crossed a porch lined with rocking chairs and approached the heavy, steel door covered with chipping paint and squeaky hinges. It gave way after a mighty shove, and he stepped directly into a game room with a few pool tables and pinball machines. Green lamps hung from the ceiling, casting a dim light about the place. He made his way across the room and over to the stairwell. The sounds of music and conversation floated down the steps, and because Stuart and Laurel were nowhere to be seen, he jogged up the stairs to the second floor.

He was greeted with a flurry of activity. A jukebox cranked out loud Southern rock, and about a dozen couples were dancing, including Stu and Laurel. It was an interesting crowd—bikers with leather jackets and beards, local factory workers and their wives, boating tourists in polo shirts and khaki shorts, and a handful of high school and college kids. He watched the room in general—and Stuart and Laurel in particular.

A peculiar emotion washed over him as he observed the two of them dancing. It wasn't that he didn't trust his friend, but…

Maybe it was because Mr. Elliot had told him to look out for her. Or perhaps he was feeling protective because he'd known her when she was a chubby, little kid. He didn't know the answer, but watching All-American, handsome Stuart laugh with Laurel and twirl her under his arm annoyed him like a mosquito bite that wouldn't stop itching. It irked him further that she was obviously enjoying herself. *What is Stu up to anyway? Doesn't he know it's bad form to hit on the ex-girlfriend's little sister?* Not that James cared or anything, but something about a guy trying to manipulate an innocent kid didn't sit well with him, even if that guy was his friend.

Laurel spied him in the corner, leaning against the wall with his arms folded. She immediately stopped dancing and waved, turning Stu around to see him. They both gestured for him to join them, pointing to a table at the side of the room. On her way to their seats, Laurel stopped at the bar.

Stuart sat down with an "oomph" and gave James his winning Stu-smile.

"Hey, how'd your first day on the job go?"

"I think I did okay."

"You'll sleep in tomorrow, I bet."

James nodded but said nothing. He was watching Laurel Elliot dance in place while she leaned over the bar. Stu followed his gaze.

"Whaddya think of Laurel, huh? Grown up nice, hasn't she?" He waggled his eyebrows, which annoyed the crap out of James.

"She looks different." He parroted her words from that afternoon back to his friend. "I haven't seen her in five years, and people change in five years."

"Yep, they sure do." Stuart was looking smug as if he knew some kind of inside information.

"You know, you shouldn't—"

"Here she comes." Stuart shushed him, and James bit back the words that were on the tip of his tongue.

"Here you go." She handed James a Coke and held hers up. "To the working man." The three of them clinked glasses.

"And the working woman," James returned.

"All women are working women," she replied.

"Hear, hear." Stu joined in.

"So," James began, taking another sip. The cold, fizzy soda hit the spot. "How's Virginia doing these days?" He cast a furtive look at Stuart to see how he'd react to the name. Laurel and Stuart exchanged startled glances, and Laurel's eyes lost a bit of their sparkle. "Um, she's fine. Why do you ask?"

"No reason." James eyed his friend. He said this morning that he wanted to catch up with Virginia. Was he just making nice with whatever Elliot girl that happened to be around? And what was that look between them?

"Well, she's taking a class in summer school at the university. It'll be over in a couple of weeks, and then you'll get to see her more." Maybe it was his imagination, but he thought her voice had turned a bit icy.

She sipped her Coke and turned toward the stage so he couldn't see her expression.

"Oh, look, they're starting open mike. I wonder who's going to sing tonight."

Stuart looked back and forth between Laurel and James. "You know, James sings."

Her head whipped around. "You do?"

"And he plays the guitar."

Whatever had been bothering her a second before evaporated into thin air. Her rapt interest made him want to tout every accomplishment he'd ever had.

"I—ah, yeah. I play a little."

"He's being modest. He's pretty good."

"You said you wanted to learn," she said, smiling.

"What?" James wasn't sure he'd heard her right.

"You said you wanted to learn the guitar. Long time ago. That time we went exploring in the tunnel, remember?"

Funny how he had just been thinking about that earlier. "Oh yeah, I guess I did say that."

"What kind of music do you play?"

James started to answer, but Stuart cut in. "Rock, country, blues."

"Acoustic or electric?" She kept her eyes trained on James.

"Both," Stuart chimed in. "Oh, sorry." He took another drink when James shot him a dirty look. "Guess you can speak for yourself."

Laurel gave him an encouraging nod. "I'd love to hear you play tonight. You should go up there."

"Nah."

Stuart leaned back and put his arm around the back of Laurel's chair. "Come on James. You play as well as any of these guys here."

"Don't have my guitar."

"Eddie will let you borrow his if I ask him," Laurel said, bouncing off her chair and over to the man behind the counter. The guy leaned his shaggy head close to hear her better while Laurel talked animatedly and pointed to James. Eddie squinted in his direction and nodded, picking a pencil from behind his ear and writing on a crumpled piece of paper beside him.

"All set," she said, plopping back down on her chair. "You're number eight on the list."

"Laurel, really—"

"No, I wanna hear you play. Stu says you're good, so I'm sure you are. Be thinking about what song you want to do because open mike moves pretty fast." She looked around the room. "I hope you don't mind using the acoustic though."

James decided it would be churlish to keep arguing. Stu was right;

he *was* pretty good. The last year had seen him practicing almost nonstop as a way to soothe his soul and forget his troubles at home. Music worked at least as well as the empty-headed co-eds he tried distracting himself with the year before, and it was certainly less messy—more lucrative, too, since he'd joined a band right before New Year's. They had taken him on even though he wasn't legal, and playing a few gigs around Dayton had been a real eye-opener.

When it was James's turn at the mike, Eddie stepped up and introduced him. "Miss Laurel Elliot says her daddy's new summer busboy plays and sings a little. Come on up here, son, and show us what you got."

James made his way up to the stage to the sound of polite applause and a whoop or two from Stu and Laurel. His heart hammered in his chest. He had no idea what he'd play once he got up there, but he was no stranger to the stage, and the moment he took the guitar in his hands, he felt his pulse slow. He plucked a few strings, tweaking the tuners and strumming a couple of chords.

"What's your name, son?" someone called out.

He cleared his throat and spoke into the mike. "James." He looked at the crowd. More people were in their forties and fifties than in their twenties, so maybe a song from a few years back would be just the thing. His eyes landed on Stu and Laurel, sitting with their heads together. Laurel leaned her head back and let out a laugh, and Stuart flashed a smirk that ticked James off. *As usual, he has his pick of any girl he wants, and he just wants whoever's handy.*

James began to strum a blues riff that led into an old Elvis song about little sisters. Just snarky enough to make them sit up and take notice of how they were acting and remind Stuart he was after Virginia, not the little sister. Not that James hadn't ever charmed a girl for whom he had only marginal interest, because he had—plenty of times—but with Laurel? Well, it seemed wrong to treat the kid that way.

He dared a look at his audience. Laurel was staring back at him with her mouth slightly open. That guarded expression was back although the rest of the crowd murmured, signaling their approval of his choice. He let the blues flow through him, making his voice rough in all the right places. It was an easy tune that let him sing his heart without thinking too much.

In short, it was his favorite kind of song.

The crowd clapped in appreciation when it was over. As he made his way back to the table, he noticed the subdued expressions on the faces of his friends and felt a little stab of satisfaction.

"Whaddya think?" James asked, his eyes fixed on Laurel's big blue ones.

"Um, that was great. Stuart was right. You're very talented." She looked down at her watch. "Guess I should get going in a minute, though. It's about eleven thirty, and Mama throws a fit if I'm late. I'll be right back." She hopped off her barstool and made a beeline for the ladies' room.

"What's the matter with you?" Stuart asked.

"What do you mean?"

"Why'd you pick that song? She thought you were accusing her of moving in on her sister's guy."

"She did not think that."

"Either that or you have some kind of thing for her sister." His eyes narrowed. "You don't have a thing for Virginia, do you?"

James sputtered in indignation. "No!"

"Good, because *I'm* asking her out."

"Fine."

"Okay."

James fiddled with the cocktail napkin under his drink. "I thought you were moving in on the kid."

Stuart's eyebrows rose, and then he sat back laughing. "Laurel? Where'd you get that idea?"

"Oh, I don't know—the dancing, coming up here just the two of you, all the sly looks." James was beginning to feel a little foolish.

"Sometimes you just take a notion and run away with it, Marshall." Stuart sat up and leaned his elbows on the table. "Laurel and I are just friends. In fact, I've been driving her crazy with questions about Virginia all afternoon."

"Glad to hear it. Because going after Laurel when you have that history with Virginia wouldn't be right."

"Since when do you get all bent out of shape about a girl's feelings?"

James frowned into his glass and said nothing.

Stu leaned over and spoke close to James's ear. "Laurel answered a lot of questions from me today, but she asked a few too—about you."

James's head shot up. "Say what?"

Stuart nudged him with his elbow. "I was trying to show your good side by getting you up there to sing to her. Girls love musicians."

"You could have told me first."

"When did I have a chance to tell you?"

"She's a high school girl, Stu."

"High school graduate, my friend—college bound. She's nice, and I know you're not blind. She's pretty, too."

James shrugged.

"And she likes you—or she did until just now. Oh, sit tight—she's coming back."

Laurel stood behind James's chair and put her hand on the back of Stuart's. "I'm heading home, I guess. I'll see you tomorrow, Stuart." She looked at the floor. "See ya round, James."

Stuart gave James a little glare and indicated Laurel with his eyes. "James, would you mind walking Laurel home? I think I'll stay a while."

"No, that's fine," she began. "I can—"

"Sure," James interrupted her.

"Great. See you tomorrow, Laurel."

"Bye."

James stood up and waited for her to pass in front of him.

"Be nice," Stuart mouthed behind her back. James just rolled his eyes.

They stepped out into the crisp, night air and walked down the hill toward the road without speaking.

When the silence grew awkward, he said, "Laurel, I—"

"You should know that Stuart is planning to visit Virginia up at school tomorrow. He's been asking me about her all day."

"I, uh—well—"

"I thought maybe you didn't know that he was still interested in her, so if you were thinking you might ask her out while you're here, you may want to reconsider, given that he's your friend and all. I mean, they do have a history. It's bad form to ask out an old girlfriend of your best friend, especially since said friend is still interested in said girl." She frowned. "Some guys think that, because Virginia's had a few boyfriends, she's easy, but she's not."

She quickened her pace, and before he could think of how to defend himself, she turned up the driveway to her parents' house. "Good night," she called without looking back.

James stood there feeling stupid. He'd just been trying to make sure that Laurel didn't get hurt! He didn't give a rip about Virginia. Then he remembered what Stu had said. *"She likes you—or she did until just now."*

So, she was interested, but how was that supposed to work? He pictured her red hair framing her face and her long legs walking in front of him and her eyes, pretty blue arrows that went straight to his heart—or his groin—he couldn't determine which.

Was he really considering asking out his boss's daughter? Bad idea —bad, bad idea.

And to top it off, she thought he had the hots for her sister. He almost laughed at the absurdity of the misunderstandings. He shook his head and resumed his walk down to the houseboat. The next time he saw Laurel, he would find a way to clear this up. He had no interest in Virginia Elliot. She belonged to Stuart.

And she didn't have the warm sparkle of her little sister.

CHAPTER 4

*J*ames climbed out of the bunk bed and eased his way toward the door at the bow, careful not to slam the screen door and wake Stuart. He sat on the boat deck and jammed his feet into his running shoes. It was just after dawn, and a fog still hung over the lake, but he knew a run would settle his head a little. He always had trouble sleeping the first night in a new place, and this trip was no different. Vaulting over the houseboat railing and onto the dock, he landed with a quiet thud and took off at a brisk walk toward dry land. As he walked up the steep climb to the road, he cast an involuntary glance toward The Loft and further up to the driveway that led to the Elliot's log house. There was no noise except the rumble of an outboard motor—an early bird fisherman putting his boat in the lake.

He turned in the opposite direction, jogging toward the state park and its winding paths. The morning air, thick with the smell of honeysuckle and locust trees, was like liquid in his lungs, and he was already sweating. He ran all around the park, until he figured he'd gotten in a couple of miles. While he ran, he mused how to fix things with Laurel. Odd how it was so important to him that they clear the air. He told himself it was because he worked with her and the summer would go a lot more smoothly if they got along. That didn't necessarily mean he wanted to date her. No matter what Stuart said, she was technically still a high school girl in James's mind, and he avoided those like the plague. He couldn't take the giggling.

But then again, Laurel was a different sort of girl. For one thing, he'd known her for years. For another, he had yet to hear her giggle. He guessed that working and living at her father's marina all her life had made her levelheaded and more mature than a lot of the girls he knew at college.

Somehow, she'd also gotten very pretty. So, should he reconsider asking her out? He liked her—a lot. If she was willing, maybe he *should* get to know her better.

He rounded the next bend and came by the playground swing set when he saw someone else up early. Sitting in a swing, staring at her feet, was the object of his morning musings. He could hardly believe his luck. They would get to talk before work.

James stopped in his tracks, and the sound of feet on the gravel must have caught her attention. Her face held no expression; she just looked him up and down. He raised a hand in greeting and settled himself into the swing beside her.

"Hi."

"Hi."

"Did you sleep well?"

She laughed a little. "You sound like my grandfather. His main concern in life was that everyone slept well. Actually, no I didn't—did you?"

"Not particularly, no."

"That's why you're up so early today?"

"I like to run early. It settles me—so I don't make stupid mistakes during the day."

"Oh?" She looked confused.

"I didn't get to run yesterday. That must have been what happened."

"Oh?" Laurel shook her head, still not comprehending.

"Last night—my assumptions and stupid mistakes."

She waited.

"That song I chose for open mike…"

"Yes?"

"Stuart said that somehow I gave you the impression that I wanted to ask out Virginia, when the truth was—"

She sat up straight, giving him a sharp look.

"I was more interested in seeing you—I mean, seeing that you didn't get your feelings hurt."

She tipped her head to the side, her eyes full of questions.

"You spent all day with Stuart, and I thought you and he—"

"Oh!" She gave an exasperated sigh. "We were talking about Ginny. He wants to go see her at college, and I wasn't sure it was such a good idea."

"Why not? Does she have a boyfriend?"

"No, she's just busy. Her class is winding down, and she needs to study. I'm not sure a distraction is a good thing right now."

"You sound like her mother. Are you your sister's keeper?" he asked with a smile.

"We're each other's keepers," she replied with emphasis. "Ever since that stupid boyfriend of hers spread all those rumors a couple of years ago, Virginia and I watch each other's backs."

James dug the toe of his shoe into the dirt below the swing. "Yeah, Stuart told me about the asshole boyfriend yesterday. I didn't know about it."

"She got rid of him pretty quick after he said those things. It made me think twice about dating any of the guys around here, I'll tell you that." She stopped. "Wait a minute. You thought Stuart was interested in me?"

"You sound surprised."

She looked back at the ground and pushed herself back and forth with her foot. "Usually guys are interested in Virginia rather than me, and I just assumed you were too."

"Maybe you assumed wrong. I recommend running to help with that." His lips curved. "I can definitely see why a guy would want to ask you out."

She smiled at him just as the sun popped over the hill across the lake, blinding and warming him at the same time. Her hair shone like copper fire under the spell of a red and orange dawn. Words tumbled out of his mouth, unplanned and unfamiliar.

"Are you allowed to date?"

"You mean go out places, to movies and dinner and things?"

He nodded.

"Well, yeah, I guess. It's never really come up before."

"So, when you said you don't date guys from around here—"

"Here is the only place I've ever been. All the guys I know are either tourists or locals."

"So, you mean—"

"Besides," she interrupted, "my parents need me to work at home a lot, and well, nobody's ever asked me except for school dances."

"Now I'm surprised."

She blushed and changed the subject. "I've been meaning to ask you—when did you learn to play the guitar?"

"I guess I started when I was about sixteen. I needed a way to combat the 'angry young man' syndrome."

"You were an angry young man?"

He nodded.

"That's hard to believe."

"All young men are angry about something or other."

"Even you, huh?"

"I've had my moments. Music helps me forget them."

"Oh." She dragged her toe across the dirt under the swing. "Did you take music lessons or just learn on your own?"

"A little of both. I started with acoustic, but I play a little electric now and then as well. I'm in this band, and we play local gigs around Dayton."

"When do you have time to study?"

James tried to keep from laughing. He never studied, but it wouldn't do to have a freshman think that's how one got through college. "We mostly play on weekends."

"Shh, be still!"

The unexpected order surprised him until he followed her eyes. He watched as a butterfly landed gently on the thumb he had wrapped around the chain of the swing. "Well, would you look at that?" he whispered, watching the creature rhythmically fold and unfold its wings. "Do you know what kind it is? Is it a monarch?"

She squinted at it. "Don't move, so I can get a good look." She paused. "No, it's a Viceroy. I think—*Limenitis archippus*."

He raised his eyebrows at her, and her cheeks grew pink. "Binomial nomenclature is a hobby of my father's. When I was a little girl, I followed him everywhere around this marina. He taught me a lot of the birds and butterflies that are native here." She watched the butterfly until it flew off.

"'Find wonder in all things, even the most pedestrian,'" she said, her voice low and thoughtful.

"Excuse me?"

"It's a quote from Carl Linnaeus, the botanist. He developed the system of classifying plants and animals. He's the father of modern ecology and my father's idol." She smiled and looked back at James.

"So, your father knows a lot about the flora and fauna around here?"

"He was going to be a biology professor, but he never finished grad school. My dad loves the outdoors—studying the animals, the insects, plants. In fact, all us girls are named for wildflowers found in the Appalachians."

"Laurel? Okay, I've heard of that. Laurel what?"

"Laurel's my middle name."

His eyebrow rose while he waited.

She sighed and rolled her eyes. "Mountain Laurel."

"Aha. Very beautiful. But 'Virginia'? That's a state."

"Virginia Bluebell."

James snorted.

"And, before you ask, our baby sister's name is Spring Violet."

"What are the boys named for?"

"Singers in the 1960's. Dylan, for Bob Dylan, and Crosby, for David Crosby."

"What did your mother have to say about all this?"

"Nothing. She pretty much lets Daddy have his way about those kinds of things."

They sat in silence for a few minutes.

"You working tonight?" he asked, already knowing the answer.

"Yep. You?"

He nodded.

"Well I suppose I best get back." She stood up, stilling the swing with her hands. "Mama will want me to help with the kids' breakfasts, and you probably want to take a shower. You know there's a public shower up at the marina, don't you?"

"Yeah, Stu showed me yesterday. I suppose I should get back too. He might be awake by now, and we're heading into town. I gotta go to the bank and open up an account."

"If he's leaving early to drive up and see Ginny, you won't have a ride."

"Hmm, I guess you're right."

"If he can't take you, I will."

"It's a deal." He stood up, holding out his hand.

She laughed and reached out, but after they shook, he didn't let her go. Slowly, hand in hand, they began the descent back to the marina and boat dock. Traffic had picked up while they were gone. Cars with trailers and fishing boats were lined up three and four deep, waiting to put into the water for the day.

"Will your father care?"

"If I take you to the bank?" She shook her head. "No, I can borrow his pickup almost anytime I want."

He slowed his pace and swung their hands up, holding hers against the center of his chest. "I meant will he mind if we go out somewhere?"

"If you've got no car, where are we supposed to go?" Her voice was a little breathless, but there was a touch of amusement under the disbelief.

James grinned down at her. "What about if I'm holding your hand while we walk? Will he care about that?"

"Worried about getting fired?"

He laughed. "A little, yeah."

"Don't worry. Daddy's not like that. If my mother finds out, on the other hand, watch out." Her tone was light, but James caught the distinct note of warning in her words. He wondered about Mrs. Elliot. People rarely saw her, but he'd heard stories about her from Stuart's mother over the years. She kept to herself. She raised an garden, preserved food by canning and drying, and sewed the kids' clothes. Except for a monthly trip into the grocery store, she didn't frequent any of the shops in town. There was no evidence she had friends outside the family either, which Mrs. Pendleton thought was odd, given how outgoing the rest of the Elliots were.

By the time he had thought all this through, they had reached the dock.

"I gotta go back up this way."

"Sorry, I guess I could have walked you to your driveway."

"No worries. I can make it on my own. Been doing it for years, Sir Galahad."

"I'm sure you have." It was an ironic choice of words—Galahad, a symbol of gallantry and purity, and just about the last words he'd ever use to describe himself.

"See you tonight then."

She started to walk away, but he kept hold of her hand, forcing her to turn and face him. He pulled her close and looked at her. James wasn't short by any stretch of the imagination, but he could almost look her square in the eye. He squeezed her hand.

"Bye, Mountain Laurel."

She blushed and took off up the ramp.

CHAPTER 5

*H*ey there—you—son—boy! What's his name again?" Phil, the shift manager, looked annoyed with his memory lapse, but the summer staff came and went like yesterday's burgers. It was tough to remember them all.

"James," Darlene said over her shoulder as she passed by with a coffeepot in her hand, cracking her gum.

"James!" Phil didn't shout in the restaurant—that would be rude—but his booming voice carried across the room to the busboy, standing idly in the doorway with a goofy look on his face. "Table twelve left five minutes ago. Clean it off already."

James jumped, embarrassed that he had been caught once again being inattentive. In truth, he was being very attentive, just not to his job. He hurried over to table twelve with his dish bin, casting surreptitious glances at Laurel as she moved between tables, smiling, taking orders, and generally being the light of the place. She winked at him, and he turned back to his task, grinning.

After five days of giving her mother the full-court press, Laurel had convinced her to let James take her out on a real date. That night they would finally go somewhere besides the walking paths around the state park next door. Granted, it was just to a burger joint and a movie, but still it was "out."

After that first day, James was alone on the houseboat. Stuart spent all his time wooing Virginia at her university about an hour away. The official story was that Stuart stayed with friends, but James had a feeling those friends rarely saw him. In fact, James wouldn't be surprised if Stuart bailed out on his parents' trip to Europe.

Unfortunately, when Stu left, so did his wheels, and that meant James had been confined to the marina for almost a week. Phil or Mr. Elliot would take him to the bank when he needed to go, but bank and store errands weren't the same as going out for a night of fun. He couldn't very well ask Mr. Elliot to drive him around on a date with his own daughter! So, the day before, Laurel asked her dad to borrow his truck and vowed *she* would drive.

She sidled up behind him, and he knew she was there without even turning around. She smelled like iced tea with a whiff of honey-suckle underneath.

He breathed deeply and smiled.

"Daddy gave me permission to stay out late," she murmured as she dropped some silverware in his tub. "Till one o'clock."

"Even then, I don't think we'll have enough time for both dinner *and* a movie."

"Well then, let's skip the dinner and just hit the drive-in."

He raised his eyebrows at her. Didn't she know what went on at drive-ins?

"And don't get any ideas, Marshall. I don't know you that well."

He laughed. "Yes, ma'am." He liked that forthright innocence she had about her—like she was naïve but still in charge of her own fate. "So, I'll meet you up at your house about ten thirty. I gotta take a shower first."

"No, I'll come down. Just meet me here."

"Laurel, are you sure your father okayed this? I don't want to have to look for another job tomorrow."

"Oh, absolutely. It's fine with Daddy. It's just Mama."

He frowned. "What did I do to get on her bad side?" Mrs. Elliot hadn't shown up anywhere on the marina since he'd been there. Usually mothers waited to meet him before taking an active dislike.

"That's not it. She's just not feeling well and won't want any company up at the house."

"Nothing serious, I hope."

Laurel bit her lip. "Oh no. She'll be fine."

Her voice indicated that she didn't want to discuss it anymore, so he decided not to press the issue. Whatever was going on with her mother, she would tell him when she was ready. He looked over at the kitchen door and saw Mr. Elliot watching them. The man had the most unnerving stare, not unlike his daughter.

"Okay. But come down to the boat if you don't mind. I don't want to be one of those creepy guys standing out under the streetlights beside the dock."

She laughed. "Fine." She disappeared into the kitchen, giving her father a bright smile as she sailed past.

JAMES WAS ready when Laurel knocked on the houseboat door.

"Come in," he called, putting his wallet in his back pocket and picking up his boat key off the coffee table.

She stepped in, looking around the place. "It's different than I remember. The Pendletons must have redecorated since I was here last."

"What? Oh, yeah, I guess. Hey, you want a Coke or something?"

Turning, she eyed him up and down in a frank assessment of his appearance that made his ears burn. It humbled him that a girl who'd never been on a date before could make a guy like him blush, so he decided to turn the tables on her.

"You look pretty." And she did. Blue jean cut-offs and a green v-neck tee showed off her svelte figure to its best advantage. Her hair tumbled in slightly damp curls about her face and shoulders. She did that girl-next-door look very well.

His compliment seemed to unnerve her a bit, but she managed to mutter, "Thank you. You look real nice too."

"Are you set then?"

Laurel nodded. "I'm glad you don't have some stupid idea that the guy always has to drive."

"I gave up stupid ideas the night I came here, remember? Besides, a guy without a car takes a ride wherever he can find it." He turned back to lock the door and they started off toward the shore, walking in silence along the dock.

"I'm saving for a car. Blew up the motor in my other one—driving too fast."

"How fast were you going?" she asked.

"Hundred fifteen."

"James! That's so dangerous! Gosh, you're lucky you didn't really hurt yourself. Driving like that on the mountain roads around here will get you killed."

"Don't worry. I learned my lesson. I've been hoofing it for a year and a half now, and I can't wait until I can afford another set of wheels. I'll take care of the car this time. That's one of the reasons I'm working this summer. I figure by the time I go back to school, I'll have enough for a decent used pickup with bad gas mileage and a reliable engine. Or a compact. Nothing fancy."

"I'll be without a car at school this fall, but Benton's a pretty small campus, so I'll just take my bike."

There was a lull in the conversation as they approached the truck. He followed her to the driver's side and reached around her to open the door.

She got in and turned to him in surprise.

He shrugged. "Just because I'm not driving doesn't mean I've lost my manners. Ladies first."

She smiled and shook her head as she put the key in the ignition. He jogged around to the passenger side and hopped in.

"Ready?" she asked, starting up the engine and giving it some gas.

"I'm at your mercy."

"I'm a good driver."

He leaned back and put his arm on the back of the seat, behind her shoulders. "I'm not the least bit worried."

"Why do you want to study art?" James asked as he slid across the truck's bench seat and reached over to grab a nacho from the paper plate. The movie was spectacularly bad, so they'd spent the time after the first fifteen minutes talking.

"I guess I don't know what else I'd do with my life. My father is really happy about my choice of major, and I'm good at art. I enjoy drawing, painting, but what I like the most is sculpting, making something and feeling it take form under my hands. How I'll shape that skill into something that buys groceries, I'm not sure. Dad says not to worry about it. If I'm true to myself, the rest will work out."

He looked at her, his expression full of doubt, and she laughed.

"I know, I know. It sounds a little hippie-trippy hokey to me too, but... Why do you want to study business?"

"I don't particularly. My dad said I had to pick a major that would be worth something, so that's what I picked." He looked at her sideways. "I'm as bad as you are. Choosing my major to suit my father."

"I can't deny that Daddy's pleased about the art thing, but I did it for myself too. I'm just not sure how to work out all the logistics of real life to go along with it, but hey, I've got four years to figure it out, right?"

"Four years that fly by," he said sagely.

"So serious."

"Realistic," he countered.

She rolled her eyes. "'Nuff about school. Tell me about something else."

"What would you like to know?"

"What's your dad like? I mean, you know mine already. I don't need to tell you about him."

James sobered a little. "He's an average dad, I guess. He goes to work. He comes home and eats dinner. He watches TV, then he goes to bed. On the weekends, he argues with my mother for fun."

"Oh, I'm sorry—bad subject."

"It's okay."

"Is it rough between them?"

He paused. "Yeah, it's bad. I honestly don't know how the two of them ever stood each other long enough to conceive two children."

"Maybe it was different for them back then. Sometimes people change." She took a sip of her drink. "What about your sister?"

"She got married last summer."

"Oh, really?"

"Yeah, he's a good guy—Navy officer. She'll be living all over the world."

"Sounds exciting. What does she do—she's older than you, right?"

"She's an accountant like Dad. She works for one of those big firms in D.C."

He paused, fiddling with the lid on his soda cup. "Let me ask you a question."

"Shoot."

"What do you think about the idea of blending business with music somehow?"

"I think it sounds like a great idea. People don't usually think about those two fields going together, but music is a business as well as an art. It makes sense to me."

"I'm not sure how all the details would work, but that's what I would like to do—if I had a chance."

"You'll find a way."

"You sound pretty sure of that."

"I call 'em like I see 'em. I think you could do anything you set your mind to."

He leaned across her to put the nacho plate on the tray hanging from her window, but as he drew back, he felt her hand caress his face, turning him toward her. He stared at her a long moment, and slowly she brought her lips to his in a gentle kiss. He pulled back, resting his arm against her car door to hold himself up.

"Very nice," he said in a low, husky voice. "What was that for?"

She looked a little shy but eager. "I've never been kissed before—not like that."

"What a tragedy."

"I wanted to know what it was like."

"And the verdict is?"

"Very nice. Although I think it has more to do with the person than with the kissing itself." She kissed him again, and he sat back up straight, returning to the passenger's side and bringing her over next to him.

"Mmm," he murmured. "Sweet, pretty Mountain Laurel. Is the flower as sweet as you are?"

She grinned against his mouth. "I wouldn't try it if I were you."

"Why not?" he asked, distracted and diving in for another kiss.

"It's poisonous, goofball."

He stopped with a sheepish laugh. "So much for my romantic sweet nothings."

She sat back and looked at him. Even in the dim light from the movie screen, he could see her flushed face and sparkling eyes. He brought his hand up to push a strand of hair behind her ear.

"You don't need sweet nothings if you can kiss like that," she whispered.

He felt his ego soar. He'd never had any complaints in that department, but then, he'd never had any particular praise either. Of course, he reminded himself, it was her first real kiss. She had nothing to compare it to. That, in and of itself, was exciting. He put his arm around her and drew her head down to his shoulder, planting a reverent kiss on the top of her head as he leaned back against the seat.

"What's this movie about again?" he asked.

"I have no idea. James?"

"Yes?"

"Kiss me again."

A shudder of excitement ripped through him. This could be dangerous. She was too eager, too pretty, and she felt too good. He had been in a months-long dry spell that left him champing at the bit, but Laurel was still innocent. Cupping her jaw with his hand, he fulfilled her request, keeping the kisses purposefully tender and sweet. When she began to shift toward his lap, he stopped her.

"I think that's enough for tonight."

She looked confused and perhaps a little disappointed. "Oh, okay."

He lifted her chin and saw the insecurity in her eyes.

"It's not you. You didn't do anything wrong. It's tempting, but I don't want things to get out of hand." He leaned back, his arm resting behind her. "You're incredibly beautiful, and you don't even know it. And it makes you that much more stunning."

"I think you just redeemed yourself in the romantic, sweet nothings department."

"Thank you. Now let's get you home on time so we can do this again real soon—and I can keep my job."

She pushed herself up off his chest and sighed, combing her hands through her hair. He made himself turn away from her.

"You're the boss, Jim Dandy."

He wound a lock of her hair around his finger. *If only that were true.*

CHAPTER 6

*T*he sun beat down on the young couple holding hands as they picked their way through the cornflowers. Queen Anne's lace adorned the path leading to the little clapboard house.

James looked up and squinted in the sun. A faded turquoise pickup, balanced on cement blocks, stuck out above the timothy and crabgrass all around the house. The truck appeared to be as old as his father.

Laurel followed his gaze and answered his unspoken question. "That was Grandpa's. Daddy never would sell the old thing."

"Does it run?"

She shrugged. "I'm not sure. Why? You want it?"

He laughed. "No, I think I'll choose something from this half of the century if you don't mind."

Laurel slowed her pace, looking up ahead at the simple house sitting all alone in the middle of a field. "I remember when Grandma and Grandpa were living, we'd come up here on Sundays for dinner. My grandma made the best green beans you've ever tasted—home-canned and flavored with ham hocks and onion."

James shuddered. "I like mine fresh or frozen please."

"Buckeye."

"Hillbilly," he teased back.

"Anyway," she went on, "after Grandma passed away and Grandpa went to live at the rest home, the old place just kind of shriveled up. We could never get my mom out here to go through any of their things."

"Why not?"

"Mama is—well—it's hard for her to leave the house sometimes. She's a real homebody."

"A homebody?" His voice was incredulous. "Laurel, I *never* see her —not since I was a kid, not at all this summer." He paused and his tone grew solemn. "Is she sick? You can tell me, you know. I won't say anything if you don't want me to. Is that why you had to cancel our dates a couple of times?"

Laurel's voice was quiet. "She's not sick physically, but I'm starting to think there's something else wrong. She's never liked to go out much. She was always fine just tending her garden and raising us and doing her sewing, but now it's like she's *afraid* to go anywhere."

He pulled her close and put an arm around her shoulder, continuing their meandering pace toward the little house.

"I don't understand her at all."

"What does your father say?"

"He's blind to it—like he can't bear to think about her having any problems. But this isolating herself? The more I think about it, the more I realize it can't be right. Some days she doesn't even leave her bed. She just sits there with the shades drawn all day. It can't be good for the boys to see her like that, or for Spring."

"Who takes care of them? You?"

"I do as much as I can. Daddy does sometimes, and Ginny. When she's home, she helps a little, but she's hardly ever home these days. They help me do what Mama can't—or won't. There are days when I get so angry at her. I wish she'd just snap out of it and get back to being the mom I remember."

He squeezed her shoulders in a comforting embrace, unsure how to console her. They ascended the steps and walked across the porch to the front door, hanging loose on its hinges.

"Daddy's started working on this place a little bit." Laurel turned the glass doorknob and pushed the front door open. "He's checked the wiring, the foundation, things like that. Ginny and I talked about staying here when we're home from college. My parents' place is kind of crowded for seven of us now that we're older." She led him by the hand through the house to the back porch, which had been built in as a sitting room with a line of windows framing a view of the foothills and valleys. Over to the right, the plateau dropped off, revealing a glimpse of the lake in the distance.

"Isn't it beautiful?" she breathed. "I would love to have a studio here. It would be an incredible place to paint and sculpt, and—well, anything."

Her enthusiasm was catching. "I could help you too," he ventured. "We could come out and paint and fix it up on our days off."

"You would do that?"

"In order to spend more time with you? Yeah, I'd do that."

She ran up to him and threw her arms around his neck, kissing his cheek as he clasped her to him. "I think that sounds like a great idea!"

They stood there for a long moment with their arms around each other, and she leaned back to look at him. "Come on! Let's go ask Dad what needs to be done next."

"Now?"

"Yes, we're both off day after tomorrow. We can get started on something if we know what to do."

"Yes, ma'am." He laughed, then sobered. "It's after six—your dad won't be at the marina now. I think Phil's covering the evening shift."

"I know. He'll be at home though."

"I don't want to barge in on your mom at dinnertime." He hesitated.

Laurel pursed her lips and huffed. "I don't care what she thinks. I'm tired of pussyfooting around her silly moods. You're my guest, and it's my home too. If she acts ugly, we'll just leave."

James was skeptical. "Okay, if you say so."

She stopped, searching his expression. "I don't want to make you uncomfortable, James. If you don't want to go—"

"No, it's fine. I'd love to go."

"I know she can be difficult, but you're important to me."

He pushed a strand of hair behind her ear and kissed her mouth. He knew the inner sanctum of the Elliot house was a place few dared to tread.

She wouldn't have invited just anyone. It was a sign of her willingness to trust him that she had offered. How could he refuse her?

"Let's go then."

THE DRIVE from the old house to the Elliots' log cabin took about five minutes, during which James fiddled with the radio, complaining about the lack of radio stations and, after giving up on that, started to tell Laurel all about Dayton and Cincinnati.

"There's so much to do. You'd love it—museums and bands and concerts and Reds baseball. You'll have to come up some weekend this fall, and I'll show you around. Maybe Labor Day we can go to the fireworks they shoot over the river."

She smiled. "It sounds big."

"And interesting, right?"

"Yeah, I guess it sounds interesting. But how am I supposed to get there without my own wheels?"

"I'll come get you in a pickup truck to be named later."

"And whisk me away to parts unknown? You'll take the country mouse to the big city?"

He obeyed an impulse and trailed a finger down her arm. "I'd love to take you there."

"I'm driving, James. You'll make me wreck."

"Are you distracted?" He tugged her hand off the steering wheel and clasped it in his.

"Yeah, a little."

"How about now?" He grinned, placing a hot, gentle kiss in the palm of her hand and then blew on it.

"Stop it!" She squirmed, but she was laughing.

"Sorry. Can't keep my lips off you." He nibbled on the inside of her wrist.

"Here," she said, sounding exasperated as she yanked her hand away. "Try to find another radio station."

He sighed in exaggerated disappointment and turned back to the dial. "Still nothing."

Laurel eased up the drive, the gravel crunching under her tires as the cabin came into view.

It looked like something out of some kind of *Popular Organics* or *Hippie House Beautiful* magazine. There was a front porch but no real yard to speak of as it was surrounded by trees on all sides. A detached woodshed stood in the side yard, and there was a makeshift tree house in the back.

Bikes and other toys—bats, baseballs, and the occasional doll—littered the rest of the landscape. Mr. Elliot sat in a homemade rocking chair, a pipe in his teeth and a whittling knife and chunk of wood in his hands. He raised his head at the sound of the truck door slam.

Laurel bounded up the steps to the porch. "Hey, Daddy."

"Hey, Punkin. What are you two up to?"

"We've been up at Grandpa's. James says he'll help work on the cabin."

Mr. Elliot gazed beyond his daughter to the lanky boy she had in tow and spoke around his pipe. "He does, eh?"

"Yep. What should we do next? He and I are both off work the day after tomorrow."

"Don't know yet, but I'm sure we'll figure something out." He squinted up at James. "Would you care to stay to dinner tonight, son, and discuss it?"

"I wouldn't want to impose, sir." Uneasy, James shifted his weight from one foot to the other.

Mr. Elliot eyed him up and down. "It's no trouble. Go tell your mother, Mountain Laurel."

Laurel grinned up at James as if to say I-told-you-so and walked into the house, leaving him outside with his boss.

"You've been spending a considerable amount of time with my daughter."

"Yes, sir."

Mr. Elliot turned back to his whittling.

"What are you making?" James asked politely.

"Walking stick. Made from hickory. You whittle?"

"No sir."

"Like to hike?"

"Maybe, a little."

"Fish?"

"Um, not recently, no."

"No whittling, no hiking, no fishing. What's your passion then?"

James was taken aback. "What?"

"What's your passion? What do you love?"

Is this a trick question? Should I tell him about playing guitar gigs? "I'm not quite sure what you—"

"To do? What do you want to do? What do you study?"

"I'm a business major."

"So, you study nickels and dimes. Yet it appears you have little interest in the natural world." Mr. Elliot muttered, "An economist without knowledge of nature is like a physicist without knowledge of mathematics."

"Pardon?"

"Just a little kernel of wisdom from Carl Linnaeus, the father of modern ecology." He paused. "A business major." Mr. Elliot looked unimpressed. "So, you love money then?"

"Who doesn't?" James joked, but then he realized Mr. Elliot wasn't amused. Laurel came out onto the porch, the screen door banging behind her.

"Mama says dinner's ready."

Mr. Elliot rose from his chair, folded up his pocketknife, and laid the half-finished walking stick against the arm of his rocker.

After a brief introduction to Mrs. Elliot, James took a seat next to Laurel at the round oak table in the kitchen. Several mismatched chairs surrounded it, and the table was set with dishes of various designs and patterns. Huge bowls of mashed potatoes, green beans, cornbread, and a plate of fried chicken graced the middle.

The younger Elliots descended on the table like hummingbirds around a bird feeder. The twins piled their plates high and shoveled the food into their mouths.

"Boys, slow down," their mother admonished.

"We're going fishing after dinner," Dylan said through a mouthful of food.

"Gotta hurry," Crosby added.

Mrs. Elliot took a sip of water. "So, James, how do you like working at the marina?"

Laurel's elusive mother certainly piqued his curiosity, and he had to force himself not to stare at her. Beverly Elliot was tall like Laurel, but that was the only physical trait they shared. Her hair was a mousy brown, streaked with gray and pulled back into a severe ponytail that reached down her back. Her nondescript hazel eyes had a flat, empty look, and her mouth was drawn into a thin, humorless line. James wondered how this woman could have birthed the beautiful, colorful creature sitting beside him, covertly holding his hand under the table. He tried to formulate what he thought Mrs. Elliot would deem an appropriate answer to her question.

"I'm grateful for the work, ma'am. It will help me a lot with school expenses."

Mrs. Elliot didn't respond.

"James is going to the University of Dayton, Mama," Laurel explained patiently. She looked up at him with an adoring smile. "He's studying business."

"How do you study business?" Mrs. Elliot looked genuinely confused. "Business is something you do"—she cast a fleeting look at her husband—"or not, as the case may be."

Mr. Elliot seemed not to notice his wife's subtle criticism. "Education is a fine thing for a young person to pursue, Beverly, as long as the knowledge gained is used to better the world." He took a bite of chicken and chewed for several seconds while the others waited for him to finish his thought. Finally, he went on. "I think I saw a copperhead today—didn't get near enough to tell for sure though."

Dylan and Crosby clamored to hear all about his close encounter with the snake, and much to James's relief, the conversation shifted away from him. Over the next several minutes, he discovered that in this family the threads of discussion changed with startling rapidity due to Mr. Elliot's abrupt introduction of obscure topics. James sometimes had trouble keeping up although Mr. Elliot seemed content to pontificate without anyone responding. Laurel chimed in on occasion, and Spring sat looking at her empty plate, listening but saying nothing. She was a chubby little girl with mousy brown hair and hazel eyes like her mother. Mrs. Elliot eyed James blankly throughout the meal. It was almost bizarre—the way she was there but not *really there*. It was impossible for James to tell whether she liked him or not, or whether she even cared who her daughter had been dating all summer. He understood now why Laurel had taken so long to bring him home with her. He hadn't thought it was possible, but her family was even stranger than his own.

After dinner, James took his plate to the sink because his mom always complimented his friends when they did that. Dylan and Crosby took off on their fishing expedition, and Laurel and her dad washed the dishes, declining his offer to help. After trying several times to start a conversation with Laurel's mom, he sat in silence on the couch. Mrs. Elliot was knitting, but in a few minutes, with an agitated sigh, she got up and left the room. He didn't see her again before they left the Elliot's house.

———

THE PICKUP TRUCK rolled to a stop on the state park playground. Laurel parked away from the streetlamp so as not to draw attention and turned off the engine. They both sat for a second: she, looking down at her lap; he, looking across the seat at her. But then she raised her eyes to his, and suddenly they were in each other's arms, kissing. He pulled her close. She shifted until she was on top of him, with a knee on either side of his hips, grinding against him as he slid his hands all over her. After a time that seemed both too short and almost too long, he made himself stop. She leaned her warm, trembling body against his while he stroked her hair and down her back in a soothing motion. Each time they did this, he came closer to losing control of the situation, and it worried him. He had never felt this way about a girl before—protective one minute and predatory the next.

Laurel had an intellectual understanding of the birds and the bees, of course, but that was different from exploring the nest and the hive up close and personal. She was both an eager student and a quick learner, and what troubled him was that he repeatedly found himself trying to make her lose control as well. Tonight, given the sounds she made and the current disarray of their clothing, he'd come very close to succeeding. He pulled the hem of her tank top down over the flat surface of her stomach, dragging his knuckles seductively across her skin.

"Okay there, sweetheart?" He felt her nod, and he chuckled. "That's good, because I'm not."

Her head snapped up from his shoulder and she pushed herself off him.

"Oh, I'm—I'm sorry. I don't know what I was thinking. I—"

"Shh." He stroked her hair and let his fingers slide down her neck and across her collarbone. "It's okay," he murmured.

She looked down and mumbled, "You must think I'm such a naïve twit or a tease—"

"No, I don't." His voice was hoarse but gentle. "It's fine, Laurel. Honest."

He couldn't seem to take his hands off her completely, but he confined himself to her shoulders and outside her clothes. "I'll never ask you to do something you're not ready for, I promise. Although," he said lightly, "I don't think I can promise not to try and convince you."

Searching his face with piercing eyes that shone in the moonlight, she reached up and ran her hand along his jaw. Wide-eyed and earnest, she whispered, "And I can't promise not to let myself be convinced."

He shivered and took her hand in his. "How about we walk a little?" He opened the passenger door and pulled her along with him. They walked to the playground and sat on the merry-go-round, facing each other.

He intertwined his fingers with hers. "Laurel?"

"Yes?" Her voice was still throaty from the rush of desire.

"I've been meaning to ask you, but it never seemed like a good time to bring it up. Have you thought about the fall?"

"What about it?"

"What we'll do about...us?"

"What do you want to do?" Her voice was subdued, guarded.

"Well, Stuart and Virginia see other people when the summer is over."

Looking solemn, she didn't answer.

All at once, words tumbled out of his mouth. "But I don't think I want that—for us. Can we try to keep this going once school starts again? I know it will be tough, being in different cities—"

She interrupted him, her voice filled with excitement and relief. "Yes. I don't know exactly how it will work, but yes, we can try." She seized his hand. "I want to try, because...I love you."

He was mesmerized by her, so mesmerized that the big scary words she uttered didn't even faze him. He wanted to bask in her smile and feel the red silk of her hair covering him while he held her. He wanted to crawl inside her skin. She made him think he could do anything—that anything was possible, even this:

"I love you, too."

$\mathcal{M}$r. Elliot swung the kitchen door open and stuck his head through, frowning.

"Mountain Laurel, stop moping around and fill the salts and peppers."

This was uncharacteristically stern talk from father to daughter, and James stole a glance at her while he stacked dishes on the shelves.

Huffing, she grabbed a tray to carry salt and pepper shakers, banged the door open with her hip, and disappeared into the dining room. Yes, she was moping a little, but then again, so was he. Summer was over. He had packed most of his things and cleaned up the Pendletons' boat. Stuart would arrive the next day around noon, and the two of them would travel back to Ohio.

A few days at home and then it was back to the grind of classes. With Laurel leaving the following Sunday, this would be their last night together for who knew how long. He never expected it would be this difficult to leave her behind.

He had a lead on a used car when he got home, but even with his own wheels, he might only get to see her once or twice before the semester break. It wasn't that he couldn't live without her—he just didn't want to.

But this was the way of things. People moved on with their lives, didn't they? It couldn't be helped. He wondered if Stu felt half as much for Virginia as he did for Laurel, how did they do this separation thing year after year?

James heard Mr. Elliot's voice, low and urgent behind the door, and leaned in closer to hear.

"Just make sure you're home on time. Your mother will—"

"I know, I know," Laurel interrupted. "She'll have a fit."

"And Laurel, I don't want you on that houseboat. Do you understand? I don't want you getting into a situation you can't handle."

James felt his mouth go dry. Torn between feeling offended and feeling guilty, he couldn't honestly say he hadn't thought about bringing her to the boat—and for the very reason her father was warning her against it.

"Dad, we're going to town to see a movie. It will be fine."

There was no response.

"James would never hurt me, Dad. Never."

"I hope you're right, daughter."

"I am right. You don't need to worry." Her voice grew louder as she approached the swinging door next to his ear, and James stepped away before she could catch him eavesdropping.

"Change of plans." Laurel smiled, but her eyes were serious. "Can you meet me at the top of the hill instead of the boat?"

"Sure. What—?"

She rolled her eyes. "I'll tell you later."

JAMES CLIMBED into the passenger seat of the pickup, and Laurel stepped on the gas and squealed out of the parking lot.

"Whoa there!" He put a hand on the dash to steady himself.

She shot him a fiery glare, making his heart pound with an unexpected burst of excitement, but then her look became tender and she shook her head.

"Sorry. Dad kind of ticked me off tonight. I guess I'm still a little miffed."

"Miffed? The woman's 'a little miffed.' Miffed about what?"

"He said..." She paused, thinking, but then she just shrugged, looking a little petulant. "Nothing."

Laurel drove up to the main highway and stopped. A lone car went past, and they were wreathed in darkness once again, with only the streetlight to illuminate them. She didn't turn onto the road, though. Instead, she turned to him and searched his face as if looking for an answer to one of life's big questions. After a few seconds, she spoke, her voice becoming stronger with each word. "I don't feel much like a movie, do you?"

"Um, okay."

"Let's take a drive instead."

"Sure, whatever you say. Where to?"

"I know a place, around the other side of the lake. It's nice, quiet. We can sit by the water and look at the stars."

"Fine by me," he agreed, wondering what this was all about.

"I put some beer in a cooler and brought some blankets for us to sit on."

"Where'd you get beer?"

"Dad's stash."

"Won't he miss it?"

"I'll just give him some money and tell him I sold it. He'll never know the difference."

They drove in silence for a good twenty minutes.

"How far away is this place?"

"We're almost there."

She pulled the truck into a path that led off the one-lane road and into a grove of trees. Without a word, she put the truck in park, turned it off, and got out. He watched her walk to the back and pull out a knapsack and a cooler.

"How about a little help here?"

He got out and took the cooler from her hand.

"What's in there?' He pointed at the bag she was holding.

"Blankets and...things." She turned on a flashlight and began walking.

He followed her into the brush, breaking twigs and ducking under branches as they went. "Are you sure you know where you're going? This looks like something straight out of a horror movie. I'm expecting Freddy Kruger or Jason to join our outing any time now."

She laughed. "Yes, Buckeye, I know where I'm going. Just wait for it. It's right over—"

They stepped through the last row of trees and brush and into the moonlight.

"Here."

James was speechless for a second. It was beautiful, idyllic—even romantic. Tall grasses gave way to silt-like sand and, several feet beyond that, the dark water lapped in quiet waves against the shore. He could see the marina lights twinkling across the lake, and a million stars of every degree of brightness littered the sky. Shimmering moonlight reflected off the water.

"Amazing spot, sweetheart. How did you ever find it?"

"Exploring on my own last summer."

She dug a blanket out of the canvas duffle and spread it out over the grass. She doffed her shoes and lined them up beside the blanket. She hooked her long arms gracefully around her bent knees and laid her chin on them.

Setting the cooler down, James dropped beside her and kicked off his own shoes. He pulled out two beers, opened one for Laurel and kept the other for himself.

"Good ole' Budweiser," he said with a sigh.

She turned her bottle up and took several swallows all at once, while he looked on in surprise. He had seen Laurel drink a beer before, but he'd yet to see her guzzle one like liquid courage. Lowering her drink, she turned to face him.

"James?"

"Mm-hmm?"

"I want you to make love with me tonight."

He sputtered and somehow managed to swallow the beer in his mouth before he spit it out.

"What?"

She looked across the lake away from him. "Please, don't make me say it again." Her voice was quieter now and less sure. He put his drink down, took hers from her, and grasped both of her hands in his. He looked in her eyes and saw love and sincerity—and apprehension—in them.

"You don't have to do this because I'm leaving tomorrow."

"I'm not doing this because you're leaving—well, not entirely because you're leaving."

"You don't seem too sure about it." He slid over beside her, wrapping his arm around her shoulders and leaning his head against hers. "I want to"—he whispered, kissing her ear—"God knows, I want to." He felt her quiver against him. "But you don't have to do this to 'keep' me or whatever stupid thing girls think about guys." He turned her face to his. "I love you, Laurel. I've never said that to any other girl—never wanted to say it before. *You* are who I love, and nothing that happens or doesn't happen tonight will change that one way or the other."

"And that's why I want to, and why I want it to be with you."

Well, hell. Who was he to argue with that?

"Laurel," he whispered. "Sweet. Beautiful." His lips met hers in a hot, devouring kiss. He eased her back onto the blanket and ran his hand from her shoulder to her hip and back to rest on her belly.

"Are you sure about doing this out here?" he murmured. "You might be more comfortable on the boat—"

"No, not the boat. Half the girls I know who lost their virginity did it on a houseboat. Too cliché."

He chuckled. Apparently, she had been thinking about this for a while.

"Okay then—not the boat."

She looked up, eyes round. "I want to, but James—"

"Yes, sweetheart?"

"I'm afraid—just a little."

He trailed kisses down her neck and below her ear. "Don't be afraid. Just tell me what you want."

Her voice was small and tentative. "I don't know what I want."

He froze, almost panicked for a second, but as he looked at her, he felt his pulse slow and his breathing calm, and his inner knight-in-shining-armor kicked in. He called up confidence and bravado from some long-subdued part of his past and promised himself he would bring her out safe and happy on the other side of this, although he didn't know exactly how. The challenge was spine tingling, like walking on a tightrope above a ravine. He felt reckless and daring and a little nervous himself. She was precious and worth all the care he could give her. He took in a deep breath and expelled it slow and easy.

"I know what you want, Laurel." He was amazed at how confident his voice sounded. "And I'm going to make sure you have it."

He started at the top of her head, pressed a gentle kiss to her hairline, and worked his way to her mouth. He lingered there while he drew a finger over her bare arm and pulled her to him in rhythmic tugs. He kissed her neck and his lips twitched when she made a little whimper. When he got to the v-neck of her t-shirt, he sat her up gently and pulled it over her head. She reached behind her back for her bra hook, but he stopped her.

"Not yet. Let's leave that alone for now." He stripped off his own shirt and nearly groaned out loud when her long delicate fingers ran down his rib cage and slid under the waistband of his jeans just an inch or two. He took hold of them and shut his eyes. "Let's leave that alone for now, too."

He eased her down on the blanket and took a long look at her. Red waves of silk radiated from behind her head in every direction. Her pale skin was luminous in the moonlight; her breasts covered in virginal white lace.

"You're amazing," he whispered. He saw her embarrassment, even in the dim light of the moon, and he brushed a finger along her jaw. "What I mean is every part of you is designed to go with every other part. You're perfect."

He leaned over and nibbled at the pulse throbbing in her throat before running his tongue along her collarbone and just inside the inner edge of her bra till his mouth rested between her breasts. She arched her back and her moan reverberated from her chest into his lips. He drew his fingers down over her stomach, feeling it move up and down as she gasped. One finger slipped under the button on her cutoffs, and he undid them in one smooth motion, drawing down the zipper and laying the fly open. The white cotton of her panties peeked out from underneath. He kissed right below her belly button and took a little nip at the hipbone jutting out.

"James?" She breathed. "What are you...?"

He slipped his hands inside her shorts and drew them down, exposing her skin to the night air and his hungry eyes. "Would you believe me if I said, 'trust me'?"

She giggled, actually giggled out loud, and his heartbeat flared and pounded in his veins for a minute. He sat beside her, simply staring at her in wonder, before reaching under her to unhook her bra and drawing the straps down her arms.

The beauty of her body beckoned him, but he found himself unable to tear his gaze from her face, intense and exquisite. Lying down beside her, he drew one hand along her inner thigh and her eyes slid shut, releasing him from her gaze and allowing him a respite so he could concentrate on the rest of her. As his fingers slipped between her legs, she started to cry out and self-consciously covered her mouth with her hand.

His touch coaxed her further into delirium, and he whispered roughly, "Let it go, Laurel. It's all right, just let go."

She broke then, her arms reaching above her head, grasping the blanket in her fingers—arching and sighing and writhing in movements so erotic, he had to drop his head and close his eyes to keep from losing control of himself. He felt as if he'd run ten miles, and he gulped the warm, humid, night air as if he were drowning. He kissed her and whispered sweet nothings, and while she recovered, he slipped a condom out of his wallet and doffed his Levi's.

He looked up to find her watching him, interest and trepidation warring on her features.

"Still afraid?"

Her eyes darted up to his face. "No," she said quickly, and then she let out a nervous laugh. "I mean, not much."

He lay down, facing her and held her close. She kissed him on the mouth in acquiescence, and he pulled her on top of him.

"What—?"

"I know what you want, remember? Trust me."

"Famous last words."

"Mountain Laurel, you're one in a million." His gaze narrowed. "Damn, this is going to feel so good." He guided her with his hands, pausing when she gasped with a quick intake of air. "Take your time. You know what to do." He moved her hips in a barely perceptible rhythm, which she slowly began to take over. His eyes closed, and he let himself sink into the warm, urgent cadence, shuddering as he felt his tenuous control slipping away. Somewhere in the middle of it, he realized she was losing her restraint too, and he wanted to shout in primal triumph as the world exploded in a white-hot burst of light.

After the resulting embers faded and floated away, he brought his hands up under the red curtain of her hair to hold her forehead against his. His voice came out low, smooth and sure.

"I will always love you, Laurel Elliot. Always."

CHAPTER 8

CHRISTMAS NIGHT, 1991

*F*at snowflakes flew across the windshield of James's Toyota Corolla as he snaked along the interstate curves leading to the mountains.

His cheeks were tight and drawn from where he'd wiped away tears shed in solitude, and his jaw hurt from clenching it for the last hundred miles. He was almost there—almost to the closest thing he had to a home now. And it wasn't a place, although the place was part of it. His home was now a person—a person with flaming red hair, dark blue eyes, and a smile that made all his troubles fade and his worries disappear.

Laurel.

He only hoped she would be there. They had been planning this interlude since October. Her weekly letters kept him abreast of the progress on her cabin, projects she completed during her weekends at home. In the last letter, she said the place was done—not fancy, but livable, and she was planning to spend her Christmas break there. She asked him to join her, and he said yes, but the plans were for him to arrive the day after next. There was no phone—no way to reach her to say he was coming early.

He still had a key to the Pendletons' boat in case her place wasn't an option, but he really hoped he wouldn't have to use it. The boat would provide shelter, but shelter wasn't what he was looking for. He wanted comfort. He wanted Laurel.

The car in front of him fishtailed in the snow, reminding him to pay attention to the rapidly deteriorating road conditions. According to the radio, the worst of the storm wouldn't hit until sometime around midnight, but he knew the snow would probably be heavier in the mountains. Once he made it to the cabin, he'd be up there for a while.

What would she say when he got there? Would she be shocked? Happy to see him? Would she see the anguish in him right away, or would he have to tell her the whole story before she understood?

Wipers stuttered over the windshield, the rough sound of rubber against dry glass. The exit sign for the lake shone like a green beacon in the dark.

He signaled and changed lanes, and soon he was on the two-lane road that wound its way to Elliot's Marina. Luckily, the snow had slacked off some although it was still hard to see. Somehow, he found the drive that led down to the dock. There were a few lights on there, and a few more a little farther up the main road that marked the entrance to the Elliot family home. He drove past, creeping along the road so he wouldn't end up in the ditch. Farther up the road, the clapboard house's gravel drive was almost completely obscured by snow, but miraculously, he found it in the dark. He shifted down into first gear, but his car ended up stuck anyway in the steep driveway about a hundred yards from the house.

He revved his engine a time or two, but the wheels just spun in place. The old car wasn't going any farther, so he grabbed his duffel and his guitar from the trunk, wound his scarf around his neck, and trudged through the falling snow. As he stepped through the last row of trees and into the clearing, he caught a glimpse of her grandfather's cabin, and his heart leapt. There were lights on, and smoke drifted from the chimney. Someone was there! Desperate optimism made him believe it was Laurel and Virginia.

Hoisting his bag on his shoulder, James walked up the steps, pulling down his scarf so she would recognize him, and set his burden on the porch floor. He opened the screen and knocked on the wooden door behind it.

The curtain slid over the sidelight for a second and then jerked back closed. The door flew open and there she stood, wide-eyed and wonderful.

"James!"

He tried to answer her, but words stuck in his throat. He held his arms open, and Laurel filled them. She pulled him inside, and a thankful groan escaped him. He held her to him as if he would never let her go.

———

JAMES SAT in the corner of Laurel's little couch, admiring her form as she approached. Her hair was pulled back and tied low on her neck, draping over one shoulder. She wore an ivory fisherman sweater and jeans tucked into brown suede boots. She looked warm and comfortable walking toward him, holding out a steaming mug of tea.

"Sorry, there's no coffee. I don't drink it very often, so I don't keep any here."

"This is fine," he said, nodding his thanks to her. "It's hot, which is the most important thing right now."

"I didn't hear you coming. Where's your car?"

"It's stuck about halfway up the driveway."

She sat in the other corner of the couch and wrapped both hands around her cup. "I bet it was a cold walk."

He gave her a one-shouldered shrug. "Where's Virginia?" he said, glancing around the room.

"She's gone back to school early. She rented an apartment up there, and I think Stu might come down from Cincinnati and visit her over break."

"Ah."

"You want a sandwich or something? I brought some ham up from Mom and Dad's house."

"No, thank you. Not right now." He set his cup on the coffee table and reached for hers, putting it on the table next to his. "Come here so I can say hello properly."

She laughed and slid over, wrapping her arms around his neck.

"Hello," she whispered and kissed him on the lips.

He sank into the kiss, pulling her to him and willing her mouth to open under his. He pulled the tie out of her hair and ran his fingers through the long, shining red locks, settling his hand on the back of her head to hold her securely in place. The pent-up emotions of the past twenty-four hours unraveled inside him, and his desperation to be with her was overwhelming. He moaned her name, inching his hands under her sweater.

"Oooh, your hands are cold."

"Let me warm them on you." He moved in to kiss her again, and she caught his face in her hands and pulled back to look at him.

"James?"

"Mm-hmm?"

"This visit is a bit of a surprise. You're here early."

"Wanted to see you."

"Mm-hmm. Wanted to see you too."

"Is there a problem?" he asked.

"No," she answered.

"Good."

"When are you going to tell me what's happened?"

"What do you mean?" he said, not wanting to talk about it when he was all charged up for other reasons.

"You look...happy, yet unhappy—happy that you're here, but unhappy about something—something big. Something that brought you here two days early."

He sighed. "I don't want to go into it just yet."

She studied him for a moment. Then she shrugged. "You're the boss, Jim Dandy." She turned so her back leaned against his chest and pulled his arm around her. "So, do you want to hear about my Christmas?"

He nestled her head under his chin and drew in a deep breath, inhaling the scent of her hair, her skin, all of her. He felt his pulse quicken but his body relax, which didn't seem possible, but there it was. "Go on."

She laughed, but there was no humor in it. "The whole Elliot crew gathered round the family homestead for the holiday. My mother planned this elaborate dinner to celebrate Christmas and Ginny and me coming home from school. It was the perfect Christmas feast—ham, mashed potatoes, sweet potato casserole, rolls, and green beans with ham hocks."

James shuddered, and she laughed at him. "Buckeye."

"Hillbilly."

"Anyway—it was going to be quite a to-do." She ran her hand down his arm as she might stroke the spine of a cat. James almost purred.

"But then, the big Christmas Day arrives"—she paused—"and Mom spends all day in her room crying."

"Oh, baby, I'm so sorry."

"So then, Virginia and I made the dinner. We fixed Mom a plate and took it in to her. We opened the presents without her, and then late this afternoon, Ginny says she's done and headed back to Lexington. It's supposed to snow, and suddenly I can't stand the thought of being trapped in that house anymore. I left my brothers playing on their new Nintendo and Spring with her nose in a book, packed up some leftovers, and hightailed it out of there."

He kissed the top of her head.

"So, here's my question: when I run off up here, what makes me any different than Mom running off to her room? Don't you think we're both hiding?"

"No, it's different, Laurel."

"How?"

"You're still changing, still growing, still doing new things—you're going to school, you're working on this cabin. Trust me—it's different than crying in bed all day. You know that."

"She wasn't always like this, you know. I mean, she was always quiet and shy, but not like this." Laurel's voice softened. "What if that happens to me too? When I get older?"

"It won't."

"You sound so sure of that."

"You won't do that. You're going to get off this mountain and go out there and do something incredible."

"I'm so glad you're here. You make anything seem possible." She snuggled deeper into him, and they sat in silence for several minutes, contented in the closeness and the quiet.

James felt his lids drooping, and he fought the urge to sleep. He didn't drive all this way to crash on Laurel's couch. He wanted her—had been waiting for her these four months—but despite himself, and without realizing what he was doing, he slipped into the welcome oblivion of exhausted slumber.

CHAPTER 9

The next thing James knew, he was awakened by sunlight streaming in the window. He lay curled up on the couch, a patchwork quilt over him and a pillow under his head. He glanced around the empty, cold room and sat up in slow motion, stretching his arms over his head.

First, he needed the bathroom. Second, he needed to find his toothbrush because his teeth felt like sandpaper.

The back door slammed, and a blast of frigid air hit him. Laurel appeared in the doorway, dressed in jeans and a thick barn jacket, her arms filled with firewood. Her cheeks were rosy from the cold, and her hair was mussed under a knit hat topped with an absurd pom-pom. She looked like a snow bunny.

"You're awake," she announced in a cheerful voice.

He rubbed his hand over his face. "Hello, beautiful."

She blushed even rosier. "I started a fire."

"Beautiful and accomplished."

She rolled her eyes. "James, I've been building fires since I was ten."

"All the more impressive."

She looked at him in sober contemplation. "I'm going to put this wood in the stove, make some tea and oatmeal for breakfast, and then

I want you to stop trying to distract me with silly compliments—although they're much appreciated—and tell me what's going on with you, okay?"

He sighed. "Okay." He got up and opened his duffle. "Shower?"

She pointed down the hall.

"Come with me?" He waggled his eyebrows at her, only half-joking.

"You haven't seen the shower yet. I doubt we could both fit."

She walked over and put her arms around him, hugging him close. "I'm so glad to see you," she whispered. He kissed her and disappeared down the hall.

She was right about the shower. It was barely big enough to turn around in. James washed in a hurry and jumped out, shivering as he donned his clothes. He ran his fingers through his hair and decided he'd shave later. When he entered the kitchen, Laurel was setting the table with two bowls and mismatched spoons. A carton of milk, some sugar and cinnamon, and a teapot made an unpretentious centerpiece.

Then she turned, spoon in hand, and gave him a smile as brilliant as sun on snow.

He sat down and picked up his cup while she spooned out the oatmeal.

"My parents are getting a divorce."

She set the spoon down in the pan, her face awash in concern and sympathy. "Oh, no!"

"Oh, yes. I knew things were bad, but it all came to a head yesterday when my mother told me that my father has been having an affair for the last ten months." He dumped two large spoonfuls of sugar on his cereal.

"Oh...oh, James." She reached over and grasped his hand. He dared a look up at her, but he saw no shock, no disdain, no censure there—only compassion.

"I guess she's known a while now, but she wanted us to have one last Christmas as a family. Apparently, the other woman didn't like that, so she called the house, complaining that Dad had promised to come over to see her yesterday, but he couldn't because Mom insisted he stay around while I was home. She goes on to ask Mom what was the point of making him stay for the holiday since Mom already agreed to the divorce.

"There's a huge blow-up. Mom is furious with Dad. She said she just asked for one little thing, for my sake, and he ruined it like he ruins everything.

"Given the state of their marriage, a divorce is probably for the best. They've been estranged for three or four years. But he should have been man enough to ask for one in the first place instead of sneaking around like a coward.

"After the cat was out of the bag, Mom threw him out, and he went to what's-her-name's house after all. Then he calls me a few hours later and proceeds to tell me there's no money for my tuition or room and board this semester. Nothing. He said he was going to break it to me gently, but when Mom threw him out, she took that option away from him. He accused her of overspending his income."

"Wow," Laurel mused, shaking her head.

"Dad says he can't pay my college bill in addition to Mom's alimony. He said plenty of other things too, but the gist of the conversation was, 'You're on your own for the bill.'"

"He actually said that?"

"Well, to be honest, I didn't give him a chance to say it. I just hung up."

"Maybe you should have let him explain."

James rolled his eyes. "Explain what? How he made a mess of my life? How he ruined our family? What's the point of listening to that?"

"I know you're angry, but he might have had a helpful suggestion or two about school."

"You don't know my dad. He doesn't give helpful suggestions, just ultimatums. It's his way or the highway."

"Well, what are you going to do?"

"I don't know. Dad says I'm twenty years old, and it's time to start standing on my own two feet. I have a little money but not near enough. I've never been too good about saving, and it's not like I had any warning or time to prepare. Maybe there's enough for tuition, I don't know, but I can't apply for a student loan in time to pay my rent, so it looks like I'm sitting out at least a semester."

James let go of her and picked up his spoon, weaving it between his fingers. He leaned his chair back on two legs. "After Dad and I hung up, Mom demanded to know what he said, and when I told her, she accused him of wasting their money on his whore—and yes, that was the word she used."

Laurel stirred her oatmeal in a slow, thoughtful circle. "Can you commute from home to the university?"

"Maybe. But I don't want to be anywhere near my parents right now—either of them."

Their eyes met, but she didn't comment further.

AFTER BREAKFAST, they ventured outside to dig out James's car and then drove down the mountain—slipping, sliding, and laughing the whole way.

They arrived at the IGA about eleven o'clock. Because Christmas Day was on a Tuesday, the day after was just another workday for the stores in town. They picked up coffee for James and groceries for a week or so, gathering items for quick entrees or for meals that made good leftovers. James made a stop at the drugstore, too, under the guise of needing some shaving cream.

"They sell that at the grocery store," Laurel said. "Why didn't you just pick some up while we were there?"

"Um, I forgot. You can wait. I'll just pop in here real quick." And he was out before she could protest. He wasn't sure what the week ahead would bring, but it would be a lot less awkward if he didn't have to run down the mountain for a condom in the middle of a moment. He tossed the bag in the back seat and gave her a lopsided grin as he put the car in gear and backed out of the parking lot.

Later that afternoon, they arrived back at the cabin with James's car safely ensconced under the carport roof. He rebuilt the fire while she stocked the pantry. When he finished, she was already curled up on the couch with a sketchpad, her feet folded underneath her, working intently. He picked up a book he found lying around and settled himself in the leather chair by the window. After reading the same paragraph again and again, James gave up, shut the book, and came around the back of the couch to look over her shoulder.

She had sketched a decent rendering of him reading in the chair, a distant smile on his face. He kissed her cheek. "I like when you draw me."

"I have other sketches of you too."

"Oh, really? I want to see them."

She patted the cushion at her side, and he vaulted over the back of the couch to land right next to her. Flipping through the sketchbook, she stopped at various portraits of him although he saw that there were plenty of other people in the book as well: her father behind the counter at the marina shop, the boys fishing, Virginia reading a book, and a haunting picture of her mother—despair pouring out of eyes encased in dark circles. There were also landscapes and a few close-ups of birds, flowers, and the like. The ones of him were from the previous summer. In one, he was leaning back, one leg bent behind him, his foot braced against the wall, a plastic bus tub in his hands. In another, he was sitting on the dock. Still another depicted him perched on a ledge high above the surface of the water, leaning back on his elbows, the corner of his mouth quirked up in a half-smile.

"I love this one—love them all. You're very gifted, sweetheart."

"Thank you," she said, blushing with pleasure at his praise.

He brought his arm around her in a tight embrace and leaned over to kiss her ear.

She trembled. "That tickles."

"Mm-hmm—nice, isn't it?"

"Yeah, I guess it is."

He turned her face toward him and brushed her jaw with his fore-finger before leaning in to kiss her again. He took the sketchbook out of her hand, set it on the coffee table, and they spent the next several minutes getting reacquainted as the cold, winter sun sank lower and lower in the sky.

The dusk settled around them and covered the room in various shades of gray that deepened as the minutes ticked by. The flames roaring in the stove stood out in sharp contrast to the gathering dusk. James lay on the couch, Laurel perched on top of him, her head on his chest as he absentmindedly rubbed her back. A fog of relaxation surrounded them, and although his body was urging him to get on with it, his mind was reluctant to let the moment go.

"James?"

"Yes, sweetheart?"

"Penny for your thoughts."

"I was wondering why I haven't chased you into the bedroom yet."

"I was wondering the same thing—not that I'm complaining or anything."

That drew a chuckle from him. "This just feels so perfect. I'm trying to etch this moment on my memory, so I can return to it again and again whenever we're apart and I miss you."

"Oh." She sighed, lifting her head to rest her chin on his chest. He played with a curl that framed her face.

"Yesterday, it seemed impossible that I would ever feel this way again."

"What way?"

"I love being here with you, but it's more than that. Since I've been here, there's this sense of belonging, like coming home after a long trip. Yesterday, it felt like that was lost to me forever—that maybe because of the divorce, I can't ever go home again. But I think I underestimated you. I should have known, though. You always make everything right. How do you do that?"

"I don't know, but I do know you do the same for me."

He pulled her up to kiss her again and felt her move against him, and the lazy moment was gone, replaced with a need to see and feel all of her. He pushed her gently and sat up. He ran his fingers through his hair and exhaled a sigh of longing and good-natured frustration while she stood in front of him. He leaned the crown of his head against her abdomen, circling her hips with his arms. Her hands combed through his hair.

"Wait here." Laurel held his now upturned face in her hands, smiling down at him. Peace suffused and settled between them. She disappeared into the bedroom and returned a minute later with an armful of blankets and pillows.

"The bedroom is cold, so I thought this might be more comfortable." She busied herself with arranging a make-do bed. "My granny would have called it making a pallet on the floor. I'm sure she never thought I'd use it for this though." Once she was finished, she sat down and held out her arms to him. He stripped off his sweater as he approached her, kicking off his shoes and leaving them beside the coffee table.

"Don't," he said in a husky voice as she started to reach for the hem of her own sweater. "I want to unwrap you."

He knelt at her feet and gently eased her back until she was lying down. Her stocking feet rubbed up and down his thigh, and he slowly pulled off her woolen socks one after the other, nibbling her ankles and massaging her arches. His hands slid up the outside of her jeans, undid the buttons, and peeled them off. He stared at her until she crossed her hands in front of herself in a self-conscious display of modesty.

His eyes sought hers, but he said nothing out loud. Instead, he continued working upwards along her body, pushing up her sweater, then slipping it over her head and tossing it away. Drawing his finger down the center of her chest, he popped her bra clasp loose with one hand. The corners of his mouth lifted, and his eyes darkened and danced with desire and amusement.

"Best Christmas present I opened this year."

He stood and unbuttoned his jeans, pushing them and his boxer briefs down and stepping out of them. After kissing up her legs and her body, he settled himself in the cradle of her hips and slid home. She rose up to meet him, again and again, and hooked her long legs around him to draw him close. He felt his restraint slipping away and tried to think about baseball, finals, anything to keep this from being over too soon. He regained some control, but at the same time, he could feel the tension building in her body, and he reached down between them to touch her. Her body tightened and then went slack with a moan and a sigh, and he let himself go.

He relaxed and then rolled to the side bringing her with him. Joy bubbled up from inside him, and he had the strange urge to laugh—to let a little of the unbearable happiness escape him. Her sweet voice called him out of his bliss, whispering words of love that he returned in kind before he lifted a blanket to cover them both. There they rested until complete darkness descended—their bodies intertwined in her mountain nest and warmed by the fire he built.

CHAPTER 10

*W*hen will this be ready? I'm starving." James was cutting carrots into pieces while Laurel peeled potatoes at the counter.

"Slice them smaller, and they'll get done faster." She reached around him and guided his hands to make a narrower cut. He leaned down and kissed her mouth.

"Oh, I gotta stir the beef." She scooted over to the stove and turned the stew meat over to brown the other side.

Out of the corner of his eye, he saw her reach for the little radio she kept in the kitchen. "Not in the mood for Hickville easy listening, Laurel."

"Sometimes at night, I can get radio stations from Knoxville."

She twisted the knob back and forth and fiddled with the antenna. "There we go. REM—how's that?"

"That'll do." His knife hit the cutting board. "I saw them at Riverfront last year."

"Where?"

"Riverfront Coliseum. In Cincinnati."

"Oh. I haven't been there, but I've heard people talk about it."

"I can't wait to take you to concerts—you'll love them. Last New Year's I went with the guys to this little hole in the wall to see..." He stopped, remembering the debauchery of that New Year's Eve. "Well, it was a really great band. What kind of music do you want to hear live?"

"All kinds. I've never seen anything but the locals around here, so it's all new to me." Her eyes were lit with a blue fire that James interpreted as a thirst for adventure that matched his own. Suddenly though, the fire went out with an abruptness that was startling.

She picked up a bowl of potato chunks and slid them into the stew pot, guiding them with her knife. "Last year, you saw a great band, and this year you're snowbound in a mountain cabin making your own dinner. This must be pretty boring compared to the New Year's Eve parties you're used to."

He mentally kicked himself for bringing it up. It made it sound like he was hiding something, but that wasn't why he didn't want to tell her about it. That New Year's happened before he spent the best summer of his life in Kentucky—before he watched as his Mountain Laurel blossomed right in front of his eyes. He was another man last year, and everything was different now.

James walked over and put his arms around his girl, nuzzling into her neck. "If I wanted a crazy party this year, I would have found one. I'd rather be with you."

She smiled at him over her shoulder and put her arm over his, holding him to her. After another squeeze, he released her and returned to his cutting board.

The song changed to a tune that had just come out and was sweeping through the dance clubs around Cincinnati. No doubt, the radio stations would overplay it, but it was a catchy song. James glanced over at Laurel in amused expectation.

"Let's see what you got, Elliot."

She held a celery stalk up to her mouth like a microphone, and put one hand up in the air, reminiscent of a Supremes' pose. Belting out the song's signature line, she began a hip gyration that had him laughing—and damned if he wasn't a little aroused again too. Even after she turned back to her vegetable peeling, her little wiggle kept going like a siren's call. He moved in behind, put his hands on her hips, and joined her in a suggestive rhythm. She tossed him a coy glance from under her lashes, and he spun her around to face him, insinuating his leg in between hers.

She laughed and broke away, singing.

WHILE THE STEW SIMMERED, James brought out his guitar and settled on the couch, picking out several tunes in a row, one blending seamlessly into the next. Laurel brought two beers from the kitchen and settled herself in the big, overstuffed armchair, one leg thrown over the arm. She listened, quiet rapture on her face.

"You've been practicing," she said, as she watched his hands move with ease over the neck of the guitar.

He noodled another second or two before he answered her. "Been writing too."

"Play me something you've written."

"Most of my stuff's instrumental. No lyrics."

"Okay, so lyrics will come later when you've got something to say. Let's hear what you've got so far."

"Well this is what I've been working on lately." He leaned back against the couch, strumming a couple of his tunes.

"James, they're wonderful! They remind of country music or Southern rock. You should head to Nashville. You could play at the Bluebird Cafe."

"You almost make me believe I could." There was a quiet pause while he sat up, looking at her intently. "This one's yours."

She cocked her head to the side, a question in her smile.

"I wrote it for you." His fingers moved over the frets and strings in an intricate, delicate melody. He couldn't look at her because a sudden, surprising shyness overtook him.

She put down her beer and moved to sit on the floor at his feet. When he finished the tune, she seemed to realize that no words were needed, only a look of adoration and a sweet kiss on the mouth. So that was what she gave him.

THE EVENING STRETCHED LANGUIDLY into night. They lingered over dinner, telling stories about school and friends, and remembering funny anecdotes from summers gone by. Afterward, they lounged on the couch, talking and completely forgetting about the time. Finally, he glanced at the clock and realized it was twelve thirty-four.

"Happy New Year, Mountain Laurel." He leaned in to kiss her.

"Happy New Year. I had no idea it was already after midnight."

"Me neither." He gestured toward the window with his head. "Look, it's snowing again."

"So it is. Let's go out." She pulled him up to his feet, led him to the door and handed him his jacket. "Just for a few minutes."

He followed her out into the front yard and studied her profile as she stared up into the sky. "Listen," she whispered reverently.

He closed his eyes. There was no sound of life around them—no birds, no insects—only the tiny whisper of snowflakes falling on the blanket of snow and gentle breezes rising and falling among the trees. When he felt her warmth pressed against his chest, he opened his eyes. She looked up at him, her eyes as bright as the stars, twinkling in the light that streamed from inside the house.

She brought her hand up and stroked his lightly stubbled jaw. "I love this place. I've always loved it, but when you're here, it's even more wonderful."

He drew her into his arms. "I can't think of anywhere in the world I'd rather be tonight."

"So, you like playing house with me?"

"Most definitely."

Her bright smile faded into an awed look of devotion. "I love you."

"And I love you too. Always." He kissed her for what seemed like the hundredth time in the last twenty-four hours. His lips were getting chapped. "But now I'm freezing, so let's go sit in front of the fire, and I'm going to show you a wonderful game—one I've never played but heard great things about."

"Oh? And what is this game?"

"It's very highbrow. It's called Strip Chess."

She giggled. "I'm not very good at chess."

"I was hoping as much."

She sashayed across the porch to the door. "I'd better keep all my winter wear on then."

"Oh no, that's cheating." He laughed and followed her inside.

HOURS LATER, James lay still in the darkness, listening to the quiet sounds of Laurel breathing while she slept. She snuggled against him, one arm and leg draped across his body. He trailed his fingers down her arm and stared up at the ceiling, just barely making out the contours of the room.

It was so dark here at night. He'd forgotten, or maybe he'd never known true dark. At home and at school, there were always street-lights, headlights, porch lights. Even at the marina, bulbs strung from overhead wires were on all night, and the other boats glowed from within. This dark, true dark, was observed not only with the eyes but with the ears as well. Different from what he was used to, where there was always a noise, an ambulance, the hum of a furnace. True dark wasn't menacing the way he had imagined it might be. Instead, it was rather…peaceful, isolating—not scary exactly but awe-inspiring in the sense that it gave him an unmistakable reminder of his insignificance in the greater scheme of things. It led James's thoughts to travel inward—or perhaps the quiet dark had just allowed them to float up and out so he could examine them. The absence of distractions turned his mind back to the decisions looming in the not-so-distant future.

Laurel stirred and lifted her head. "Are you still awake?"

"Just thinking," he replied. "Go back to sleep."

"What are you thinking?"

"It's nothing, sweetheart."

"Tell me," she murmured, stifling a yawn.

He sighed and waited a long minute, to see if she would drift back off. When she didn't, he spoke. "I'm just wondering what I'm going to do next month. I spent half the drive down here railing against my parents. The usual angry stuff: How could they be so selfish? Didn't they at least owe me a college education? After all, they had promised me that from the time I could understand what college was. That's what parents do—what all my friends' parents do. And then I started to think, and being here with you has kept me thinking."

"About what?"

"Well, you're doing college on your own. Your parents give you very little financial help."

"Well, they *can't* help much. They've got Virginia in school too, and then the boys and Spring to take care of."

"That's it, in a nutshell. You make your own way. So you make your own decisions."

"Well—"

"No, I admire you for it. You study what you want to study, chart your own path. When I think about it, it's the only way to be happy."

"Okay."

"So, like I said, I've been thinking. I've been wondering what the hell I'm doing at the University of Dayton anyway. Why do I care so much about going back there? I hate business classes. I don't want to be an accountant or an insurance salesman or a banker. So, why am I busting my ass to do something I hate?"

"You can study other things there."

"I know. I just think maybe I need to start over. I mean, why did I go there to begin with? To please Mom and Dad? Why should I worry about pleasing them when they're too wound up in their own problems to give a damn about me anyway?"

"I'm sure they love you, James." She hugged him tightly. "You're very lovable."

He smiled in the dark and could feel the air around him grow warm, but the warmth faded as his smile did.

"Maybe it's not in the cards for me to go back at all."

Laurel leaned up on one elbow. "Quit school? You want to quit school? In the middle of your junior year?"

"Maybe."

"What will you do instead?"

He shrugged. "Anything I want. For the first time in my life, I feel free—like my life is in my own hands. Maybe I'll backpack through Europe. Maybe I'll go to Nashville and write songs. I don't know. I can go anywhere—do anything. You know, the more I think about it, the more I think this may be the best thing that's ever happened to me."

She bit her lip, deep in thought. "Perhaps."

He stopped to gauge her reaction. Even in the darkness, he could feel the wary look, the stiff posture of her body. A sudden realization dawned on him.

"I won't leave you behind, Laurel—not in a million years. I want you to come with me."

"But I'm in the middle of my first year in college. I can't just pick up and go." Distress colored her voice.

"Well, you can finish your first year. I'll go ahead to wherever, get settled, and then you could transfer. People do it all the time."

"But Benton College has what I want to study."

"Lots of places have art programs, sweetheart."

"But I can't do work-study lots of places."

"We can work something out. Don't worry. I'll find a way for us to be together."

She lay down on her back, beside him, facing the ceiling. His side felt cold without her against him, and he rolled closer to her, resting a hand on her tummy and sliding it to her hip. He tugged her toward him.

"Let's not talk about it anymore right now. We have lots of time to work out details and talk about things. Right now, I just want to be with you."

"Okay." She seemed relieved to be changing the subject and he couldn't blame her. Why wallow in consternation when there was so much else to do?

"Come back, Mountain Laurel." He kissed her shoulder. She wiggled around, until she was nestled with her back against his chest and brought his arm around her. She cradled it in her own two arms and kissed his hand. "I'm here."

Silence fell over the house, each lost in their own thoughts.

Finally, he spoke again. "I'm going to Nashville, I think. If I want to try my hand at music, that's the place—either that or California. But I think Nashville's more our speed."

"I suppose."

"It will take me a few weeks to get everything together, but I'm going to use my savings to relocate."

"What will you do once you get there?"

"At first?" He kissed the back of her head. "Wait tables, probably. Then, start trying to make some connections with musicians in the area."

"It sounds like a lot of changes all at once. You don't think it's—I don't know, a little reckless?"

He shrugged. "I think it's a helluva chance to get my life back. Live it on my own terms. You don't agree?"

"I don't know."

"We could be together."

"Could we?"

"I hope so." He leaned up and rolled her toward him. "Is there something you're not telling me, sweetheart?"

"No." She sighed, turning back around and wiggling her rear end back into him. "I just don't know what my parents would say if I came home and suddenly announced I'm up and moving to Nashville."

"I know it's an adjustment, and your dad was happy about you going to Benton, but transferring schools will be fine. I'll go first—you can follow later. We can even go talk to your folks about it before I leave."

"I'm not sure that's a good idea."

"Why? Your dad knows me. He always seemed pretty open-minded. I'm sure he'll discuss it with us."

"It's not him I'm worried about—it's Mama."

James rolled his eyes. "What is her problem? How can she say anything to you, give you any kind of advice—when she never leaves the house?"

Laurel lifted her chin. "Mama and Daddy love me—and they're going to be concerned about this. They only want what's best for their children."

He hugged her close. "Of course they love you." He kissed her neck. "Why do you think your mother will be against the idea?"

Laurel shrugged. "She's worried about your influence over me."

"What?"

"It's not your fault. It's because of what happened the night you left."

He sat straight up. "What happened?" Surely, she hadn't told her mother.

"I was late coming in as you might remember. She was waiting up, and she was upset with me for missing my curfew."

"What did she say?"

"She was worried, and I guess she overreacted. She said I was wasting my time with you because you were leaving the next day, and I'd never see you again."

He caressed her jaw and turned her face toward him. "I guess I proved her wrong then, didn't I?"

She held up her arms and drew him close once again. "I guess you did."

"Don't worry, sweetheart. I can be charming when I want to. We'll convince them that we're good together."

"Maybe we will but not until we've got some kind of realistic plan. So, let's not test the waters just yet, okay?"

He paused, holding her close, and a niggling sense of foreboding stole across his mind. He pushed it away and answered her in a soothing voice.

"Whatever you say, Laurel. They're your parents, and you know them better than I do. We'll do this your way."

CHAPTER 11

NASHVILLE, TENNESSEE

FEBRUARY 1992

*C*ome on, come on! Pick up, will ya?" James cradled the receiver against his shoulder and blew on his chilled fingers. Sleet pelted against the glass of the phone booth, and the February cold made him irritable and impatient. It was Tuesday night, and he always called Laurel on Tuesday nights. Why wasn't she waiting for him? He wished one of those co-eds whose room was near the only phone would hurry up and answer. He had places to go and people to see, and he was freezing his ass off.

"Hello?"

Finally! "Hey, yeah, can I talk to Laurel please?"

Although she covered the phone with her hand, the girl screeched loud enough that he had to hold the phone away from his ear.

"Hey, Elliot! Your Tuesday night guy is on the phone." She took her hand off the mouthpiece. "She said she'll be down in a second."

"I'd better be her guy every other night too."

The girl just laughed.

"What was your name again?"

"Adrienne."

"Yeah, Adrienne. Look, I hate to bother you, but I'm kind of in a rush right now. Do you think you could ask her if she's going to be a while? Or does she want me to call her back?"

Her voice carried again. "He says to hurry up!"

He grimaced. "That wasn't what I said." He couldn't be too upset though because he had the supreme pleasure of hearing his girl on the phone a few seconds later.

"Hey, Jim Dandy. Sorry it took so long. I was studying for a sociology test in the lounge at the other end of the hall."

He felt his pulse slow. Laurel's voice always had that effect on him. Like the smoothest bourbon, she relaxed him, and whatever was wrong faded into thin air.

"Hello, beautiful," he crooned. He swore he could hear her blush over the line, and he smiled.

"What are you up to?"

"Nothing much. Just on the way to meet some guys who are looking for a temporary bass player."

"That's great! I didn't know you played bass."

"I've been trying my hand at it lately. How are you, sweetheart?"

"I'm okay, I guess."

"Just okay? That's good," he joked.

"What do you mean?"

"Well, I wouldn't want you to be deliriously happy without me."

She laughed, but then her voice grew somber. "I do miss you a lot."

"I miss you too."

"How are things in Nashville?"

"Going pretty well. Lots of stuff going on right now."

"Did you write any music this week?"

"I haven't had much time for writing lately. Got a couple more pick-up gigs though."

"That's good. Have you made it to the Bluebird Cafe yet?"

"Not yet, but I'm still holding out hope for a lucky break. Good news on another front though. I got that job at the Coke bottling plant. I just started yesterday. It's pretty boring, but it's a steady paycheck. Now I can pay the rent and still have evenings to play music —not like when I was waiting tables and couldn't get gigs because I had to work."

"Sounds like a good plan. How's the new place?"

"It's great! Just two rooms, but there's a kitchen corner, a bedroom with a door, and I finally got a bed to go in it. I bummed the one from my mother's guest room. Susan and her husband brought it over in their truck when they were passing through. They're on their way to San Diego."

"They're moving again?"

"Yeah, that's where he's stationed, so they'll be there for a while."

"Is your mom okay with that? It's pretty far away."

"I think she's good with it. She knows that's how it is with the Navy. The divorce still isn't settled, so that's taking most of her attention right now. She did get a job, though, as a secretary in a church office. Not much money, but with the alimony, she should make it all right."

"Good for her. How's your dad?"

"Beats me. We haven't spoken since I left."

"I'm sorry, James. Is he ever going to get over you leaving school?"

"Who knows, but I'm not sure what he expected me to do when he yanked his financial support out from under me. Where does he get off telling me that this move to Nashville was a 'foolish notion'? I say he lost his right to any opinion about my decisions when he stopped paying my bills. Wouldn't you agree?"

"I suppose so, but I can sort of understand why he's disappointed. He probably expected you would, you know, figure something out— do whatever you could to stay in school."

"Yeah, well he figured wrong, didn't he?"

"Are you sorry you left? Was it worth leaving school and everything behind?"

"Oh, definitely worth it. I mean, I won't lie to you and say the last two months have been easy, because they haven't been. But I don't have to tell you pretty lies, sweetheart, to get you to join me. You know the way the world works."

There was a silence of several seconds. "Laurel?"

"I'm here."

"I thought we got disconnected or something."

"Tell me more about the apartment."

He knew she'd be excited about that. "It's not spacious but roomier than a dorm, I'll bet!"

"Everything's roomier than a dorm."

"The rent is reasonable, too, so we'll have a little bit of a financial cushion while you sort out work and school for yourself. Middle Tennessee State is here close, and then there are some community colleges as well. Vandy's probably not an option because of the expense, but I know we can carve out a workable solution for you."

"I hope you're right."

"You'll love Nashville, darling. There's so much life and energy here. All the mainstream crossover into country music has breathed new life into the whole place. It's really a city for young people now, not just for the Grand Old Opry crowd of a few years back."

"It sounds like you're happy there."

"Oh, I am, but I'll be happier when you're here too. I hope it won't be much longer before I can hold you every night and wake up beside you every morning."

"That was one of the best parts of last winter, wasn't it?"

"Have I told you how much I loved living on the mountain with you during Christmas break?"

He heard her smile from almost two hundred miles away. "A few times."

"I know I have, but I'll say it again anyway. I'll never forget it. It was one of the best times of my life. An island of sanity away from all the craziness, and you were the center of it all—my sanctuary amidst the chaos."

"My boyfriend, the poet." Her voice grew serious. "I'll always be here for you, James."

"I love you so much, and I can't wait to have you with me every day. I wish I could come get you now."

"I can't leave in the middle of the semester, you know that."

"You could do it." After a pause, he added in a hopeful voice. "I'll help you find work, apply to schools, whatever it takes to get you here."

"I—I can't. How would I explain to a new school that I was a drop out? And throwing away all the money Benton's given me for this semester? It seems wrong. Don't ask me to do that, James. I just can't."

Disappointed but not surprised, he sighed. "Yeah, I know. I guess I'll have to wait, maybe even until the end of the summer if you need to work and save up some money."

"Waiting will be best in the long run."

A pall of silence settled over him, and he fought to find a more cheerful subject. "I hear from Stu that Ginny is burning up the pre-dentistry program."

"She really likes it."

"Stu says he's thinking about transferring to Lexington for dental school too after he graduates."

"They seem to have it all worked out. But then, Ginny always knows what she wants."

"So, how are your classes going?"

"Pretty good."

"It's a shame you don't get to do any real art yet. It's still all that general studies crap, isn't it?"

She laughed. "Well, that general studies crap is part of the liberal arts education."

"I hated that about college. Why don't they just let you study what you want to do with your life?

"I don't know, but maybe all this will come in handy someday."

"Doubtful. Well, I suppose I'd better go. It's almost time to meet those guys at the club. I'll call you next week, okay?"

"Okay."

"You sound sad, Mountain Laurel."

"It's hard to be so far away from you."

"I know, sweetheart. All the more reason you should come to me sooner, rather than later. Don't worry. It will be a grand adventure, not a tightrope walk without a net. I'll be your fail-safe, and you'll be my muse. Sweet nothings, etcetera, etcetera." He tried to joke, but the loneliness he felt was real. He could hardly wait to see her—be with her—all the time.

She sniffed. "I'll write you this week."

"I love you."

Her voice sounded so, so far away. "I love you too."

End of Part One

INTERMEZZO 1

The music pounded in James's head as he took a sip of his very expensive champagne. It was bubbly and dry, and it tickled his nose. The best champagne money could buy—like his suit and tie, like the coveted party tickets he bought for the most exclusive New Year's soiree in San Francisco.

A sudden bump on his shoulder nearly made him spill his drink all over his shoes. He turned and grinned at his friend's tipsy, happy expression.

"Eric! Having fun?"

"A blast. Best New Year's Eve bash in the city, bar none."

"Who's watching little Trevor tonight?"

"Millie's mother. God, I love that woman! It was part of our Christmas present this year—a New Year's Eve out on the town, *sans enfant.*"

"I'm surprised you got Millie to go out so soon after—what is it?—a month since she had him?"

"Six weeks. Look at her." Eric sighed, lowering his glass to gaze, love struck, at his wife. She was laughing and swing dancing with their good friend John, while John's girlfriend, Fiona, cheered them from the sidelines. Every time John made a misstep—which was frequently—Fiona and Millie laughed.

"You'd never know she just had a baby six weeks ago," James offered generously, giving his friend another opportunity to brag on his wife.

"She's amazing, that's for sure." Eric's chest seemed to swell with pride. "So, buddy, what are you doing standing here all by your lonesome? I know you can swing dance—better than John anyway."

"Just hanging back and watching the crowd."

"Watching or scoping?"

"Maybe a little of both."

"I thought you were going to bring Monica tonight."

"We broke up."

"Oh, geez, James, I didn't know. I'm sorry."

"Yeah, me too." James wasn't particularly sorry, though.

"Well, there are plenty of women here tonight. Take your pick—brunette, blonde, redhead. You could probably have all three at once if you put your mind to it, you handsome sonofabitch. You know, I hate you for that."

James's mouth twitched as he popped an hors d'oeuvre in his mouth.

"That is, I hated it before I caught Millie. Hey, come into the bar with me for a sec. I need a manly beer to counteract all this girly champagne."

The men took two empty barstools and ordered a couple of beers and a club soda for Millie.

"So—spill. What happened with you and Monica?"

James shrugged. "Nothing to spill, really. She wanted to take the relationship to the next level. I didn't. So, she walked."

Eric held his friend with a steady gaze. "James Marshall, the perpetual bachelor."

"Looks that way, doesn't it?"

"It's too bad about Monica. Millie and I really liked her."

"She's a great gal." James turned his beer bottle on the table, drawing a large circle of condensation.

"Beautiful, smart—"

"Best attorney in town."

"Who was the one before her—Tracy?"

James shook his head. "Stacy."

"That's right. The cellist with the San Francisco Symphony."

"Yep."

"And before that was Christine."

"Mm-hmm."

"Napa Valley vintner."

"Divorced twice, and I can see why." James shuddered. "Ba-a-a-ad temper." He paused. "Your point is?"

"You, my man"—Eric pointed his beer bottle at James—"are too picky."

James shrugged. "Can we talk about something besides my love life?"

"You should start thinking about settling down."

"Spoken like a happily married man with a kid. Alas, *mon frère*, there just aren't that many Millies out there in the world."

"She's one of kind. But there are plenty of good women, James. Look at John and Fiona."

"Not that many Fionas out there either."

"I can't believe John. After waiting all this time, he popped the question on Christmas Eve."

"Said he had to make something of himself first...so he would deserve her."

"As if she cared anything about his money or the rest of it."

"Well, it mattered to him, I guess."

"They'll have the rest of their lives to enjoy it."

"Yeah."

Eric took a pull off his beer. "You ever think about tying the knot? Getting married?"

"Who me? Perpetual bachelor, remember? I'm a child of divorce, and I have commitment phobia—or so I've been told by many well-meaning women."

"No one even came close?"

James knew Eric was pumping him for information. It wasn't the first time he'd done so either. It all started a few months earlier when Eric spied the charcoal drawing in his office and asked about it. He told him it was drawn by a childhood friend. Then, when he was moving from his apartment to the townhouse, Millie teased him about the girly flower painting in his room. She had stared at him, puzzled, when he told her it was just some wildflower that reminded him of home, so he moved it with him wherever he went. Then there was the time they asked him about that little melody he was always playing on his guitar. He managed to avoid answering that one and tried not to play it in front of them anymore. Unfortunately, he fiddled around with the melody so often that sometimes he didn't even realize he was strumming it.

Apparently, Eric had been taking nosy lessons from his wife. On another night, James might even have resented it, but he had enough drinks in him to loosen his tongue and stave off any ill feelings toward his inquisitive friend. Besides, he'd been thinking along those lines himself since his breakup with Monica, and the answer to Eric's question just sort of tumbled out of his alcohol-numbed brain.

"There was one girl, back East, years ago. Man, I was sprung on her. Guess I was young and stupid. If I'd had my way, I'd have married her in a heartbeat. Probably been divorced by now too."

"What was her name?"

"Get a load of this—Mountain Laurel."

"You're joking."

James shook his head, laughing. "No, that was really her name—Mountain Laurel Elliot. Her father was an aging hippie from the Sixties."

"Where'd you meet her?"

"Southern Kentucky. I worked down there one summer bussing tables at her father's restaurant when I was in college."

"First love, eh?"

"She wasn't my first that way." He paused. "But she was my first here." He touched his beer bottle to his chest and looked away.

"Ah. What happened?"

James smirked. "I wanted to take the relationship to the next level —she didn't. So, I walked."

"I'm sorry, man."

"Water under the bridge, my bro."

"What does she do now?"

"I haven't got a clue. She was studying art. I'll bet she's got a husband and two point three kids and a minivan somewhere in suburbia." James downed the rest of his beer. "Come on, enough sentimental bullshit. Let's go take your wife her club soda and join the party."

He walked unsteadily into the ballroom to an old pop tune about partying like it's 1999.

He laughed as a pretty party-guest grabbed both his hands and did a little shimmy against him. Then he tossed his friend a wink and led the woman to the dance floor.

James groaned and rolled over to swipe at his alarm clock, but even after repeated hits, the noise went on. He realized it was the phone ringing and swiped at it, knocking it off the stand before he was able to grab it and push the talk button.

"Yeah?"

"Good morning, slacker. It's almost noon."

"Jesus, Eric."

"No, it's just plain Eric. Get up and get some coffee. I'll be over in an hour, and we'll take a run."

The phone clicked, and James swore again. He dragged himself out of bed, took a piss, and pulled on some shorts and a t-shirt. He remembered his running shoes were still downstairs, so he snagged his socks and slowly descended, yawning widely.

While the coffee was brewing, he stepped out on the front stoop to grab the paper. The new neighbor across the street opened her door at almost the same moment.

"Good morning!" she called, waving to him.

"Good morning."

She looked like she was about to come out and start a conversation, so he turned and went back in without delay. She was nice enough—recently divorced, kind of attractive—but the last thing he needed right then was woman trouble.

Maybe it was time to move on, head off somewhere else. Seattle, maybe? Or Phoenix? Somewhere back East perhaps. No, he cut his final ties there and had become a permanent West Coast man six years earlier. Going back to school was a smart move, probably the best decision he ever made once he knew what he wanted to study. California had the added bonus of being closer to Susan and Gary who had been so good to him since he'd left home for keeps. Because of his estrangement from his parents, they were the only family he had left—well, them plus Eric and Millie, and John and Fiona. They were some of the best friends he'd ever had, and they were family to him too. Sometimes he missed Stuart, his best friend from childhood, but even before he left Tennessee, they hadn't seen each other much anyway.

Maybe it was inevitable—what life did to their friendship, how it pulled them apart—but a lot of that probably had to do with who Stuart married.

Stu and Ginny wanted him to be an usher at their wedding, but the idea of meeting up with Laurel Elliot again, even two years after their breakup, was extremely unappealing to him. He didn't think he could contain his anger if he saw her again, and what good would that do any of them? The die had been cast. So, he begged off groomsman's duties, giving Stuart some lame excuse about finals week. He didn't even attend as a guest.

James ambled into the kitchen, poured a cup of coffee and headed into his study. The sketch Eric had commented on rested on the antique secretary.

Why do I keep that thing around?

He stepped over and picked it up, holding it over the trash can in a moment of indecision. There had been several moments like this over the years. His heart gave the familiar momentary squeeze when he thought of Laurel—her long, jean-clad legs, flaming red hair in a braid down her back, brilliant, dark blue eyes, her amazing smile. But as always, the recurring anger quickly covered the fond memories. *Sentimental rubbish, Marshall. You only think about her because you couldn't have her. Maybe she wasn't what you wanted anyway. One thing was painfully obvious though: she sure as hell didn't want you.*

Like a speeding car spinning out of control, the memory of the last time he saw her roared into his mind. Could it really have been all those years ago? Sometimes it still pissed him off as if it had just happened last week...

He turned into the familiar, gravel drive and began the long trek up to Laurel's little cabin. She had done some work on it since she'd been home from college. There was a new coat of paint on the outside, and shutters now adorned the windows. He felt the draw of the place, the draw of her, and the rapid pace of his heart began to slow. It was like the whole world slowed down when he was there. He hoped she was home, but in this, as in so many other things that day, he was disappointed.

He found her in her father's little office at the marina, working on a ledger of some sort. He walked in without knocking and shut the door behind him.

She looked up, her blue eyes wide in disbelief.

"James?"

"Hello, sweetheart." He leaned over the table and kissed her, but it was a business-like peck on the lips rather than the all-consuming kiss that was inside him waiting to be unleashed.

"Why are you here?"

"I wrote you I was coming. Did I beat the letter here? I really wish you'd get a phone up at the cabin."

"No, I got it—the letter, I mean. I just—" She looked out the window. "I just hoped you'd think better of it and not come after all."

"How could I not come? First of all, I find it impossible to believe that you would dump me through the mail without even the courtesy of a face-to-face discussion. You don't have a callous bone in your body, so I assume that somebody got to you. Is it your father? Your mother? What have they said to convince you that we shouldn't be together? Tell me, so I can refute it and relieve your mind."

"James, it isn't just what they said. It's the whole situation."

"I promise you, we can make this work. I can do anything if you're beside me. I've been composing a ton of songs the past few months. They just keep rolling off my fingers, and I've gotten more jobs as a studio musician too. I'm learning about recording and mixing music from other musicians. Yeah, I'm not going to college, but I know that all this experience is going to pay off in the end. It won't be a hand-to-mouth existence forever. Tell your parents that if they're worried about it."

"I don't care about living on a shoestring, but you'll be at work all day and out at clubs all night, and I'll be alone in a strange city."

"So, you'll come with me to the clubs. Look, I know you. You're not some kind of pampered princess, Laurel. You can roll with the ups and downs of being with a musician, and I'm not worried about you taking on any challenge we face. I've seen you handle everything life has thrown your way. You've never backed off from what you want, and after everything we've meant to each other, I can't believe breaking up is what you want. Don't run away from this—from us. We're meant to be together."

She was near tears. "Please don't say these things. It just makes it worse—"

"I need you, and I love you, and that's why I drove all this way to talk some sense into you!" He paced back and forth in the little office and stopped in front of her, holding out his hand. "Come for a drive with me so we can talk."

Her expression was hidden, wary. It unsettled him the way she retreated behind that frozen façade. It looked too much like her mother's face; the lack of animation made her look like a mannequin. Her eyes darted to the office window, and he followed her gaze to see her father looking in on them with an unusually stern expression. What a time for the man to start acting paternal!

"We'll go to our little clearing by the lake." His heart beat faster just thinking about the idea of being alone with her. "We'll have some privacy there."

Her eyes darkened, just for a moment, and then the cold, blank stare was back. She looked down at the papers on her desk.

"We can talk here, although there isn't much else to say. I can't move to Nashville with you."

"Yes, you can. You just won't—and I'm here to find out why."

The blank stare was gone, finally, but her crestfallen expression was sad in a way he'd never seen before. "It's impossible. I can't leave school."

"But you can! I've told you. There are other schools—good schools —around Nashville."

"Not where I have work-study already lined up. Not schools that I can afford. My parents have no money for college, James. This is my only chance to get an education."

"People make their own chances. There's always another way if you want something badly enough."

She sighed. "Not for me."

Anger boiled up inside him at the defeated tone in her voice. "Those are your mother's words. What on earth did she say to you?"

"The truth."

"Oh, really! And what is the truth according to the Hermit on the Hill?"

"That leaving school now would be a terrible mistake—that this whole plan is crazy—and I won't let you provoke me about my mother. This isn't about her."

"Bullshit!" he hissed. "This is all about her and him." He gestured toward her father, still watching through the glass. "When is it going to be about you, Laurel? Sometimes you have to stand up for what you want!"

"I can't," she whispered. "I'm not like you. I can't just pick up and leave everything I've ever known without a second thought. Why can't you understand that?"

He decided to change tactics. Something inside him screamed that this was one of the big Crossroads of life—with a capital C—for both of them. He had to change her mind or at least make her see what she was giving up.

He gentled his voice and tried again. "I know it's a big step, darling, but it will work—I know it." He sat on the desk and covered her hand with his, trying to entwine their fingers.

"I know you believe that, but it's not that simple."

"Yes, it—"

"No. It's not." She jerked her hand back and folded her arms protectively across her chest. "Have you considered that me tagging along is not in your best interest either?"

"How can you say that? How could being without you ever be in my best interest? I love you. What could be more important than that? And you love me."

She said nothing.

"Don't you?"

Her face was frozen in place. An icy cold wind whipped around his heart in spite of the hot July day. He waited a long minute. "I see."

She swallowed hard.

"Yes, I see now. Apparently, I've made a huge mistake coming here. In fact, I've made a complete ass of myself." He shot her a withering look and turned his back on her as he put his hand on the doorknob. He looked over his shoulder. "But you've made a mistake, too, Laurel Elliot," he said in an ominous voice, "and you'll regret it. I promise you that." He threw open the door and strode out.

Mr. Elliot followed him outside to the dock and called after him. "What did you say to my daughter, Marshall? She looks upset."

James turned around, anger radiating from every pore in his skin. "You're killing her spirit, you know, persuading her to stay here so she can be near you. It's selfishness on your part. You of all people should know better than to keep an exotic bird in a cage and expect her to stay beautiful and brilliant. I'm telling you, it won't work. She'll end up a shadow of what she could have been. Sir." The last word was smothered in sarcasm.

"And I suppose you're the one who can save her from a horrible fate out here in the sticks," Mr. Elliot said, his face contorted in anger. "I know your type. You're a materialistic hothead, and you'd be the ruin of her. You're all big plans and dreams, but you're doing nothing —working a day job at a bottling plant. Go out and find your life, such as it is. Leave my daughter alone to find hers. She's made her decision."

"She made that perfectly clear. Goodbye, Mr. Elliot. Rest assured you won't see me around here ever again."

After that, James hardly knew how he made it to his car. He barely remembered any of the drive back to Nashville, except for thinking that he knew what a broken heart felt like.

After Laurel cut him loose, he coped by forcing himself to think only of the future, and it had been effective. He threw himself into learning more about music. He went to college in California. Now, more than seven years later, James had constructed a new life for himself. A life that had taken twists and turns he never expected. He had embarked on more than one new adventure, striking out on his own time and again, and he had done well—succeeding beyond his wildest dreams—and Laurel had missed out on all of it.

He sighed and put the sketch back on the desk. It was beautiful work, and James was an artist of sorts too. He couldn't bear to throw it away.

The doorbell rang. He turned his back on the picture and went to answer it. Eric was jogging in place.

"Come on, big guy. Let's pound some pavement."

James rolled his eyes. They set off at a brisk pace, but the previous night was catching up to him, and after a while, he had trouble keeping up. His friend stole a look over at him.

"We'll go through the park, and then we can turn back toward home. You doing okay, buddy? You seem a little sluggish today."

"I'm just fine, Mom. I like a run in the morning." He wheezed. "It clears my head."

"Let's walk a little and catch a breather." Eric didn't wait more than a minute before he dropped his latest bombshell:

"Laurel Elliot."

"What about her, Eric?"

"She doesn't have two point three kids, and she's not married. Don't know about the minivan though."

"What?" James stopped, staring at his friend.

Eric stopped too and turned back, breathing hard from running. "She's still in Kentucky—some place called Uppercross Hollow."

"How do you know all this?"

"A miraculous entity called the Internet."

"You little stalker—"

"This is all according to a website from some forward-thinking craft fair in West Virginia back in the fall. They had a web page with artist bios listed on it. I can't believe you haven't looked her up your-self—out of curiosity."

James plopped on a bench and hung his head down while he rested his elbows on his knees. "I'm not going back there. And I'll thank you to butt out of my love life."

Eric sat beside him. "Look, I'm not trying to tell you what to do. But I saw your face when you talked about her, man. Something's still there, and I think you need to either face her or let her go. You're at a standstill. You can't make things work with any other woman—"

James Marshall sprang off the bench, hands on his hips as he glared at his friend. "Okay, thanks for the advice, but if I need a life coach, I'll hire one."

"You need to come to grips with this," Eric persisted. "You've conquered the world, genius, but now you've got some decisions to make—like what you're going to do with the rest of your life and who you want to do it with."

"I'll tell you one thing I'm not going to do"—James turned and started running—"I'm not going to track down Laurel Elliot."

PART II

CHAPTER 12

UPPERCROSS HOLLOW, KENTUCKY

JUNE 2000

*L*aurel Elliot shut down her potter's wheel and wiped the back of her hand across her sweaty forehead. It wouldn't be summer for another month, but it already felt like it. She loved her studio, but with three of the four walls made of floor-to-ceiling windows, it was sweltering in the afternoon. She walked into her kitchen, a room eliciting a feeling of homespun comfort with its lemon-yellow walls and French-blue accents. When she remodeled, she had splurged on a retro-looking fridge with a guilty, modern *secret* hiding inside the freezer door: an automatic icemaker. That little device had saved her a ton of frustration because she was forever trying to get a stale ice cube or two out of a tray that she had forgotten to fill.

She stepped to the sink, filled her glass with cool well water from the tap, and downed it in one breath. Throwing pots was thirsty work, especially without air conditioning.

Listening closely, she heard the rumble of a Jeep just over the hill signaling the imminent arrival of the day's mail. Laurel wiped her hands on her apron and went out the front door and down the drive to the mailbox. She was expecting a letter from the craft fair people in Knoxville, and it was supposed to arrive today. She liked the excuse that the phone company still wouldn't install phone lines up to her cabin but now with cell phone technology, she would probably have to invest in a cell phone at some point. The world moved fast these days, and people complained all the time about not being able to get hold of her in a timely manner. Yet Laurel still resisted the idea. She told herself it was because she didn't want to be a slave to a device. Or that a cell phone was too expensive. Mostly though, she balked at the idea of being instantly accessible to people. Living alone on the hill had taught her to keep her own company, set her own schedule, and live by her own rules. A cell phone would upset the predictable rhythm of her life, and she found it difficult to sacrifice her independence for other people's convenience. Besides, if her parents could call her on a whim, she'd never get any work done.

Hilda, the mail carrier, was long gone by the time Laurel reached the end of her driveway. She opened the box and pulled out a small wad of envelopes: a bill for art supplies, an advertisement for the IGA, and a letter addressed to her with a large curly *P* on the return address label.

"Ginny." She smiled to herself. Tearing open the letter, she began reading on her way back to the house.

Hey Sis,

I hope you are doing well. Dad writes that you are still up on your mountain throwing pots and living off the grid. Mom is about the same, I gather.

Stuart and I are both doing well, and we have pretty incredible news on two fronts. One is that after a lot of soul searching, we've decided to move back to Kentucky! Old Dr. Dawes is retiring at the end of July and has agreed to sell us his practice, such as it is. It will need some updated equipment, but the location is ideal, and Stuart is happy about the move. We love a lot of things about Cincinnati, but we've been talking about striking out on our own, and this seems like a good time. Stuart has always loved that area around the lake. It's a good place for a dental practice, given the recent growth in population, and it's a quiet, family-friendly atmosphere.

And that leads me to the other good news: I'm expecting a baby! Finally! After trying for so long, we actually did it! We're a little nervous about telling people until the first trimester is over, so keep it under your hat for now. I haven't even told Mom and Dad yet. I'm about six weeks along, and so far, so good. I would have loved to call and tell you the news, so I could hear you squeal with delight, but you don't have a phone! Grrr...

Anyway, we are leaving Cincinnati on Memorial Day weekend and plan to take an extended vacation down on the lake. We've rented a huge vacation house for the summer, so we can look for a permanent place to live and set up the practice to open the first of September. And we'll have lots and lots of time to see you if you have time for us. If I remember right, most of your big craft fairs are in the spring and fall, right?

We're planning a nice leisurely summer, the kind we used to have when we were kids, and we're inviting Stuart's sisters to stay with us, sort of a "last hurrah" before settling down to be boring parents who talk incessantly about their offspring.

So, how do you think you'll like being an auntie? I'm sure you'll be incredible at it. Well, I gotta run. Hope to see you real soon.

Love,

Ginny (& Stu)

Laurel couldn't help grinning. Stuart and Virginia were going to be parents! They were moving to the lake. What a great summer she had to look forward to now instead of the hot, muggy, and endless days of the last few years. She had kept busy remodeling the cabin, working, and traveling around to sell her pottery, but hopefully, Virginia's arrival would provide a welcome respite from the other task that had inadvertently fallen in her lap—de facto maternal figure of her family.

Mrs. Elliot's emotional problems had worsened over the years.

Now that she was older and had seen a little more Oprah, Laurel knew that her mother was struggling with a full-blown case of agoraphobia. She rarely left the house or yard, spending most of the day in her room with the TV on. Her physical health was deteriorating too, and she'd gotten quite heavy from lack of exercise. Her only activity was sewing beautiful clothes for Laurel to sell at the craft shows and fairs where she showed her pottery. The family had been unsuccessful at getting her to try therapy or medication. She refused to see any doctor, and Mr. Elliot was afraid to push her too far for fear of what she might do to herself.

It was an impossible situation. Laurel knew this but felt powerless to help. Maybe now that Virginia would be around, things would change. Laurel was pleased but very surprised that her sister was coming back to their hometown. Once Virginia left for college, she had essentially never looked back. Since she and Stuart married, she came home only once or twice a year, citing her busy schedule with dental school, then work.

The Elliot boys had moved out a couple of years ago. Neither of them had gone to college, electing to get an apartment and stay around their old stomping ground. Dylan was an electrician, and Crosby sold real estate.

Spring would graduate high school next year. She was an incredible student, putting even Ginny to shame with her college entrance scores. Thankfully, she would probably get a full ride to college because the family business was struggling. Mr. Elliot was a nice man, but he was no businessman. A new, modern facility was going in across the lake, so the old Elliot's Marina desperately needed, if not a full upgrade, at least a facelift. He said a remodel would be giving in to commercialism at its worst, but Laurel suspected the real reason was that the renovations would cost money that he was unwilling to part with. Her father was stubborn enough that he wouldn't take any advice from his children—the ones who were willing to give him any —and Laurel wasn't sure the marina could take many more summers like the last and still stay open.

She had learned to cope by separating her life from her parents for the most part, keeping her own company in the solitude of her mountain cottage. It was not "off the grid" as Ginny liked to say—she did have electricity—but it was quiet there, and she could think without the distraction of everyone else's problems. She had been squirreling away money too. As an artist, she was only a step above the poverty line, but Laurel had always lived a frugal existence, and that allowed her to be financially independent.

Every week she helped her father with the payroll and made the obligatory check on her mother, but she never stayed long. On holidays, she went to her parents' house and cooked family meals to give her brothers and sister some semblance of a normal family life. At those times, her mom often stayed in her room because the noise was so "discombobulating."

Laurel had given up being angry when she realized her mother was truly ill, and she wondered sometimes if that illness played a part in her mother's almost terrified insistence that she not move to Nashville when she was eighteen. It was hard to say, but Laurel Elliot took responsibility for her own decisions. She wouldn't blame anyone but herself.

So, while she might wish for a different life, that didn't mean it was going to happen. Laurel had made her choices—good and bad—and she was resigned to live with them. Unfortunately, the isolation of the mountain prevented her from broadening her horizons except for brief sojourns for business. Her natural reserve made it difficult and exhausting to meet people at the craft fairs she attended. And men? There were no single men around her little corner of the world—none that interested her anyway. There hadn't been anyone, anyone since...

Unbidden, he came to mind: handsome, dashing, and determined. The eight years of separation had faded any flaws she ever saw in him, and now he was almost larger than life to her. He had been right to believe in himself and in his ability to make his mark on the world. He had made it, too—perhaps not in the way he intended but still successful beyond his wildest dreams.

She still remembered the day she had discovered it. She had gone into the public library to see whether they had a new copy of her favorite art magazine. As she perused the shelves, she glanced at the February issue of Forbes. The name in the headline drew her eyes like a magnet:

John Benwick, Eric Harville, and James Marshall: From musical toys to business with the big boys. A tale of three high-tech millionaires.

Hurriedly, she scanned the Table of Contents and flipped to the article. She felt numb all over as she backed into a wooden table and fumbled for the chair:

"I don't know exactly how it happened. We met, we started talking and that led to working, and that led us to starting the company."

Thus began the saga of one of the year's most surprising business success stories. It's the Cinderella tale of a company founded by three college buddies —a software development firm that turned the music industry on its ear. "Easy Music Producer", or EMP, is a user-friendly computer program enabling any technology-challenged layman to record and mix music tracks. Now, amateur musicians no longer have to beg, borrow, or steal time in a recording studio, opening doors traditionally guarded by music industry professionals. Industry pundits speculate this issue might be the reason a large entertainment conglomerate, eager to get in on the ground floor of this major paradigm shift, purchased the rights to EMP for an undisclosed, yet reportedly staggering sum.

"We are lucky. No doubt about that," says EMP front man Eric Harville, looking like the quintessential modern father, participating in this interview with his infant son in his lap. "We were in the right place at the right time, but we put in a lot of work, too, and sometimes people forget that part."

When asked how they came up with the idea, James Marshall speaks for the first time. Harville credits him as the inspiration behind EMP's development.

"It all started one night after a grueling circuits' exam. We were playing quarters with a pitcher of beer and talking about music to try and forget about school for a little while."

"James is a musician and a composer," Harville cuts in.

"Okay, I was talking"—Marshall gives a disarming smile—"and Eric and John were tolerant enough to listen. I said, 'Wouldn't it be great if ...?' and John said, 'Why couldn't we...?' and we were off. It was John who developed the original code. He's a brilliant programmer."

Benwick is conspicuously absent, and it is obvious his business partners feel it. They explain that he is caring for an ill relative. Both men spend several minutes raving over John Benwick's abilities, as well as his character.

The future of this close-knit team, however, is uncertain. The terms of EMP's sale agreement prohibit the three from developing any competing software for five years.

"We're not sure what we'll do next. We're just taking things one day at a time," Harville says, skillfully evading the question of EMP's next phase.

Marshall continues, "We started this as friends having fun, and we would love to continue working together. We'll just have to see what life has in store for us and make our decisions accordingly."

Whether they form another formidable software team or strike out on their own, one thing is certain: these three young men took passion and skill and turned it into a pot of gold at the end of the rainbow. They're set for life.

After that, Laurel couldn't get enough. She scoured the press for information and found out that James earned a bachelor's degree in engineering from San Jose State University. He met Benwick and Harville at college, and they started their company the year before graduation. Another article announced that software whiz kids James Marshall and John Benwick had made a list of the most eligible bachelors in Silicon Valley, with James being touted as the better catch, given that Benwick was engaged.

Later, Laurel read that John Benwick was grieving the recent loss of his fiancée to a rare and aggressive form of metastatic melanoma.

Laurel had fallen in love with James Marshall when he had nothing but seeing evidence of his success made her both proud of him and, if she were honest, a little wistful too. At times, it was hard not to regret her decision to stay at Benton all those years ago. She reminded herself that she was a young girl of eighteen at the time, and what he wanted her to do was rash and fraught with the potential for disaster. Her mother's advice was reasonable to give a teenaged daughter— although in those first awful months, Laurel wondered whether her mother's motives might have been more than a little self-serving.

With the perspective of experience, however, Laurel's views on her decision changed. She now wished that she had been brave enough to take that chance and follow her heart or, at least, try to find some middle ground.

Unfortunately, Laurel could not see any compromise at that time in her life, and her doubts, along with the persuasive arguments of her parents, convinced her to let James go. In many ways, her life path was set when she made that choice. The older people in town called her "another Elliot hermit," an unfortunate recluse in the making. The rest just called her odd or eccentric—the lady who lived all alone at Uppercross Hollow without a phone, modern conveniences, or anyone to keep her company.

She was a little surprised that some blonde, California girl hadn't snapped up James already. She had never met another man like him. He was right when he had said she made a mistake, but it wasn't because he was now rich and successful. It was because no one else had ever touched her heart the way he did.

CHAPTER 13

"So, what do you think about the place?" Virginia Elliot Pendleton twirled around the living room of the house she and Stuart would call home for the next few months.

"I thought you said you rented a cabin," Laurel replied. "This is like a palace."

"A palace is not made out of logs. With the wood floors and stone fireplaces, it's positively rustic, don't you think?"

Laurel wandered to the wall of glass that opened out to a second-floor deck and an incredible view of the lake. "It's lovely, Ginny."

"Thanks." Her sister seemed pleased with Laurel's praise, yet she was nonchalant about the relative opulence in which she lived compared to the rest of her family.

"Oh"—she went on—"I meant to tell you earlier, but it slipped my mind—pregnancy brain, you know."

"Yes?"

"Stu heard from James Marshall, and he invited him down here to stay a couple weeks this summer."

Laurel felt her stomach sink to her sandals. "James?" she whispered.

"Yeah, you and he had that fling a while back, I remember, and I told Stuart it might be a little awkward for you, but he was so thrilled to hear from him again, and he'd already asked him, so—"

"How did Stuart find him?"

"James found us, if you can believe that. It was weird the way it happened. Crosby was looking for a place for us at the same time he was helping James's sister, Susan, and her husband find a vacation home around here."

"Oh?" Laurel said weakly, trying to mask her expression and fiddling with some papers on the counter.

"James told them how much he loved the lake when he was growing up, so when Susan's husband retired from the Navy, they started looking here for a place. We met them while we were house hunting and struck up a conversation. We made the connection, and she told James, and the rest is history. James called Stuart that weekend to catch up."

"I see."

"You can handle this, can't you? I can't imagine it would be awkward for you now. That was so many years ago, and you were just kids. It might be kind of fun to get to know him again since he's a big millionaire now."

Laurel said nothing.

"With Carrie and Heather, and now James, too, we're going to have a full house for the month of June," Virginia went on, wiping off windows with a Windex-soaked paper towel.

Laurel mentally rolled her eyes at the mention of Stuart's younger sisters. They were nice enough and fun to be around, although they could be a little silly at times. Heather had just graduated from college —tall, slender, and very beautiful. And boy, did she know it. Carrie was her faithful sidekick, one year younger and slightly more animated in personality.

"The whole month, huh?" Laurel picked up the window cleaner bottle and read the label. "Hey, are you sure you should be breathing this stuff? Is it good for little Junior?"

"I'm not breathing it, sister dear. I'm cleaning with it, and it's fine. And don't call him or her little Junior. I'll get in the habit of it, and I'll never be able to think of a name. Mrs. Pendleton's already trying to get me to commit to traditional family names like Opal and Harvey."

"Junior's better than those," Laurel quipped.

"So, the girls are arriving in a couple days." She led Laurel through the hallway to one of the bedrooms. "I'm going to put them in here. They'll have to share because James will be in the other guest room here." She walked further down the hall. "This is the master bedroom, and it has a bath off to the side. Isn't it great?" Virginia's voice was full of excitement.

Laurel nodded, smiling at her sister. She put an arm around her shoulders and squeezed. "I'm glad you're here."

Virginia returned the one-armed hug. "You know, I worry about you up in that cabin all by yourself, especially given Mom's problems. I don't want that to happen to you."

"Oh, don't worry about me." Laurel waved her hand in dismissal. "I've been told that as long as I'm growing and changing, it's not the same as hiding away."

Virginia flopped down on the bed. "But are you growing and changing? Or is it just more comfortable to stay here?"

"Mom and Dad need me, and I hate to spend too much time away from home until Spring is out on her own. She's going to need help with college applications and all that. We both know Mom is no good with those things—she's already crying about her baby leaving home. And Dad doesn't do details—you know how he is. He's got so much on his plate with the marina..."

"It's that bad?"

"Well, I mean, he's scraping by, but the marina is old, and things need repairing. The restaurant needs a menu update and new décor. There are only so many times I can re-paint the walls to freshen up the look a little bit. It's just all starting to look shabby, especially compared to the new place they're building across the lake."

"Sounds like you've got a lot to keep you busy then. If I were a good daughter, I'd help more. But now I've got the move to deal with, and the practice to keep track of, and the dental office to re-do—"

"And the baby in the oven," Laurel reminded her.

"Well, there's that."

With a shrug, Laurel went on. "It's fine. You gotta do what you gotta do." *Besides, it's not like I have anything better to do.* She tried not to let bitterness creep into the back of her mind.

Virginia rolled over onto her back. "It's a risk, you know, moving back here. Not a financial risk—I think the dental practice combined with the orthodontics Stuart wants to develop will be a great success, but I don't want to get embroiled in all that Mom and Dad mess like you have. I don't mean to criticize you—honest, I don't. It's just—it's just not for me. I can't deal with them."

Laurel shrugged. She'd like to get out of that mess, too, but somebody had to help, and somehow it had fallen to her. She supposed it was just her lot in life.

CHAPTER 14

The next week saw the arrival of James Marshall at the lake. Virginia and Stuart were excited about seeing their old childhood friend, and Carrie and Heather felt all the anticipation that the appearance of a rich, single guy could bring. Plans were made for a celebratory dinner at the Brownsboro Inn, the nicest restaurant in the nearby town. There they would meet up with Susan and Gary, James's sister and brother-in-law, who had recently moved to the area. Laurel dreaded that first meeting with James, but it ended up going well enough.

She waited along with Stuart's sisters, who were already on the deck at Pendleton Place, as they were beginning to call it. Before long, they spied a black BMW snaking its way up the mountain road. The excitement from the girls was palpable, but Laurel kept her emotions hidden from view.

"I wonder if he's as handsome as his picture in that magazine Stu showed us," Carrie wondered aloud. "I don't remember him being that attractive when we were growing up. Didn't he used to clean tables at your father's restaurant, Laurel?"

"Hmm? Oh, yes, he did—one summer."

"Was he good looking then?"

"I suppose."

"Well, you know they always stage the photos in magazines to put people to their best advantage." Heather sniffed. "But I always say money makes men better looking."

Carrie laughed.

Heather went on. "I'd be more interested in whether he has any personality at all or if he's just one of those engineer geeks who can only talk about computers and Star Trek."

"He's not like that," Laurel said in a quiet voice.

"Oooh, really?"

"He's a musician, actually—a guitarist. The software his company developed records and mixes music tracks."

"How interesting," Carrie remarked. "Maybe he'll play the guitar for us. I wouldn't mind having a millionaire serenade me around a summertime campfire." She giggled.

They heard the crunch of gravel down below and the slam of a car door. The sound of men's voices and warm greetings drifted up when Stuart and James saw each other for the first time in several years. The door below opened and banged shut. Laurel felt her heart beating against her ribs, but she forced a neutral expression and followed the girls inside to face her past.

"Heather! Carrie! Laurel!" Stuart called up the stairs. "Come say 'hi' to James. The prodigal friend has returned!"

The girls bounded forward with welcoming embraces and exuberant hellos.

"And of course, you remember Laurel."

James stepped around the girls, and Laurel had to stop herself from gasping. He looked good—really good. He'd always been tall, but he had filled out the way men do in their late twenties. His shoulders were broader than she remembered, but his hair was still that rich brown color. She had forgotten how pretty it was. He looked at her with those captivating eyes she remembered so well, but in them, she saw only intellectual interest.

There was no anticipation, no emotion. Well, that was to be

expected, she told herself. He had surely moved on years ago from whatever attachment he had to her.

With a brief smile, he said hello, and made a vague "good to see you again" comment. Then he turned to Stuart. "Where do you want me to put this bag, Stu?"

"Oh, here, I'll take it. Heather, get James a beer, would you? I'm going to go see what's keeping Virginia."

"Sure thing." Heather took James's arm and led him into the kitchen area.

"Wait till you see the view from the deck. Laurel and I were just talking about it when you drove up."

Laurel watched him as he walked, but she stayed put, unable to follow. She sat down on the couch with a heavy thud.

Stuart came down the hall a couple of minutes later and gestured to her. "Hey, Sis, come here a sec."

"What's wrong? Is she okay?"

"She's sick. It's like morning sickness but not in the morning. It isn't a problem normally, but today seems to be a bad one. I guess she overdid it with the cleaning or something." He glanced over at the clique in the kitchen.

"I'd stay with her myself but… It's just that with James coming in today and the dinner at Brownsboro tonight…" He hesitated.

Laurel got the hint, and to be honest, it was fine with her to stay and play nursemaid to Virginia. It would have been much more difficult to sit at a dinner table with James when he seemed so disinterested in her.

"I'll stay with her. It's not a problem."

"Oh man, that would be great. I hate to ask you because you don't get to go out that much." He stopped short, looking awkward and a little embarrassed by his last remark. "I didn't mean that the way it sounded."

"I don't mind. If Virginia's fine with it, I'm fine. Just bring me a slice of cheesecake, would you?"

"Sure, sure, I'll do that. Thanks a million, Laurel. I know it's just morning sickness, and it's normal, but it's unusual for her to be sick, and this is all still uncharted territory for me." He paused. "Umm, this situation isn't too weird for you, is it? I mean, James being here. I know you guys dated for a while back in school, but it was a long time ago, so—"

"I'm sure it will be fine," she said lightly, turning away. "I better go let Virginia in on the plan for tonight."

"What's going on?" Carrie asked.

Stuart walked over to them. "Virginia's not feeling well. I didn't get a chance to tell you before, James, but we're expecting."

"Oh!" James's voice showed his surprise. "Well then, congratulations." He set down his beer, shook Stuart's hand, and clapped him on the shoulder.

"Thanks."

"She's okay, isn't she?"

"Yeah, she's okay—just that morning sickness thing. Or I guess evening sickness in this case. Laurel's going to stay with her."

The way the four of them turned and looked at Laurel as a unit made her feel like she was on display in a glass case. She gave them a weak smile.

"Aww," Carrie whined. "Laurel, that's too bad." She turned to James. "We love getting together with Laurel. She always has such interesting stories to tell about life in the mountains."

"Oh?" James answered nonchalantly, looking over at Laurel's flushed face.

Heather interjected. "But maybe you'll have some interesting California stories for us. Have you ever met any celebrities?"

"A few, a very few," he said in a self-deprecating tone. "I'm sure my stories aren't all that exciting."

"Oh, I'm sure they are," Heather said, gushing. "You've done so many things and been so many places."

Stuart rolled his eyes and took a swig of his beer. "Damn, girls. Don't scare him off his first day here. We'll never get him to come back if you put him on the spot like that. Don't worry, James, they do this to everybody."

Heather and Carrie giggled.

Laurel looked past them and caught James staring at her closely. After a second, he spoke up. "You're sure you don't mind staying?"

"No, it's fine. Stuart's bringing me a great dessert. I'll just go get Ginny some saltines and a glass of water. You all have fun, okay?"

She left the room a little abruptly then, but she didn't trust her expression to stay neutral much longer.

STU, James, and the girls arrived back at the house about ten thirty. Laurel heard the car door slam, and laughter drifted in the open door as they made their way up the stairs to the great room. She and Ginny smiled at each other and shook their heads.

"Hush, you two. Ginny's probably sleeping," Stuart admonished.

"Oops, sorry." Carrie lowered her voice as she led them into the room. "Oh, there she is. She's not asleep at all. How are you feeling, Ginny?"

"Better. I think I was just tired." Ginny put down her magazine. "Did you have a good time?"

"Great time, wasn't it, James?" Heather looked at him with admiration.

"Yeah, good time." He directed his attention to Laurel. "My sister was sorry she missed meeting you—and seeing Virginia again, of course. She hopes maybe you two will be able to get together with her another time."

"Oh, okay," Laurel said, surprised.

"She's a fan of yours, as it turns out. She went on and on about your pottery."

"I see."

"And she wanted to talk to you about it. So...maybe some other time."

"I'd like that."

Virginia stood up and stretched. "I think I'm turning in," she began, then stopped suddenly when the phone rang. "Who could that be this time of night?"

Laurel glanced over as her sister answered the kitchen phone and then plopped down at the counter. When she looked back around, she found James watching her again.

Quickly, he looked away and said to Stuart, "I'm pretty tired from the drive down here. It won't offend you if I turn in a little early, will it?"

"Oh no, not in the least," Carrie replied. Her face told the whole story: She was completely besotted with James Marshall.

Ginny covered the receiver with her hand and beckoned her sister. "Laurel, come talk to her." Her impatience came through loud and clear.

"Who?"

"It's Spring. When she found out you were here, she only wanted you." Laurel moved to take the phone, and Ginny rejoined the group in the living room. Laurel spoke to her sister in low, soothing tones, and after a few minutes, she hung up and made her way to the couch.

"Everything okay?" James asked.

She nodded, careful not to meet his gaze. "Mama's"—she paused —"she's not feeling well." She turned to her sister. "You know how it upsets Spring when she gets like that."

Ginny just sighed and gave Stuart a resigned look.

"I'm sure she'll be fine tomorrow," Laurel cut in. "I'll stop in on my way home and check on them."

James cleared his throat. "Well, good night, I guess."

"'Night," Heather and Carrie chorused.

"See you in the morning," Stuart said. He reached for Ginny's hand and led her out of the room.

After they left, the sisters plopped down on either side of Laurel, alternating excited whispers between them.

"He's the cutest thing!" Heather began.

"I'll second that," Carrie added. "Not a drop of geek in him."

"He told us all about California and all the things he's done there— hiking and sky-diving and touring Napa Valley."

"And he told us about living in Nashville before he went to California. Why didn't you tell us that? He said you knew about it."

"Um, I don't know. It didn't occur to me, I guess. It was so long ago, wasn't it?"

"Long enough, I suppose," Heather went on. "You know, he said he wouldn't have known you, Laurel, if he met you on the street. He said you'd changed that much."

"He did? I don't think I look that different."

"A little older maybe," Carrie said soothingly.

Ouch, that hurt! Laurel knew Carrie wasn't trying to insult her. She just said thoughtless things sometimes. She had gotten to know the Pendleton girls fairly well, especially since Stuart had married her sister, and for the most part, she liked them. Sometimes, though, they just acted…young.

"Well"—Laurel put her hands on her knees and stood up—"I guess I'll head back up to my cabin in the hills."

"Don't forget your cheesecake," Heather said helpfully. She handed Laurel the box.

"Thanks. I'll see you all. Have fun at the lake. Don't hound the company too much."

"Good night, Laurel," they said in unison.

Laurel walked out to her old Jeep sitting in the driveway. She felt a little prickle on the back of her neck as if she was being watched. When she turned around and glanced up at the house, she expected to see Heather or Carrie there, but there was no one—only the movement of a curtain from one of the guest bedroom windows.

CHAPTER 15

Over the next few days, Laurel and James were often in each other's company. The culmination of the week found them all on the Pendleton family houseboat cruising around the lake to dock at the state park picnic grounds for a cookout. Laurel had staked out a spot on the roof where the wind could drown out the sound of girlish laughter and James's easy-going speech from below. He was charming the pants off the Pendleton girls—well, Laurel hoped not literally, for their sakes. What would happen to sisterly affection if he showed an interest in one of them over the other or, heaven forbid, both at the same time? Laurel clung to the little bit of resentment that thought produced. It would do her no good to let herself become enamored of James again. She was a great believer in karma and timing, and her time—her chance for a future with James Marshall — had come and gone.

As if summoned by her thoughts, James's head popped over the edge of the roof. She couldn't see his eyes behind the Ray Ban Aviators he wore, but he stopped, and his body stiffened.

"Oh, sorry. I didn't realize anyone was up here."

She started to reply, but he cut her off.

"I was just looking for a quiet place to read. I'll go somewhere else though."

And then, he disappeared down the ladder.

It was obvious he was avoiding her. What she didn't know was why. He couldn't still be angry after all that time, so it must be indifference. Maybe it was just too awkward to socialize with an old flame. Maybe he was congratulating himself on escaping and not tying himself down. After all, his life apparently turned out better without her, just as she predicted. Would he ever have gone to California if she had been with him? Would he ever have gone back to school or had the time to start EMP? Now he probably saw what he'd gained by going on alone.

Seeing him in person confirmed what she'd presumed after reading about him. He had become a fascinating, amazing guy. It was to his credit that he'd managed to pull himself up from nothing. A self-made man like him was a rarity in this day and age. *No, Laurel,* she berated herself, *stop thinking about how much you admire him. You're supposed to be indifferent to him—the way he's indifferent to you.*

They arrived at the picnic grounds in the late afternoon. Stuart and Laurel built a fire while the rest of the party carried coolers of food off the boat and over to the picnic table. James volunteered to start the charcoal grill, and Ginny arranged chairs around the campfire.

"I'm glad they have the grill here," James said as he lit the coals. "I wouldn't want to try cooking on the open fire pit."

"I've done it both ways. The grill's much easier though." Laurel fished a beer out of the cooler and headed over to the fire to tend the flames.

"Sit here, James." Carrie patted the chair between her and Heather. "We want to ask you about earthquakes in California." He chuckled and plopped down while Laurel smirked into her beer.

"That was a little lame, Carrie," she murmured to herself.

It seemed the sisters were trying to outdo each other for James's attention. Laurel took a chair beside Ginny and Stu and stretched her long legs out in front of her. James's comment the other night had stung a bit, so she had dressed a little "younger," in cut-off jeans and a tank top, and she'd painted her toenails a dark red that clashed with her hair—just to be a rebel.

James sat between the two girls, grinning like the Cheshire cat, and Laurel couldn't blame him for being flattered by the attention. Although he had matured into a very handsome man, he had spent most of his youth in the shadow of Stuart, who was worldly, charming, and rich by middleclass standards. James had always had his own brand of charm, but he'd never garnered the level of female interest that Stu did with his "Ken doll" looks and his sports car.

He was trying to explain the Richter scale to the girls, when Stuart finally had enough of their foolishness and interrupted.

"So, what are your plans now, James? Are you going to continue working on the EMP now that it's been bought out?"

James took a sip of beer and set it on his knee, staring into the fire for a second before he answered.

"No, the EMP project is over for me. Belenos Music & Media bought it, and they can do what they want with it. I suspect what they want is to shelve it. I can't develop any competing software for five years at least, so most companies aren't interested in hiring me. I'm at a crossroads, I guess. My friend Eric seems to think it's time for me to settle down..." The thought trailed off awkwardly, and James let out a half-hearted chuckle. "I might go back to playing music for a while or designing some other type of software. I don't know."

"Laurel said you were a professional guitarist in Nashville."

"She exaggerates my talent," he said. "It would be more accurate to say I was a factory worker who played around on the guitar on nights and weekends."

"But you brought your guitar with you, right? Will you play for us a little later?"

He shrugged. "If you want. Do any of you play? Or sing?"

"Laurel does both," Carrie piped up. "She sings at her dad's restaurant sometimes and plays the acoustic guitar."

Laurel's eyes went wide. "Just accompaniment chords—nothing spectacular."

"It was spectacular enough for Brian Fisher." Heather waggled her eyebrows.

That brought an instant blush to Laurel's cheeks. "Heather Pendleton! You stop right there!"

James looked at her but aimed his reply at Heather. "Do tell, Heather. This sounds interesting."

"Crosby let it slip, but then he said we had to ask Laurel for the scoop."

"Big-mouth Crosby," Laurel muttered.

Carrie laughed. "Yeah, big-mouth Crosby. So, Laurel, what's the scoop with Brian Fisher?"

Heather's eyes opened wide, and she sat up on the edge of her seat. "I think I remember that guy! He's a real Grizzly Adams type—beard, flannel shirts, the whole bit, right?" She slumped back against her chair. "He's sort of cute in that blue-collar way."

"Yeah," Carrie joined in. "He's a carpenter, a man who'll build you a cupboard or fix your leaky roof."

"He must have been enchanted with your famous rendition of 'Where Have All the Flowers Gone.'"

Laurel rolled her eyes. "I was trying to help my dad drum up some business for the marina. Other people sang too. And that's Dad's favorite song."

"Well, I guess it was Brian's favorite song after that," Heather said, mercilessly teasing her. "Did he wait around after the performance to get your digits?"

"There are advantages to not having a phone," Laurel quipped.

"You still don't have a phone?" James asked, incredulous.

"Did you give him the dreaded 'let's be friends' speech?" Heather asked.

"Or did Crosby and Dylan have to run him off?"

James was smiling, but tension rolled off him.

"He's married to someone else now, and that's the end of it," Laurel insisted.

"I guess he just decided it was time to settle down, kind of like your friend Eric said." Heather shot James a winning smile.

James looked embarrassed, and Laurel was mortified at the direction the conversation had taken.

"Think I'll go see if the coals are ready," she said, and she was off like a shot.

James watched her go. "Shouldn't we go help?" he asked the sisters.

"Oh, Laurel always cooks when we grill out. She's good at it, and she doesn't mind at all."

James said nothing, but a quick look behind her told Laurel he was surveying her backside, she hoped, in appreciation. She swatted a mosquito off her calf, relieved that her shorts did something more for her figure than the hippy-girl skirt she'd worn the other night. It made her feel better to see that at least he noticed her a tiny bit.

She set the burgers on the grill, grabbed another beer, and rejoined the crowd around the fire. Thankfully, the conversation had shifted. Stuart, Virginia, and James were deep in a discussion about software to run billing for medical and dental practices while the Pendleton sisters set out the condiments, chips, and fruit salad.

Laurel checked her grill a couple more times. After several minutes, a swirl of charcoal-scented smoke clouded around her head, and she waved it aside with her spatula. "Burgers are ready," she announced.

The crew gathered around her, filling their plates and grabbing drinks. Heather and Carrie sat down amid an intense conversation about whether stilettos were better than platforms. James approached the grill and held out his plate.

"Worcester or no Worcester?" she asked, transferring the last burgers onto the serving plate.

"Worcester, thanks." His voice was deep and rich and ran down the length of her spine and out her toes. She took his plate and put a burger on it, and when he took it back, his hand brushed hers. She felt a little jolt, and against her will, she looked up. There was confusion in his eyes, and he shifted his weight uneasily from one foot to the other.

"Thank you," he murmured.

"You're welcome."

He gave her a shadow of a lopsided smile, and damned if she wasn't in love with him all over again.

June was going to be a long month.

CHAPTER 16

*L*aurel was in the kitchen when she heard a knock at her front
door. Before she could dry her hands and get to it, the door
opened, and a voice called out, "Hello, is anybody here?"

"Oh, hey, Ginny. I'm in the kitchen. Come on in." Her sister
appeared in the doorway. "What brings you here? You want something to drink?"

"Some water would be great." Ginny accepted her glass with a
smile of thanks. "I hope you don't mind me just popping in like this. I
haven't seen the new kitchen, and I wanted to check out the place
where my sister spends so much of her time." She looked around. "I
really like what you've done here. You're so...artistic."

Laurel rolled her eyes good-naturedly at the joke. "Well, I am an
artist. But thanks." She indicated a chair and sat down. "So, how's it
going with your houseguests?" Laurel asked, trying to sound disinterested.

"Well, we're down by one."

"Oh?"

"Yes, James is gone."

Laurel swallowed hard and tried to think of something to say that
wouldn't convey the strange combination of relief and disappoint-

ment she felt, but Virginia continued before she could come up with anything.

"Yeah. He rented a cabin over near his sister's for the rest of his stay."

"I thought he was only staying a couple of weeks."

"He told me he likes it here. He likes being able to see his sister, and since he has no job to get back to, he's talking about hanging around for the rest of the summer."

"Oh?" Laurel's ambivalence instantly changed to apprehension. She was not looking forward to running into James Marshall all summer.

"Yes. And he's invited his former business partners for a visit. They're arriving next week."

"Really?"

"Yeah. The married one, Eric, he's only staying for a couple of weeks, but the other one might stay a little longer."

"That's nice."

"Laurel, can I ask you something?" Virginia sat down and fidgeted, turning her water glass in circles on Laurel's tiny kitchen table.

"I suppose you can ask. Do I have to answer?"

Virginia smiled. "Not if you don't want to, but after watching the two of you the other night at the cookout, I'm beginning to wonder what happened between you and James. I was gone that summer, but Stuart says you guys were always together. He thought James really had it bad for you. But then he just up and moves to Nashville the next winter and then to California a couple years after that, and Stu doesn't hear from him for ages. And now, all of a sudden, he turns up again. Do you think he came back to see you?"

"No. In fact, I'm pretty sure I was the last person he wanted to see."

Virginia looked at her and waited.

"We had a...relationship, I guess you'd call it. He wanted me to move with him to Nashville."

Virginia's eyebrows went up. "Wow, I had no idea it was that serious. Why didn't you tell me?"

Laurel shrugged. "Like you said, you were gone, and after things with him ended, what would be the point in discussing it?"

"I don't know—for a sister's sympathy, maybe?"

"I guess I just didn't want to talk about it much."

"That sounds just like something you'd say. You're so stoic." Virginia gave her sister a sad smile. "So, he asked you to go to Nashville, and you turned him down."

"Well, not at first. I said I would, but a few months later, when I told him it was impossible, he was pretty upset with me. He thought I had led him on—and maybe I did, I don't know. But mostly, I think I lied to myself more than him. Part of me wanted to go, but..." She huffed, impatient with the tenacity of her feelings. "What did I know? I was eighteen years old and in the middle of my first year in college. He was so headstrong, so sure he was doing the right thing, and everything would work out fine, but I wasn't convinced. I mean, he quit school and moved to a new city where he didn't know anyone or anything. It just seemed so...reckless. I was afraid, I suppose, and then Mama said—"

"You told Mama? What were you thinking?" Virginia's eyes were round.

"Well, I was planning to move away, so I had to tell them. Daddy was unhappy about it, although he never really said that in so many words. But Mama, she didn't hold back."

"What did she say? I can't imagine."

"The gist of it was that I was throwing myself away at eighteen. And if I left school, I'd never go back and finish my degree. And that one day twenty years later, I'd be stuck on a mountain somewhere with five children and no prospects for anything better."

Virginia winced. "Ouch. Did Dad hear that?"

"No, thank goodness."

"I've never heard her speak that strong an opinion about anything."

"Me neither. That's one of the reasons it worked. I listened to her instead of James, and he never forgave me for it."

"Now I feel guilty. I didn't mean to make things awkward for you. I had no idea you two were that involved. Why didn't you tell me all this when Stuart invited him to stay with us?"

"Well, it was kind of late by the time I knew anything about it. Besides, he's Stuart's good friend. How could I deny you all a reunion with him? Just because of my mistake." She fiddled with the box of tea bags.

Ginny reached over and covered her hand gently. "So, it was a mistake? You loved him?"

"Oh, I don't know." Laurel got up and walked over to the sink. "It doesn't matter now. He probably hates me. He can barely stay in the same room with me. Not a very auspicious beginning for a reunion of two star-crossed lovers, is it?"

"Hate isn't the opposite of love, Laurel," Virginia said, using her quiet, big sister's tone.

"It's not?"

"No, the opposite of love"—Virginia stood up and took her glass to the sink—"is indifference."

Laurel leaned back against the counter, absorbing those words, remembering how he'd reacted to finding her on the roof of the houseboat. If indifference was the opposite of love, that episode certainly illustrated it.

Virginia's voice broke in on her thoughts.

"Well, I best get back. Stuart will worry. He worries all the time now. It gets a bit annoying."

Laurel shook her head. Virginia was used to doing her own thing on her own schedule. A baby was undoubtedly going to change her life! "Yeah, I need to get some work done too. Gotta get ready for that Woodland Arts Festival this week." She paused. "Virginia?"

"Yes?"

"Don't worry about me. I'll be fine."

"Yes, I know. You're always fine. I just wish you could be happy too."

Laurel couldn't think of a thing to say.

Virginia sighed. "Okay, I'll mind my own business now." She leaned over and kissed her quiet little sister's cheek. "See you later,

Sis." Then she turned the opposite direction and headed out the front door.

Laurel sat down at the table and tried to concentrate on her art supply catalog, but restlessness overtook her. She tossed the catalog aside, and went out to her studio, getting out a lump of clay and dumping it on the potter's wheel. As it turned, and her hands worked the clay, she let her mind wander. Usually, pottery took her on a soothing journey, but reliving her history with James had left her unsettled, and instead, she traveled back in time to the conversation that had forged the direction of her life...

LAUREL WATCHED as her father stalked toward the front door of the house.

"Where are you going, Walter?" Mrs. Elliot asked in agitation.

"To the marina." His reply was terse, and he glared at Laurel as he went. Once the door shut behind him, Mrs. Elliot turned on her daughter.

"Now, look what you've done. You've upset your father."

"I'm sorry he's upset."

"Well, I'm upset too." Her mother went over to the sink and started on the breakfast dishes. "I knew it was a mistake letting that boy stay with you last winter. Your father should have run him off then, and we wouldn't be dealing with this problem now."

Laurel's mouth gaped.

"Did you think we didn't know? Did you think no one saw you shacking up with him at your grandparents' cabin for three weeks? I told your father he should intervene, but he just said you had to sow your wild oats like any other young person. Now look where we are." She rinsed a handful of silverware and dropped it in the dish drainer.

"Mama, I love James, and he loves me. We've been planning this for six months now. I finished out my first year, and I can transfer to a school around Nashville. He says—"

"He says, he says. He'll say a lot of things, Laurel. Young men are just like that."

"He's not like that." Laurel's voice was quiet but steady. She picked up a dishtowel and began drying the plates in the drainer. "I wish you'd get to know him before you said those kinds of things."

"I know his type. He came to dinner that night, and I talked to him then."

"One evening, Mother. You can't get to know someone in one evening."

Mrs. Elliot sighed and put down her dishrag. She took the towel from Laurel and dried her hands, then took her daughter's hands in her own and led her to the kitchen table.

"I know you think you understand everything. You've basically raised yourself since you were seven years old. By the time you were twelve, I didn't think I had anything left to teach you. But I know something about this, so please, please, hear me out."

Laurel said nothing, but she nodded reluctantly.

"I've been where you are now, Mountain Laurel. I met someone when I was eighteen years old. It was 1970, and I was waiting tables, planning to go to college in the fall. He had just graduated from the university and was staying here with his uncle and aunt for the summer. He was going to graduate school to be a professor.

"Almost every morning, he came into the diner where I worked— got a cup of coffee and a stack of hotcakes and sausage." Mrs. Elliot's eyes were far away, remembering. "That man was everything I thought I wanted: handsome and friendly and smart. I was shy and quiet, and he seemed perfect for me. Lord, I was a fool for him. We had this incredible, whirlwind romance.

"When the summer was over, I discovered I was pregnant."

Laurel sat, shaking her head in disbelief. That smitten, naïve girl her mother described just couldn't be the tired, haggard-looking woman sitting in front of her now.

"I didn't know what to do, but he said we should get married. I asked him about his graduate school, and he said he'd go back after a couple of years. I was worried about my college, but he said when the baby got older, I could finish school.

"As you've probably already figured out, that man was your father.

That baby was Virginia Bluebell. The years went by, and he never went back and neither did I, and it became pretty obvious that neither of us was going anywhere when I got pregnant with you. So, I gave up on the idea, but your father was always dreaming about what he was going to do next. He read a hundred books, talked to dozens of people 'in the know,' made all sorts of plans and promises, but in the end, it all came to nothing. When his uncle died and left him this broken-down marina, he promised things would get better, but I've lived this hand-to-mouth existence ever since. So, you see, what they say doesn't mean anything, Laurel.

"Is this what you want? Look around you. Do you want to end up like me?"

"Is it so awful being you?"

Her mother held her gaze for what seemed like an eternity. "Yes," she said simply. "Yes, it is."

Laurel's eyes filled with tears.

"Finish your education, Laurel. Don't follow this boy on a crazy path to nowhere. You might think you love him, but you can't live on love. The only person you can rely on is yourself."

THE POT TOPPLED over on the wheel. Growling in frustration, Laurel scooped up the clay and smashed it into a blob before throwing the whole mess into her scrap bucket.

If only she had met James when she was a senior in college instead of a freshman. If only his parents hadn't gotten a divorce and he had stayed in Dayton or kept in touch with Stu. If only she had been brave enough to defy her parents' wishes. If only she had known that he was planning to leave Tennessee. If only, if only, if only...

If only he had asked her—just one more time.

The sorrow of it made her sick to her stomach. It seemed as though their love was jinxed at every turn, and all the wrong things had happened at the worst times. Why couldn't her life ever work out for the best? And why, when she'd managed to carve out a bearable existence for herself, did he have to show up in the middle of it and remind her of everything she lost?

She put on her day hikers and punched open the screen door. This desperate sadness inside her now was the reason she never told anyone about James, and a stab of resentment tore through her that Virginia's questions had just made her relive it all. She chose a path that would take her through the woods. A nice long walk would help her get her head together. Then perhaps she could be productive for the rest of the afternoon.

CHAPTER 17

*L*aurel decided to take her brothers and her sister Spring with her to the annual Woodland Arts Festival. Dylan always enjoyed the woodworking booths, Spring loved the jewelry, and, of course, Crosby loved to talk to anybody and everybody about the beautiful and competitively priced building lots down by the lake that just happened to be listed by his real estate company.

All kinds of vendors attended the festival. Great local food was available, and it brought together many local artists. Since it was only about an hour and a half drive, Laurel borrowed Dylan's trailer to haul her pottery, shelves, and other paraphernalia, as well as a few of the brochures Crosby had designed for her. She hoped that attending this year would have the added bonus of taking her mind off James Marshall.

But it was not to be. Laurel had no sooner set up her booth and sent Spring off to get a couple of sodas, when she turned to find a woman standing at the next booth looking at her name with interest. While her companion, a tall, broad-shouldered man with a crew cut, talked to the wood-burning artist next door, the woman approached her.

"Good morning," Laurel began, smiling.

"Good morning. Your work is beautiful."

"Thank you. Is there something in particular I can show you?"

"Something for my brother, I think." She chuckled. "He's just moved into a new house down the road from us. It's a temporary arrangement, and I'm trying to get him to stick around permanently. Do you think a housewarming present for a single man is a bad idea?"

"Hmm," Laurel replied. "Let's see. A bachelor might use a big bowl —you know, for chips or pretzels or something. You could get a smaller bowl to hold dip. It would be sort of a set."

"That's a marvelous idea."

"I think I might have something back here." She stepped around the table and looked through a couple of crates. "Ah, here it is. And there's a small one just like it on the shelf there."

The woman took the bowl and turned it in her hands. "Yes, it's lovely and good quality too. Just like the potter." The woman's eyes twinkled in her tanned face. "You're Laurel, aren't you?"

"I am. I'm sorry, but have we met?"

The woman's face broke into a wide smile. "Not exactly, but I do feel as if I know you from your sister Virginia's description and…" She held out her hand. "I'm Susan. Susan Murtowski. My husband and I met your sister when we were buying our house on the lake. Of course, I've known her husband, Stuart, for years—since we were kids really. He's my little brother's oldest friend."

Laurel's eyes flew open wide. "You—you're Susan Marshall," she stammered. "I mean Murtowski, of course. Ginny told me about meeting you, and James said—" She broke off, her stomach dropping. "He said you were living in the area now."

So, this was James's beloved sister. Now that she looked more closely, Laurel could see a family resemblance in the green eyes and the engaging demeanor. She took a deep breath and shook Susan's hand. "It's good to meet you."

Susan's laugh had a musical lilt to it. "Right back at you. I've been waiting quite a while to make your acquaintance, although to tell the truth, we actually have met before."

Laurel tilted her head and smiled, confused. "We have?" She didn't remember Susan ever coming to the Pendletons' boat when they were growing up.

"Gary and I came to an art show where you were displaying your pottery last year in Tennessee."

"Really?"

Susan nodded. "I didn't make the connection then. I—" She stopped again. "Well, I finally put it all together when Ginny and I were talking."

"I wish I remembered meeting you. The Tennessee show was a madhouse."

"There were at least a couple of thousand people there that day. I'm not surprised you don't."

"Well then, I guess it's good to meet you again."

"I bought one of your vases at that fair, and I just love it. Not only is your work beautiful, it's durable too. You know, Midwestern girls like me appreciate that. We have that practical streak."

Laurel blushed at the compliment. "You're very kind."

"Do you have any new designs this year? I might just need to get something for myself as well."

"Oh, of course." Laurel indicated her display, stepping back and gesturing with her hand. "Look all you like and let me know if you have any questions."

After a few minutes, Laurel asked, "So, how do you like the lake area? Are you settling in?"

Susan looked her directly in the eye—the way James used to. "We absolutely love it. After Gary retired from the Navy, we wanted a place to put down some roots. Kentucky is close to my parents"—she leaned over and whispered in a knowing tone—"but not too close, if you know what I mean."

So, she was blunt like James too. "I think I might."

"And Gary doesn't have any family still living, so anywhere quiet was fine with him. Now, if only we could get my brother somewhere on this side of the country, I'd be happy as a clam."

Susan turned and called to the man who was with her. "Gary! Come meet Ginny Pendleton's sister."

A man who was maybe ten years older than Susan strode up to the booth. He was rugged in appearance, not especially handsome, but he had a smile that was warm and friendly. His graying hair was cropped close to his head, apparently a holdover from his years in the military, and his sky-blue eyes were striking in his weathered face. He held out his hand and gave Laurel a hearty handshake.

"Hello!" he said in a booming voice. "Gary Murtowski."

"Laurel Elliot."

"Ah yes, the famous Laurel Elliot. Your sister sings your praises, and my wife loves your work."

"Thank you."

"You from around here?"

"No, Gary," Susan cut in. "Remember? She lives in our neck of the woods, in a cabin above Uppercross Hollow."

"That's right, that's right. You're a neighbor. I have to say, I really like the neighbors around our new place. Nice people." He winked at her. "Present company included. My brother-in-law, James, said he knew you, but he neglected to say how pretty you are."

"Gary, you're an awful flirt! You're embarrassing her."

"Aw, surely not," he insisted.

Laurel laughed through her blushes. "Don't be too hard on him, Susan. It's not hard to make me self-conscious—really no challenge at all."

Spring returned then, handing Laurel her soda and her change. The Murtowskis introduced themselves and began a conversation with Spring about her college plans. Normally, Spring was tight-lipped with adults, but Susan and Gary's engaging personalities made it easy to speak with them, regardless of the age gap.

Susan turned to her husband. "Best drag out your wallet and pay for my purchases, Gary. I'm sure Laurel has other buyers that need her attention." She nodded toward a clique that was making its way up the row.

"Oh, no please," Laurel replied. "Consider them a welcome gift."

"Nonsense," said Gary. "We insist. We remember the struggling artist scenario. James lived it for a couple of years, didn't he, my dear?"

Susan nodded. "I worried about him constantly. Still do, but that's what big sisters are for. You know how that goes, being a big sister yourself."

Laurel put her arm around Spring's shoulders. "Yes, I can relate." She turned to her money box. "Here, let me get you a receipt."

As she wrote out the slip, Susan invited her to have lunch one day next week. They set a date, and in a whirl, the Murtowskis were gone.

Laurel sat down with a thud, her face flushed and her heart beating rapidly.

"You okay?" Spring asked.

"Just hot." Laurel reached over, grabbed her soda off the table, and took several swigs.

After that, the sisters sat under the canopy tent, fanning themselves with programs and listening to the murmur of conversations as people strolled by.

Laurel answered questions from a group of women who stopped to look and, therefore, was completely unaware that she was being watched. Spring nudged her and surreptitiously pointed to a man standing a couple of booths down, looking intently at the two of them.

"Who is that, Sis?"

"I'm not sure." Laurel squinted. "Hmm, I know the face, but I can't quite place him. He's too old to be a classmate. Maybe he docks at the marina? Or used to?"

"Oh, shit, he's coming over here."

"I wish you wouldn't use that kind of language. It isn't becoming in a girl your age."

Spring rolled her eyes. "Whatever. *Oh, darn,* here he comes."

Laurel pursed her lips in maternal disapproval, but she was stopped from any further comment by the man's approach.

"Laurel Elliot. I can't believe it. It is you." His face broke into a dazzling smile, and he held out his hand. "I'm Cooper Edwards, a friend of your father's from his university days, but I also teach history at Benton College."

"I thought I recognized you. How are you, Dr. Edwards?"

"Cooper, please. No need to be so formal." He clasped her hand in both of his. "I'm fine, just fine. And you're doing well, I see."

"Yes."

"How's your father?"

"He's good—still at the marina of course."

"I haven't seen him in ages. I remember when he wrote me you were coming to Benton, but I never had you in class."

"I'm not much of a history buff, I'm afraid. I took the bare minimum requirements, and I was out of there. I think I had Dr. Pinehurst for those."

"Yes, well, you're forgiven if you spent your time learning to make this beautiful pottery. May I look?"

"Oh, of course." She gave him the spiel about lead-free glazes.

"Are you living here in Lexington now?" he asked, turning a pitcher over and looking at the price on the bottom of it.

"No, I'm still living in the same area where my family is. In fact, this is my younger sister, Spring."

"Hello, Spring, how are you?" He gave her a friendly but disinterested nod.

"Yeah. Hi."

"And my brothers are around here somewhere."

"Ah, yes—the mischievous twins. I've heard some great stories about them."

Laurel laughed politely and took in the appearance of her father's friend while he looked over her work. Cooper Edwards was handsome for an older man. About her height or maybe a wee bit taller, his dark hair was trimmed short and streaked elegantly with gray at the temples. A goatee and wire-rimmed glasses gave him a scholarly appearance. He was fit—he looked like he might be a runner, and his slender hands had a manicured, well-kept look to them.

"I think I'll take this one." He held a pitcher out to her. "It's lovely."

"Thank you. It's one of my favorite designs, too. I love the blues and greens in it."

He fished out his wallet and paid her in cash. "I'll have to get down there to see your father sometime soon. You'll tell him I asked after him, won't you?"

"I will. I'm sure he'd be happy to hear from you," she said in an absentminded manner as she wrapped and bagged his purchase.

"Well, take care then." He took her hand in both of his and winked at her. "It certainly was good to see you again."

"Bye." Laurel stood and watched as he walked away, looking once over his shoulder and tossing her a final charming smile.

"Well, he seemed nice." She turned back to her pad of receipts and put the carbon between the next two sheets of paper.

"I didn't like him." Spring wrinkled her nose in disdain.

"Why not? He was friendly."

"He creeps me out."

"Oh, Spring, you're just being obstinate. He's a friend of Daddy's."

"Hmm," Spring said noncommittally. "Whatever…"

"Boy, I'm starting to hate that word," Laurel mumbled under her breath.

"Who was the old dude holding your hand?" Crosby bounded up and picked up an orange and red bowl. "Oooh, I like this one. I haven't seen it before."

"He said he's a friend of Dad's from school, and he teaches at Benton."

"An old prof of yours, then?"

"No, I wasn't ever in his classes."

"How did he know you?"

"Well, my name is on the front of the table. And I think I met him once or twice a long time ago."

"You doing any good today? Sold any dishes?"

"Yeah. How 'bout you? You get any leads on prospective landowners?"

"Got several interested in the new development that's opening up across the lake—you know, next to the newer, bigger marina. Gave out a bunch of my cards too. Maybe something will come of it."

"We can hope."

On the drive home, as Crosby and Dylan slept, and Spring buried her nose in a book, Laurel considered her new acquaintances. What different feelings they provoked in her! Susan and Gary were very nice but stirred up a fevered kind of anxiety inside her. It was hard to talk to them without constantly remembering their connection to James, but with time, maybe she could overcome that. She was glad she'd met them and could see why James was so fond of them. Like him, they were good people—forthright, plainspoken, and yet, kind too.

In contrast, Cooper was a bit of an enigma, and somehow, that also drew her interest. Her father would be glad she had spoken with Dr. Edwards. She believed they once had been great friends although, over time, they had drifted apart.

Laurel had to admit she was charmed by the man. He was pleasant, well mannered, and probably quite interesting to talk to. She wondered though—he had asked after her family but hadn't mentioned any family of his own.

But that intriguing train of thought was interrupted when Dylan woke up and put in a cd, and the two of them had a great time belting out eighties tunes all the way home.

CHAPTER 18

*T*he next weekend, Laurel went out on Dylan's boat with Ginny, Stuart, and her brothers. As Dylan steered past a couple of jet skis and a pontoon, a sudden shout from Stu startled her out of the pleasant lethargy brought on by the sun, the drone of the motorboat, and the wind in her face.

"Hey, Dylan, turn the boat around! It's James."

Laurel's eyes popped open and she squinted in the direction Stu pointed. Another boat bobbed in the wake and Laurel's eyes were immediately drawn toward one of the boaters, shirtless and leaning over the stern, pulling in a ski rope. He turned in response to the shout and held up his hand in greeting. James had developed quite an outdoorsy look to him since he'd arrived, and Laurel thought it suited him. She turned her attention to the rest of the group and saw two men and a woman she didn't recognize, but it was difficult to discern their features given the distance. Laurel surmised they could only be the famous EMP think tank and found herself very curious about the people who knew more about the man James had become than she did. She was interested—but undeniably apprehensive—when Dylan indicated a small beach where they could all meet up.

They tied up at a little dock floating just a few feet from an area of brown sand, flat enough to hold a few chairs and maybe a little hibachi grill.

"Hey, Stu, imagine meeting you here!" James came up and the two shook hands, James reaching up to clap him on the shoulder. "Hi, Virginia," he nodded. He looked at the rest of the party. "You guys need to come over and meet the California crew."

He led them over, and Stu whistled. "Nice boat, James."

"Oh, it isn't mine. I rented it for a couple of weeks. Not much use for it when it's just me, but I thought it might come in handy while I had guests. Had to show them the best of the area, and a boat's the best way to do it."

He turned to his friends.

"Stuart, this is Eric Harville and his wife Millie, and this is John Benwick. Guys, meet my old buddy Stuart Pendleton. This is his wife, Virginia, and her brothers, Dylan and Crosby Elliot, and her sister Laurel."

Eric startled at Laurel's name and cast a quick surreptitious look between her and James. Then he stepped forward and held out his hand to her. He was an average-looking guy with a pleasant aura about him. "It's nice to meet you." He turned to the others and shook hands with them as well. "This is quite a big crowd for just one family," he remarked.

"We have another sister too," Laurel replied, "but she's seventeen and too cool to come out with us old folks. She went to the movies with some friends."

"Wow, lucky you. I have no sisters or brothers at all—except for these two bucket-heads. Millie and I think of them as the brothers we never had. She's only got one sister."

Millie Harville stepped forward then. "Hi, it's so good to meet you. Any friends of James, you know, and all that. I'll be glad to have a couple of women to talk to finally! I can only stand computer and sports talk for so long before I just wig out!" She was the classic California girl: blonde hair, perfectly straight teeth, bubbly personality, and a cute figure.

"Are you the ones with the baby?" Virginia asked, suddenly interested. "Is he with you?"

"Oh no, we got a babysitter for today." Millie shook her head. "We couldn't bring him out here. All this hot sun and deep water—that life jacket would have just made him miserable. And you know if he's miserable, we're all miserable!" She giggled. "I heard you're expecting your first."

"Yes." Virginia smiled, patting her barely rounded middle.

Millie took her arm, already forming the alliance of two women sharing the experience of new motherhood. "Have you been feeling well? Oh my gosh, I was so sick at first, but then it got better later on."

Laurel, having nothing to contribute to that conversation, turned to the last member of the party.

Of the three men, John Benwick was the most stereotypically "nerdy." Thin and pale, he wore retro-looking, horn-rimmed glasses and stood at the edge of the crowd. His hairline was starting to recede a little, but he was far from unattractive. He was very pleasant-looking in that gentle, beta-male sort of way.

"So, you're Laurel Elliot. James hoped we'd get to meet you while we were here."

"He did?" Laurel was genuinely surprised. She thought James would have done his best to avoid her and make sure his friends did the same.

"He said you were an artist—a potter."

Laurel nodded. "Guilty as charged."

"My fiancée was an artist too. She worked in graphic design, but she painted china as a hobby."

"Yes, I heard that she passed away recently. I'm so sorry."

"Thank you. It's not been an easy time. Fiona was a wonderful woman. The world lost an incredible person when she left it. She was Eric's cousin. Did you know that?"

"No, I didn't."

"Yes, I guess it's one of the reasons the three of us have stayed close, even after the buyout."

"I can imagine. It's good to have friends to lean on in times like that."

"I have a book that Fiona published. A coffee table book of her work. Would you like to see it sometime?"

"Yes, of course I would. Did she have a certain style that she preferred?"

"Her favorites were Asian designs. There's so much Asian influence in art on the West Coast."

Laurel felt a prickle on her neck and turned around, only to see James eyeing her and John as they talked. When he caught her looking, he quirked his lips in a little smile and turned back to his conversation with Crosby.

"James has a lot of fond memories of this area from when he was a kid. He's talked about it a lot over the years. That's why Eric and I couldn't say no when he invited us to join him. I wouldn't be surprised if he decides to settle down here someday."

Laurel groaned inwardly. Watching James settle down with a wife and kids in her back pocket sounded like hell on earth to her. Unable to think of a fitting reply, she was relieved when Virginia called to her.

"Laurel! Hey, come here a sec."

"Excuse me." Laurel smiled apologetically at John, and then went to join her sister and Millie, who had been chatting with their heads together for several minutes.

"Millie has invited all of us for supper tonight. Isn't that nice?"

"That's all right with you, isn't it, James?" Millie called over her shoulder.

"Is what all right with me?" he called back.

"If we all descend on your place for supper," Virginia answered.

"I don't know what you'll find there to eat, but it's fine with me otherwise," he replied.

Millie rolled her eyes in mock exasperation. "We'll stop and get something on the way home—maybe pasta and salad? Oh, can you do pasta, Virginia? Will your stomach take it?"

"It sounds great. What time?"

"About seven thirty or so?"

"We'll be there. Laurel, can you stop at Dad's and pick up a couple bottles of Chianti?"

"You can get wine here? I thought it was a dry county."

"Oh, um, our dad—" Virginia began.

Laurel chimed in. "Dad keeps wine on hand for company. He won't mind a bit."

"I mean, I know *I* can't have any," Virginia went on, her equilibrium returning. Even after all those years, the mention of her dad's contraband still unsettled her. "But I thought everyone else might enjoy some."

"Sounds wonderful. I think I'll splurge on one glass tonight, even though I'm still nursing." Millie giggled again. "Speaking of Trevor, we'd better be getting back soon. You know, time to feed the little prince. If I don't get there in time, I'll be pretty miserable and so will his babysitter."

"I imagine so," Virginia replied. "Thanks for the supper invite. We'll get some wine and dessert together and see you around seven thirty."

"See you then." Millie waved. "Good to meet you, Laurel!"

The rest of the party said their goodbyes and parted ways.

Laurel climbed in the boat and sank down onto the rear seat.

"I can't believe we ran into James," Stuart said. "What luck."

"His friends seem okay," Dylan ventured as he untied his boat and shoved off the dock.

"You'd never know they were all obscenely rich just by talking with them," Crosby put in.

"Well, they haven't always been wealthy," Virginia said, smiling and shaking her head. "They're people just like the rest of us."

"It's a shame Heather and Carrie didn't get to meet them," Stuart went on. "But James wanted me to be sure and bring them tonight. When we get back, I'll tell them. They'll be thrilled, I'm sure."

Laurel kept her thoughts to herself because she couldn't help feeling a little melancholy. She wasn't surprised that James Marshall had picked good friends for himself. It occurred to her that they might have been her friends, too, if she and James had stayed together, but then she pushed that thought out of her mind. It was entirely possible that James never would have met them if he'd stayed with her, and it was entirely possible that even if they had met, she and James might not have stayed together. Would've, could've, should've thinking was not going to serve her well. She had to force herself to remember that.

CHAPTER 19

*L*aurel climbed out of Stu and Virginia's SUV and looked up at James's cabin, conflicting thoughts volleying back and forth in her head. Spending the evening at his house would be awkward, but at least he seemed to be trying distant civility this time rather than ignoring her as he had done the last time they were forced together. He had even said nice things about her to his friends. But then again, he hadn't wasted any time in making sure Stu would call Heather and Carrie and invite them as well to make it, in his words, a "lively party." Obviously, her company was no longer exciting enough for him.

She made her way up the stairs, listening as Heather's and Carrie's exclamations about the house overran every other greeting. As Laurel approached James, arms full of Chianti and store-bought cake, he gestured to the counter without a word.

"Here, let me help you with that." John Benwick sprang forward from his spot behind the kitchen island and took the bottles from her hand.

"Thanks." She reshuffled her load and set the cake on the counter. "I hope I didn't mess up the icing."

"Looks fine to me," John said. He pulled out a corkscrew and opened the wine, pouring a glass for all who wanted one.

"So," Virginia asked, sipping ice water with lemon, "what do you all think of Kentucky?"

"We like it," Millie started. "It's different than San Francisco, that's for sure."

"It's more isolated than we're used to for one thing. I'm not used to having such spotty cell phone service," Eric chimed in. "But I can see why James would like the privacy of his little hideout."

John turned to Laurel to explain. "We've had a little bit too much attention from the press lately."

"Oh? How so?"

"Nothing too intrusive, but there's always a picture or a blurb coming out in some gossip rag or community paper. That's what a little money and a little fame will do. Makes it hard sometimes to know who your friends are."

"That's a shame."

"It was worse after that 'most eligible bachelor' garbage was published last year, especially for James. Eric's married after all, and I was with Fiona for years, but he's had to be more careful. You wouldn't think it, but that really hurt his social life."

Laurel gave James a quick glance. He was preparing the impromptu feast with Millie and laughing at something she said. Her heart gave a little twist at the idea of people taking advantage of him. As she turned back, she noticed Eric Harville giving her a frank, curious stare while he bounced little Trevor on his arm. He smiled and joined them at the bar.

"Now here's a woman who likes her privacy, John. I hear you live in a cabin up in the hills without even a phone."

"Haven't seen the need for one yet, but sometimes I have to admit, it would be handy. I've thought about it, and I'll probably succumb to the technology beast sooner or later."

"No computer, I suppose."

She shook her head, smiling. "No, don't have one of those either."

"You'll have to forgive us geeks. We can't imagine living without one."

Laurel laughed. "Well, I can't imagine living without a potter's wheel, and I'm pretty sure none of you has one of those."

"And you would be right."

"We all have our essentials, don't we?"

"That we do—this little guy is one of mine." He kissed the top of Trevor's bald head. Eric looked around at the crowd gathered in his friend's house. "I think this is going to be an interesting evening. Good food, good wine, good music, and good company—I can't think of anything better. It was right for James to come back here."

"Oh?" Laurel couldn't help her gaze traveling toward the topic of their conversation.

Eric looked directly in her eyes when he spoke. "James has this restless energy about him, like he's always looking around for something—or someone. Since we've been here, I haven't seen that look. It's like he's come home at last."

"The mountains and the lake have a way of doing that," Laurel agreed.

Baby Trevor gurgled and babbled at her. She lifted her hand and he grasped her finger while she cooed to him.

"Do you mind?" she asked Eric, holding out her arms. "Gotta practice for the auntie thing, you know."

"That's my boy." He handed the baby to her. "He likes pretty women."

Laurel walked the baby around, talking to him and pointing out the window. The back of her neck prickled like mad, but she ignored it. She took Trevor out on the deck and settled into the big, cushioned chaise lounge, where he fell asleep on her shoulder within a minute or two. She looked around for Eric, but only saw Millie, who was busy cooking, so she sat back and relaxed, holding the baby and listening to the quiet sounds of birds and insects around her. She dozed a little herself, waking a few minutes later to the sound of male voices rising from beneath the deck.

It was Eric's voice she heard first. "...and available according to

Stuart. Striking woman, great smile—don't you think, James?" There was an unintelligible mumble, and Eric laughed. "Boy, it's fun to watch you squirm a little bit. What do you think, John?"

"If I were in a better place, I might be interested myself. As it is, I'm not ready, so I'll just settle for a good friend. She's easy to talk to and seems really nice. I like your friends, James."

The voices moved out into the yard, out of earshot. The baby stirred, and Laurel went in to ask Millie if she ought to put him down in his crib.

Millie directed her to a playpen in the living room, and then Laurel joined her in the kitchen. "Mmm, the sauce smells wonderful."

"Thanks. It's kind of my specialty. I spent a semester in Italy and learned to make it from the family I stayed with."

A knock at the door, followed by, "Hello? Anybody in here?" announced the arrival of Susan and Gary Murtowski.

"Hey, Susan," Millie called. "Come on in!"

"Hello, everybody!" Gary's voice reverberated through the house.

"Shh! Gary! You might wake the baby!" Susan elbowed him in the ribs.

"Oh, sorry," he said in a stage whisper, while he looked around. "Where's the menfolk?"

Millie laughed. "Outside, last I knew."

"Well then, let me grab myself a beer and join 'em."

Susan watched him go, shaking her head and smiling. "I brought bread." She held up a couple of Italian loaves wrapped in plastic.

"Great, just set it"—Millie looked around—"on the bar, I guess. There's so many of us, we may have to eat buffet style tonight."

"I told James he might need a couple more chairs in the dining room, but you know men. They never think of things like that."

"Oh, by the way, thanks for helping him settle in and get ready for the Harville Invasion. I'm assuming you're the one who made sure we all had clean towels and the kitchen was stocked. He said you were a big help. This is better than any hotel."

Susan waved her off. "Oh, you're welcome. He looked a little over-whelmed when he asked me what he'd need to have on hand for a visiting baby." She set the bread on the counter and turned around. "Laurel! How are you, dear?"

"I'm good. How about you?"

"I so enjoyed our lunch the other day. We went to a tearoom over in Summerville, Millie, and it was marvelous. You'll have to go sometime while you're here."

"Sounds like fun."

Susan turned the wine bottle around and read the label. "Think I'll have a glass of this."

Laurel handed her a wine glass.

"Thanks. Now, what needs doing?"

"You can probably start the water for pasta."

"Can I do something to help?" Laurel asked.

"Hmm. Do you want to cut up the salad veggies?"

"Sure. Just let me wash my hands first." She headed toward the half bath, washed up, and was on her way back when the sound of Heather speaking her name startled her. It seemed opportunities for eavesdropping lurked around every corner.

"I know Virginia worries about Laurel. We all like her so much—it just seems a shame the way she wastes away up in that cabin of hers."

"Well, it's her decision, isn't it?" James replied. "If living up there isn't what she wants, the ball's in her court, and she's the only one who can pitch it." His voice rose a little with agitation. "I refuse to feel sorry for people whose lives aren't what they wanted because they were afraid to take a chance."

"You really think Laurel's just too timid to come down off her mountain?"

"I don't know. Like I said, maybe that's what makes her happy. I'm just saying that there are a lot of people in the world who have their fates handed to them. Makes it hard to feel sorry for the ones who are persuaded to take a path other than the one they really want. I mean, look at Benwick. He got a raw deal that he had no control over. He found the life he wanted and went for it—but then he lost Fiona. Laurel, on the other hand, could have anything she wants if she had the fortitude to stand up and go for it. I know for a fact, she's had at least one chance to leave, and she turned it down flat, apparently without any regrets."

Laurel stepped back, startled and, for the first time in a long time, angry. How dare he gossip like that about her with Heather, of all people—shallow Heather with her school-girl giggle, low-cut halter tops, and shoe obsession.

Furthermore, he voiced a brazen opinion that her situation in life was all her own choosing. What a condescending jerk! And what self-absorbed bitterness to assume that she had not been hurt by what had transpired between them and had no regrets. Well, if he wanted to play the martyr to make himself feel better, so be it. Her eyes stung with tears. Perhaps the old James was really and truly gone for good. Life and the passage of time had changed her, so it stood to reason that he had changed as well—and maybe not for the better. It bothered her, though, to think he still viewed her decision all those years ago as some kind of cop-out, when it was more about caution and being there for her family.

"Look, I'm not saying anything bad about Laurel," James was saying, "or about you all for being concerned about her. That's nice of you. But what I admire is someone who knows what she wants and then goes for it. It's the only way to truly live a full life."

"Oh, I agree with you completely." Heather concurred with the blind enthusiasm of youth and infatuation. "I would much rather be resolute and determined than wishy-washy."

Laurel could hear the smile in his voice. "No one could say you aren't determined, Heather, once you decide on something."

"I'm glad you think so."

"I'm going to get another beer. You want one?" His voice was coming closer and closer, and, before Laurel could gather her wits and get away, she came face to face with him in the hall. He looked startled.

"Oh, excuse me. I didn't see you there."

All she could do was to stare at him wide-eyed and vulnerable. He raised his eyebrow. "You all right?"

"Fine." She pushed past him and down the hall to the kitchen, intent on busying herself with salad and forgetting all about James Marshall.

AFTER DINNER, the dishes were cleared, the baby was put to bed, and the new group of friends decided on a game of poker to round out the evening, using pennies to make the game interesting. Laurel didn't care to play, however, and started making noises about heading home when John Benwick approached her, a large book in his hand and an earnest look on his face.

"I dug this out of my suitcase. It's Fiona's work—the coffee table book of photos she published. Would you like to see?"

"I'd love to see it." She walked around the back of the couch and sat down, propping her feet on the edge of the coffee table and setting the book at an angle on her knees. John sat beside her, pointing out various pieces as she perused the pages.

"That one was a favorite of hers." He indicated a cup with cherry blossoms on it. "She loved flowers."

Laurel ran her finger over the photo. "It's lovely work—so intricate."

"She was very talented." He cleared his throat. "I guess it's a little maudlin to haul this thing around with me wherever I go."

Laurel reached out and patted his shoulder. "You miss her, of course. It's normal that you want to remember."

As they leafed through the book, Laurel could feel a palpable grief simmering just below the surface, leaving her with the distinct impression that John Benwick, understandably, was heading for a significant depression. She wondered whether his friends had seen this tendency in him. He talked incessantly about his fiancée, not always in sadness, but she was almost always the focus of his conversation. After a while, he even seemed to realize this himself.

"You're very kind to listen to me talk about Fiona. It's hard for Eric and James to hear me miss her like this and know they can't do anything to fix it. They loved her too. Everybody loved her. Sometimes I just feel like I'm going to buckle under the weight of losing her. So, thank you. It feels good to talk about it—to get it off my chest."

"I'm convinced it always helps to work through your grief somehow, but people do that in a variety of ways: through talking, through exercise, even through art and music." She paused. "Don't you have any family to talk to, John? Or other friends to help you cope that weren't so close to Fiona?"

"No family to speak of. My father died when I was a teenager, and my mother tries, but she lives far away from me, and we aren't very close. No brothers or sisters, and as for other friends, well, I'm not exactly the best company right now, am I? Making friends seems like an insurmountable challenge."

"It's a challenge worth taking though," Laurel went on. "You might consider a support group. Grieving is a process, and it takes time to move through it. Have you ever heard about the stages of grief?"

"Maybe I heard about it—in college perhaps?"

"I think it would help you to do some reading about it. There are five stages, and we have to progress through them all, although it takes people different amounts of time to move through each one. What you don't want is to get stuck. You want to keep moving through them until you finally reach acceptance, and then you're ready to move on with your life."

"The idea of moving on with my life seems impossible right now, but I know you're right. I really have no other choice."

"And, from what you've told me about Fiona, she was a woman who loved life and loved you, and she would have wanted you to live it to the fullest. She would want you to be at peace."

"You're right about that too. She was a very caring person."

"So, don't you think you owe it to her to try?"

"I suppose when you put it that way, it makes perfect sense."

Laurel was vaguely aware of the irony of counseling someone to get on with his life when she had spent the last eight years pining for a man who had left her far behind.

A burst of rip-roaring laughter assaulted them from across the room, and Eric called out, "What are you two talking about so seriously over there?"

"We were talking about books," Laurel replied, swirling the wine in her glass and drinking the last of it down in one big swallow. She smiled at John, and he sent a tentative smile back, but it was genuine, tinged with humor rather than sadness. It changed his face, and she could see how a woman might fall for him. Feeling that familiar prickle on her neck, she turned to look at the card players. Sure enough, James was watching her curiously, but somehow her earlier trepidation had lessened. Now that she knew what he really thought of her and how he had no use for people like her, she needn't worry about trying to impress him. She felt the stranglehold of anxiety loosen, and she stood up in a decided fashion.

"Is there room for one or two more? I think I'd like to try my hand at this game." She walked over to the table.

"Sure," Eric answered her. "Pull up a chair. We're always ready for another sucker—I mean another player, right, guys?"

"Right," came the chorus of replies.

She beckoned to John and pulled up a couple of chairs. "Well then, somebody deal us in."

THE NEXT MORNING, Laurel was up early, feeling stronger than she had in a long time. Sure, there would always be some regret about James, but having inured herself to his presence for the most part, she felt that perhaps now she could move on. Counseling John Benwick to do the same had reinforced her resolve. It was time to stop hiding on the mountain and go live the rest of her life.

She fixed tea and oatmeal, worked a couple of hours on ideas for new pottery designs, and then decided to head over to the marina. It was Thursday, so she needed to do her father's payroll. While she was at the marina, she would also drop by the Pendletons' houseboat and touch base with Ginny. They had invited her to go along on their outing, but this time, she declined. Despite her newfound resolution regarding James Marshall, she wanted to keep a little distance between them.

The four Pendletons, minus Heather, were at the boat when Laurel arrived. She and James had gone out for a walk along the docks. Laurel hadn't been there five minutes when Virginia commented that she needed some supplies from the marina store and asked Carrie to walk up and fetch them.

"I'll go with you," Laurel volunteered. "I can help with the bags."

They set off and soon saw Heather and James strolling leisurely toward them from another pier. Heather was talking, her hands moving in wide, animated gestures, and James was smiling. He looked relaxed, walking with his hands behind him, wearing khaki shorts, a polo shirt, and topsiders. Laurel's breath caught in her throat as she watched him stroll toward her. He was beautiful, there was no doubt about that, and she couldn't help but look at him.

Carrie called out, and they looked up at the same time.

"Hey!" Heather greeted them cheerfully. "Where are you two going?"

"Just up to the shop to get some things for Virginia."

"Here, we'll join you." Heather took James's arm and pulled him in behind the two women.

They had almost reached the marina store when they met a man heading out to the shore. He stepped aside for the ladies to pass on the narrow dock and started with recognition.

"Well, hello, Laurel."

She looked more closely, and then her face broke into a smile. "Dr. Edwards!"

"Cooper, please." He held out his hand to her and clasped hers in a warm grip, using both his hands to hold her fingers fast.

"Yes, Cooper, of course. What brings you here?"

"Came to see your father. After you and I met up at Woodland, I realized it had been far too long since I'd seen him and decided to make the trek down from Benton. There's really no excuse—me being as close as I am. Shameful I haven't come before."

"I'm sure he was glad to see you." A gust of wind took a wisp of hair over her face, and she brushed it back with a delicate hand. Cooper Edwards' gaze warmed, and his eyes slid down her form with admiration.

"And now I run into you as well—my lucky day. I would have come by to visit you, too, if I'd known how to contact you."

"Oh, I don't have a phone, but you can always reach me through Dad." Laurel rarely told anyone where her cabin was. Anyone close enough to visit her at home knew where it was already.

At last, Cooper noticed her companions and paused, expecting an introduction.

"Oh, these are some friends of mine. This is Carrie and Heather, and this is James."

Cooper nodded hello to the other three. "Well," he said, turning back to Laurel, "I guess I'll be heading out. Have to be back to teach my summer school class by three."

"Of course. Don't let us keep you. I'm glad you came to see Dad though. I'm sure it was the highlight of his week."

Cooper laughed and looked down in an attempt to appear humble, but it rang false on him. "The pleasure was mine, I'm sure."

"Goodbye then."

"Au revoir." He leaned over then and, to her surprise, took her elbow and kissed her cheek. James stiffened slightly, and so did she.

"Who was that?" Carrie asked after he was out of earshot.

"A friend of Mr. Elliot's, of course. Weren't you listening?" Heather replied in an exasperated voice.

"He's cute for an old guy—very distinguished."

"He's a professor at my old college." Laurel, more than a little curious at this spontaneous visit, turned to watch him walk away. "I ran into him last week at a craft fair."

"And he drives all this way to see your dad for the first time in years, and then he drops a little lip love on you?" Carrie said, giving her a speculative look. "Have you been holding out on us, Laurel?"

"Don't be ridiculous. He's my dad's friend and, therefore, mine."

"He didn't look at you like he wants to be friends. I didn't see a ring on his finger either. You should think about it," Carrie said in a sing-song voice.

Laurel waved her off and continued toward the marina store so quickly that she almost didn't catch James's scowl as he watched Cooper Edwards disappear into the distance. After a second, she glanced back, and he followed along behind the girls, but the easy-going expression he sported earlier was long gone.

CHAPTER 20

Because the Harvilles and John Benwick planned to leave for California right after the Fourth of July holiday weekend, Stuart and Virginia decided to invite everyone on a two-day, houseboat excursion. The weather promised to be hot and sunny, so Dylan and James said they would also bring their motorboats along for skiing.

"I'm terrible at skiing," Carrie pouted. "It's all I can do to get up on two skis. I'm not like Stu, who can slalom. Even Heather's better than me."

"I don't know about that," Heather answered. "I haven't skied on one in a few years. I might have forgotten how."

"It's like riding a bike—you never forget," James reassured her. She beamed a wide smile at him.

"Do you ski a lot in California?"

"Yeah, we go when we can."

"I'm sure you'll do fine, Carrie," Virginia encouraged her as she packed a cooler into the ski boat. "I'm going to ride in the houseboat with Stu, Eric, Millie, Susan, and Gary." She counted them on her fingers as she listed each one. "Dylan, Crosby, and Spring will take

Dylan's boat and meet us at the campground, and John's going with James and the girls in his boat. What do you want to do, Laurel?"

"I don't care. I'll ride with you—"

"Why don't you ride with us?" John asked as he approached the boat with a slalom ski under one arm and a couple of life jackets under the other. "You know the lake better than any of us. You can make sure we don't get lost on the way."

"Sure, if you like."

"Great, that's settled, then." John gave her an affable grin. They had developed a comfortable friendship over the last several days, and the results were not lost on Eric Harville.

Yesterday, he had pulled Laurel aside and said low in her ear, "I don't know what you said to John that night at James's house, but whatever it was, I'm eternally grateful to you. He's been better this past week than I've seen him in months—since Fiona got sick."

"I'm sure it was nothing you hadn't said to him before. Sometimes it just takes an objective person from outside the situation to validate a close friend's opinion."

"You're a wonder, Laurel Elliot. Why hasn't some lucky guy snapped you up yet?"

"You know, I wonder that myself sometimes." She laughed, not completely at ease but better. Now that she knew James's true opinion of her, she was doing her best to let go of the past and her lingering feelings of regret. She patted Eric on the shoulder and went into the other room before he could read too much into her expression.

Now, she told herself, she hadn't a care in the world. The boat ride was marvelous, and in the bright morning sunshine, the five of them looked like something out of a beer commercial. John drove with James sitting beside him at shotgun, and the Pendleton sisters stretched out on the side seats, sunning themselves. Laurel lounged along the rear seat, reading the new John Grisham novel. She might not be as sexy as the Pendleton girls were in their bikinis, but she felt pretty enough in her violet one-piece and the gauzy cover-up tied about her waist. That feeling was validated when she saw James's aviator-covered eyes turned her way. His mouth hung slightly open and she cocked her head to the side as if to ask "What?" He closed his lips with a snap, sat up, and turned toward the front, pointing out something in the landscape to John.

On the way to the campground, they all took turns skiing. Laurel had already been out a few times with Dylan and Crosby that summer, so she was fine after a couple of initial spills. John was charged with spotting for a while, but then he grew tired of watching the others and offered to drive.

Carrie did her stint on two skis, just barely making it up and quickly signaling that she was ready to stop. Heather clamored for her turn, so James and John obliged her next.

"I want to slalom ski," she insisted.

"Are you sure you want to try that right off the bat?" James asked while helping adjust the straps of her life jacket. "Two's a little easier, especially if you haven't been on skis in a while."

"No, I can do one." She threw the ski in the water behind the boat and jumped after it. As she wrestled with putting her left foot in, he called to her, "Not so tight on the boot. You want your foot to come out of it if you take a spill."

"I don't like the way it slips around on my foot."

James shook his head but said nothing. John moved forward slowly, tightening up the rope. She grabbed the handle when it reached her, and the boat pulled her slowly through the water.

Laurel and Carrie shielded their eyes from the sun and watched as Heather tucked her right knee behind her left and curled into a little ball in preparation. She gave the thumbs-up, and John punched the gas. She disappeared behind the water spray for about ten seconds, but then she popped up to the surface, grinning. They clapped and shouted as she got her bearings and leaned back.

James signaled to ask her whether the speed was okay. *Faster!* she gestured, and John increased his speed accordingly. She was doing well and started to swing out over the wake, but she hesitated and drifted back behind the boat. She gestured again—*Faster!*

"She wants me to go faster?" John asked, incredulous.

"She just thinks she does." James shook his head no, but Heather insisted, signaling again—*Faster!*

James rolled his eyes. "Fine! Speed up."

John tossed him a wary look. "I don't know, James."

"That's what she wants—let her have it."

John bumped up his speed, and Laurel turned back from her spotting post. "Maybe you should slow down, John," she shouted over the whine of the boat motor.

James shrugged. "She said she wanted to go faster."

Laurel turned back around and resumed watching Heather, who responded by giving the okay signal. She was growing braver by the minute, moving from side to side, and expertly jumped the wake. As she picked up momentum and swung around almost beside the boat, Laurel scanned ahead of her for debris in the water that John, who was concentrating on driving, might miss. Suddenly, Heather swept back across the wake, racing to the opposite side.

Laurel saw the log, but her shout of warning was a second too late. She whirled around to get Heather's attention, but her frantic gestures were futile. Heather never heard her or saw it coming. The next few seconds went by in sickening, slow motion. Heather hit the log and catapulted into the air, the rope flying out beside her. She crashed onto the surface of the water and somersaulted end-over-end as Laurel watched in horror. Then, with a terrific spray of blue-green water, she disappeared. When she resurfaced a few seconds later, time resumed its normal pace, and Laurel's senses returned.

She could hear James shouting at John to turn back. Carrie was screaming. John whipped the boat around and raced back to Heather, reducing speed as they approached her. She was face down in the water, limp and unmoving.

When they were close enough, Laurel dove into the water without a second thought, turned Heather over and shouted back, "Someone, help me! Hurry! She's out cold—come help me!"

It was James who dove in and was beside them in a matter of

seconds. They kept shouting to her to wake up even as they pulled her toward the boat. Carrie stood with her hands over her mouth, crying in silence. John killed the motor and helped them gently lift her up over the side and lay her flat. Thankful that her dad insisted they all keep their Red Cross training current, Laurel dug deep in her memory and went through the CPR assessment.

"Heather, Heather, wake up!" She bent down and listened for breath. "She's not breathing, but maybe the wind just knocked her out or something." She gave two rescue breaths.

"Jesus Christ, look at her foot!" James's voice was low, but his face was pale and his eyes wide with fright. Heather's foot jutted out at an unnatural angle.

"Never mind that. We've got to get her conscious first," Laurel insisted.

James moved up to do two-man CPR.

"No," she ordered in a calm but firm voice. "Does John know CPR?"

"I don't know," James answered, momentarily confused. "John?"

"Yeah!" John jumped up.

"Good. John, you help me. James, you know the lake better, so you drive. You remember Carter's Ford dock—where it is?"

"Just up on the left, isn't it?"

"Yes. Get us there. They've got a landline phone."

The men switched places. Laurel was concentrating, her fingers on Heather's wrist. "I'm getting a pulse—we won't need compressions." Carrie let out a sob.

Laurel gave another rescue breath, and there was a convulsive cough. They rolled Heather to her side and water leaked out her mouth.

"That's good," Laurel whispered. "She's breathing now." She heaved a sigh of relief.

"Almost there," James shouted from the front. As they approached the dock, John took the wheel while James leapt out and took off toward the building about halfway up the hill. John and Carrie held the boat next to the dock while Laurel continued to monitor Heather for any change. She was breathing but still unconscious. Laurel didn't dare move her for fear of doing more damage.

James ran back down the dock. "The ambulance is on its way. How is she?"

"No change," Laurel replied.

John's calm voice soothed Laurel's jagged nerves. "You're right to move her as little as possible. It's best to let the professionals do that."

After the ambulance arrived, Laurel and Carrie stepped back out of the way to let the EMTs tend to Heather. Laurel stood watching for a few seconds, her arm around a shaking Carrie, and then turned around to find James pacing back and forth in agitation, muttering to himself, a furious scowl on his face.

Laurel hesitated, but then she approached him, touching him on the arm.

"James, we need to find Stu."

"What was she thinking?"—his voice rough with anguish. "How could she be so careless? She hadn't been skiing in years!"

"She just didn't have enough experience to dodge the log, or she saw it too late."

"I shouldn't have let her go so fast. I shouldn't have encouraged her."

"James, it was an accident. It's not your fault."

He shook his head and swore.

"We need to find Ginny and Stu," she repeated. "Can you take the boat back and look for them?"

A burly EMT with a handlebar moustache approached them. "Ma'am, she's set to go. She's stable, and we've got the foot immobilized, but she might have a concussion from hitting the water so hard. Who's going with her to the hospital?"

"Well, that's her sister over there—" Laurel began.

James interrupted. "No, Laurel, you're going with her. Carrie's too upset to answer questions or anything." He looked at the EMT and said with confidence, "Laurel will know what to do."

Laurel glanced up at James in surprise. He looked back at her with a grim intensity. "I'll take John and Carrie, and we'll find the houseboat. We'll meet up with you at the hospital as soon as we can get there, okay?"

She nodded.

"Take care of her." James touched her arm, slid his hand down to hers, and squeezed it gently. "See you soon."

CHAPTER 21

Once at the hospital, Laurel ended up with little to do besides wait for Heather's family. The ER nurse asked her a few questions about Heather's medical history, most of which she didn't know, and about whether she was allergic to anything, which she also didn't know. She sat in the ER waiting room for what seemed like hours until Stuart and Virginia arrived, followed by Carrie and James. Stuart rushed toward Laurel, worry covering his handsome face.

"Where is she? How is she?"

"They took her into surgery a while ago. Her ankle's broken, and they've called in an orthopedist to set it. She also has a concussion, but even though she was still unconscious when we got here, they said there's no reason to suspect a more serious head injury, according to the CT scan."

Stuart closed his eyes in relief, and Virginia put her arm around him.

Carrie exclaimed, "Thank God!" and threw her arms around the two of them. James stood back, watching Laurel with a strange expression. Was it awe, admiration, discomfort? When the surgeon came out, he talked to Stuart, Virginia, and Carrie and then led them back to see their sister in the recovery room. James and Laurel stood, alternately glancing at each other and then looking away in uncomfortable silence. Finally, Laurel sat back down. After several minutes, Virginia came out.

"How is she?" James asked.

"As well as can be expected. Stu and Carrie are going to stay for a while, probably overnight. Their parents are in Greece, so Stu is going to call and tell them what happened. I don't know if they can get back very fast though.

"James, can you take me home? I'm going to leave them the car and get some rest tonight. My husband is worried about me." She smiled, but her expression was weary. "I told him I'm fine, but maybe this is best anyway. He and Carrie will be exhausted tomorrow morning, and I can come back and take a turn staying with Heather while they rest. I have a feeling that's what we'll be doing for the next few days."

"Of course." He turned to Laurel. "I assume you want to go home as well?"

"Yes, if you don't mind the longer drive."

"Not at all."

They rode home in virtual silence until Virginia broke the quiet. "Carrie told me everything you did to help Heather today, Laurel. I'm so glad you were there."

"I was more than happy to help, of course, but I don't think I did that much."

James looked at her in his rearview mirror. "How can you say that? You had the coolest head of all of us."

"We grew up on the lake, and sometimes emergencies happened. I guess I just kind of went on autopilot. Ginny would have done the same."

"I overheard Stuart talking to the doctor who admitted her. He said probably the most dangerous time was when we first pulled her out of the water, and she wasn't breathing. It would have been so easy for her to go into respiratory arrest, and then we might have lost her." His voice cracked a little. "You saved her life, Laurel."

Virginia reached back for Laurel's hand and gave it a gentle squeeze. They continued riding in silence until they reached the Pendleton place.

"Thanks for the ride," Virginia said as the car pulled to a stop.

"You're welcome. Try to get some rest," James answered.

Laurel moved up to the passenger seat, feeling as if she could cut the tension in the car with a knife, but she had no idea what to say to make it better, so she said nothing. James waited until Virginia was inside the house before backing out of the driveway. He drove without speaking, glancing at her every once in a while. Laurel stared straight ahead.

"It's been quite a day, hasn't it?" he finally ventured.

"Yes, one I wouldn't want to repeat—ever."

"I keep waiting for you to have some kind of little break down, tears, angry words, something—but I don't guess you will, huh?"

She looked at him. How could she tell him that she had to hold her emotions tightly when he was around—that there was no way she could let her guard down even in a situation like this?

"What would be the point of that?"

"What indeed," he muttered to himself.

Laurel felt exhaustion creeping over her. The idea of a hot shower to wash off the hospital smell and the lake, followed by falling into bed, sounded more appealing by the minute.

"You'll have to help me find the turn in the dark."

"Oh, okay. It's just a couple miles ahead—on the right." After a few more minutes, she pointed. "Right here—see the reflector?"

"Yep."

He turned in and began ascending the long slope up to the cabin. When the car popped over the hill and her house came into view, he remarked, "It doesn't look much different."

"I didn't do too much to the outside—new paint, a new roof, a new deck. The inside is where the biggest change is."

"You must be doing well with your pottery to afford remodeling."

"Oh, I get by. I've been renovating on a shoestring. Dad helps quite a bit. He knows a lot of people and gets me labor and materials for a very reasonable cost."

"I see."

"And Dylan and Crosby help too. Dylan did all the wiring." They were getting close to the cabin, and, in a rush, she asked, "Hey, do you want a cup of coffee or something?" She had no idea what she was thinking, except, all of a sudden, she didn't feel like being alone.

"Sure."

His answer was quick, making her suspect he felt the same way. Laurel shuffled up the porch steps, fishing in her bag for her keys. A couple of steps behind her, James caught up while she fumbled with the lock. He held the screen door open while she forced the key to turn. The door opened so unexpectedly, she nearly stumbled over the threshold. He reached out to steady her at the elbow.

"Okay there?"

"Yes, thanks," she mumbled. He left his hand on her arm for longer than he needed to, and her skin burned where he touched her. She tossed her things on the couch and headed for the kitchen, turning on lights as she went. She heard his keys drop on the end table by the door, and then he was in the kitchen with her, just standing there as if he didn't know what to do next. She got out a couple of coffee mugs and pulled out the teakettle.

"I hope instant is okay. I don't have a coffee maker because—"

"Because you don't drink much coffee," he finished for her.

She crossed the room to the pantry door, standing on tiptoe to reach the jar of coffee at the back of the top shelf. She froze when she realized James was close behind her, his voice bathing her in warmth as he said, "Here, let me get that." He leaned one hand on the door frame above her head, and she thought he would reach to get the coffee with the other, but...

His hand touched her shoulder and slid in a sinuous motion down her arm to her hand. He was close behind her now, so close she could feel his breath on her neck and the heat emanating from his body. He whispered her name, and she turned as if in slow motion. They stared at each other for a long moment, and then he leaned in and kissed her. It was slow and sweet at first, like honey, and as he pulled back, she opened her eyes. Her hand came up to caress his face and his eyes closed. Suddenly, they popped open again, green like the trees that lined the lake. He yanked her toward him, covering her mouth in a fierce kiss that took her completely by surprise. He pressed against her and she could feel the hard planes of his body—well, everywhere.

He murmured her name between kisses, reverently—as if he were praying it. "Laurel," he breathed. "Laurel. Sweet." His lips traveled to her jaw, then to her neck. "Beautiful." She braced herself in the door frame to keep him from pushing her into the pantry. "Want..." he whispered, "want so much..."

He kissed her again, and she whimpered—a stunned, vulnerable sound. She was defenseless against her long-buried feelings for him, but then, he froze. He pulled away, and, with his eyes still closed, he groaned in frustration and slammed his palm against the door. The blow reverberated through the walls. She didn't dare move.

"Damn it!" He turned his back on her and ran his hand over his face in consternation. "God, Laurel, I didn't mean...I'm sorry." Without looking at her, he stalked out of the kitchen. The front door slammed, and the car motor roared as he sped away.

Sliding down the wall, Laurel hugged herself into a little ball and buried her head in her arms. The knot inside her started loosening, and her defenses unraveled at a frightening speed.

Only then did the sobs finally come.

THE NEXT MORNING, Laurel groaned, and rolling toward the edge of the bed, pulled up and looked at the clock. Then she groaned again and fell back on her pillow before she dragged herself to the bathroom and showered. Her eyes were puffy and red, and her face felt tight and stretched. Brittle and fragile, she felt as if she might shatter into a million pieces and simply drift away. She had no idea what she should be feeling, so instead, numbness prevailed.

Over tea and toast though, rational thinking began to seep in little by little. She replayed the previous night's events in her mind, looking at them from every possible perspective. She and James had both been exhausted, physically and emotionally, and Heather's accident had been a visceral reminder of life's fragility. So, they had sought each other's company—old friends, old comforts; that made sense. That must have been why she invited him in. But then he kissed her, and oh, what a kiss it was! It felt like she was leaving her body and floating when he held her. And he whispered her name and called her beautiful and sweet. She could hear the words, and then "want...want..." It had made her roar to life inside her lower belly. *Yes,* she thought, *I want too.* But then he left. Why? Was he feeling guilty because Heather was lying in a hospital bed while he was locking lips with her? Could there be something between him and Heather? As far as she knew, he'd never asked out either of the Pendleton girls, in spite of the fact that he'd been there almost a month and they had flirted with him almost nonstop. But neither could she deny he'd acted interested at times. And the way he reacted to Heather's accident—how he blamed himself and had grown pale when he recounted how they might have lost her...

Or was she reading too much into it? She considered her own history with James. Never had he given her mixed signals back when they were together. She always knew what he wanted from her because he was bluntly obvious about it. But years had passed, and they'd both changed, and now she was having trouble reading him. Why had he stormed out without talking to her? Did he think she didn't want him? Despite her recent attempts to convince herself otherwise, she realized now she'd always wanted him. Even though she wasn't ready to upend her whole life and go with him all those years ago, it didn't mean her feelings changed. After all that time, nothing had changed. It was so sad—pathetic, really. Oh, how she regretted that she'd found the love of her life when she was eighteen and didn't have the discernment to realize it! And what now? Was it really too late?

She replayed the previous night one more time. She hadn't exactly welcomed his advances with open arms. She was too exhausted, too shocked to respond the way she wanted with proper and genuine feeling. With sudden realization, she nearly dropped her mug. He must have thought I didn't want him to kiss me. That's why he said, "I'm sorry." Well, she damn sure wasn't sorry, and she was going to make sure he knew it too!

She left her breakfast on the table and practically ran out the door, pausing only to grab the keys to her Jeep.

The black rental car was nowhere to be seen when she arrived at James's cabin. Her frantic knock echoed in the quiet morning air. After a minute or so, she heard footsteps, and for a moment she wondered what in the world she was thinking to be pounding on his door at that time of the morning. When it opened finally, she was both relieved and disappointed to see John Benwick on the other side of the threshold.

"Oh, hey, Laurel. How are you this morning?" He took in her expression. "Are you all right?"

"Yes, I'm fine," she said, breathless. "But I need to see James. Is he here? Did he go to the hospital already?"

"Yeah, he left a couple of hours ago. He was going to stop at the hospital for a few minutes, and then he said he was leaving from there. I'm sure he's gone by now."

"Leaving? Where's he going? When's he coming back?"

"He didn't say. He's driving up to see his parents today and flying back to California tomorrow."

Laurel felt her blood run cold. "California? Tomorrow?" She cleared her throat in an attempt to control the wobble in her voice. "What about the cabin here?"

"He said he would deal with it later. It's paid up through Labor Day. He asked if I'd stay and house-sit for him."

"Oh. Um, that's nice, John."

"Yes, it's so peaceful here. I don't know how long I'll stay, but I think the time away will be good for me—you know, communing with nature and all that. Maybe I'll try a little writing."

"I see." Laurel felt a surge of panic in her breast. She had to get away before John saw her true feelings, but she didn't want to hurt his. They had so much in common—favorite books and movies, a love of art, a certain reserve that people often misunderstood, and…the pain of a lost love.

"I need…I need to go. I'm expected up at the hospital. Virginia wanted me to help her sit with Heather today."

"Sure, I understand. Hey—are you sure you're all right? You look upset."

"Just tired. It was quite an ordeal yesterday."

He nodded. "It sure was. Tell the Pendleton's I said hello and I hope Heather is better soon. I'll come and see her as soon as she's up to having visitors."

"I'll ask. Umm, I'm going to go now."

"Okay, talk to you soon."

"Bye."

She hurried down the steps and almost ran to her Jeep. She had lied to John. She wasn't going to the hospital right then. She couldn't listen to the inevitable talk about James and speculation about his sudden departure without losing her mind. Nor could she go back to her cabin yet. His presence lingered there so strongly that she could almost see him standing in the kitchen and smell the aftershave he typically wore. How could this have happened? How could she have lost him again?

No, she reminded herself—this time she never had him. She had made her decision long ago, and despite last night, there was no going back to what they were to each other then. There would be no second chance for Laurel Elliot and James Marshall after all.

She got behind the wheel of her Jeep and headed toward the only place that could bring her comfort. She went to the lake.

End of Part 2

INTERMEZZO 2

Laurel peered over the top of Café Livre's lunch menu, scanning for her companion, who had just appeared in the doorway. The hostess pointed in her direction, and he nodded his head in recognition as he wound his way around the tables.

"Hi there. I'm not late, am I?" His quiet voice was barely audible over the restaurant crowd.

"Not a bit," she replied. "I was a few minutes early."

John Benwick unrolled his silverware and put his napkin in his lap. He leaned forward with a smile and asked, "How are things?"

"About like they were the last time we met. Things don't change that fast around here." She studied him more closely. "You look good, John. I missed talking to you last week. Are you doing well?"

"Actually, yes." He sat back and pushed his glasses up with his forefinger. "I have you to thank for it, too, because you were the one who told me about that grief counselor at the hospice center. I'm getting a lot out of those sessions. In combination with my writing and this amazing place, things are really starting to look up. I feel like maybe I turned a corner this week."

"That's wonderful. I'm so glad for you."

"I've even been out visiting a bit—you know, trying to be social."

"Really? With who?"

"Oh, just folks from around the neighborhood there—Susan and Gary—you remember James's sister and brother-in-law—and the Pendletons mostly."

"I think they would be just the right kind of company. Stu is always so optimistic, and—"

"And Virginia is kind to everybody, no matter what. And it's been really good to get to know the Murtowskis this summer after hearing James talk about them all this time."

"You can't help but be cheerful around Susan and Gary. And Heather is so bubbly and fun. How is she? I haven't talked to Ginny in a couple of weeks. She's been so busy with everything."

"Well, Heather's ankle is healing—slowly. Cast comes off in about three or four weeks, I think." He laughed, and Laurel marveled at how it changed his appearance. The brooding John Benwick vanished right before her eyes. He went on, chuckling. "She's getting impatient with all the restrictions that come with a cast and crutches. There are all those stairs at Virginia and Stuart's house, and she can't get around very easily. When James called the other night, she got a little snappish with him."

Laurel's heart sank. "Oh? James has been calling pretty often then?"

"Every few days to check on her. He even sent her flowers and a 'Welcome Home' balloon when she got out of the hospital." John shook his head, amused. "James always takes responsibility for everything. Heather told me every time he calls, he apologizes all over again for letting her get hurt—or at least he did until the other night when she told him... How did it go again? Oh yeah, she said, 'It was my own fault if it was anyone's, and I wish you'd just shut up about it already.' That Heather—she's something else."

Laurel somehow summoned a weak smile and took a sip of water. "I was surprised she didn't go back to Cincinnati after they released her from the hospital."

"I guess her parents decided not to cut short their trip to Greece since she's in good hands with Stuart and Virginia. I gather it was some kind of business trip, and it would be difficult to get away before the end of August. That's a lot of responsibility on Stu and Ginny though. The dental office renovations are taking more time than they realized."

"Those things usually do. But they have Carrie to help out."

"I suppose, although Carrie's leaving in a couple weeks. School's starting soon, and she's doing student teaching this year. But, boy, Heather can't wait to get out of that cast. She's anxious to start interviewing for jobs as soon as she can."

"That's right. She graduated this past spring. I forgot."

The conversation paused while the waitress took their order.

"How are your mom and dad?" John asked, picking up his drink.

"They're doing fine." But that wasn't entirely true. It had not been a good summer for the Elliots. Mrs. Elliot withdrew and became even more a shell of the woman she once was, and Mr. Elliot barely managed to scrape by and hold on to his business. He was losing customers by the droves to the new marina on the other side of the lake. Somehow, he made ends meet, mostly due to his illicit bootlegging operation, which was just as strong as ever.

"You still helping out with the books?"

"Oh, that's a given." She laughed. "I've been doing that for years now. Mostly I do the payroll. Dad prefers to order supplies and food from the distributors himself. That way he gets to talk to all his buddies. In fact," Laurel said, glad for some pleasant news to share, "he's just recently reconnected with an old friend from his college days—a professor from Benton College."

"That's your alma mater, isn't it? Did you know him?"

"Not really, but I saw him earlier this summer at Woodland. That's how he caught up with Dad again."

"I guess it was the season to reconnect with old friends."

"I guess so."

"And make new ones." John tipped his glass toward her, and Laurel nodded.

It was good to see John moving through this grief and begin the process of rebuilding. If only she could do the same. She'd had no direct word from James. She knew he was back in California because Susan told her when they ran into each other in the grocery the other day. John mentioned talking to him now and then, and, of course, today she'd found out he was checking in with Heather on a regular basis. Laurel had seriously considered asking Susan or John for his address, but then she worried they might ask her why. The thought of broadcasting any of the feelings she held close to her heart for so long was mortifying. Even if she had the address, what would she say to him in a letter? She never got up the nerve to ask, so she never got the chance to tell James anything or ask him for any answers. But what was he doing? Did he have feelings for Heather? Her heart sank at the thought of it, but she couldn't dismiss the possibility. But, if that was the case, what business out in California kept him away from her?

Whatever it was, he'd better not stay away too long, or he risked stretching Heather's attention span to its limit. She might forget all about James Marshall in a week or two. Laurel smirked and then berated herself for her sarcastic inner monologue. Ugly cynicism would only make her feel worse. With considerable effort, she pushed the bitterness out of her thoughts. Regardless of what happened in her kitchen that night after the accident, she had to be strong and find a way to carve out an ordinary life for herself. Again.

Laurel looked up from her payroll when she heard the restaurant door slam. Her father entered, an excited look on his face, followed by Cooper Edwards.

"Hi, Dad. Hello, Cooper." She'd finally reached the point where calling Dr. Edwards by his first name didn't seem quite so strange. Her father closed the office door behind him.

"Cooper has some good news."

"Oh?"

"Tell her." Mr. Elliot sat down in one chair and gestured Cooper into another.

"Well," Cooper began with a dramatic flair, "I have a friend from the Benton College Alumni Association who is an art dealer—owns a number of galleries around this region of the country—very successful. His name is Neil Crenshaw."

"I've heard of him," Laurel replied.

"I thought you might have. We ran into each other earlier this week, and he mentioned searching for an artist to display at his gallery in Asheville the first weekend in October. You know what happens in Asheville in October, don't you?"

"There's a large regional arts and crafts festival there," Mr. Elliot interrupted.

"Yes, Dad, I know." The Craft Fair of the Southern Mountains was one of the best-known showcases for arts and crafts in the entire region.

"He was going to try to find a painter again, but I said he should do something unexpected and consider an exhibition of ceramic art instead. He was intrigued by the idea and asked if I knew any talented potters. Well, the gist of it is, he wants to meet with you about the possibility of doing a show there." Cooper watched for her reaction, a smug smile on his face.

"I've never done anything that…involved before. I don't know."

"Laurel, dear," Cooper said in a patronizing voice, "Neil Crenshaw is a very influential man. Networking with him would be a tremendous boost to your career. Many artists he's taken an interest in have gone on to be very successful."

"How do you mean?" she asked, interested despite herself.

"Selling designs for mass production, for example, invitations to prestigious national shows, opening their own galleries. I've taken it upon myself to do some research for you, and there's quite a market for quaint Appalachian keepsakes. Apparently, they elicit some kind of mawkish nostalgia and induce a subsection of the intellectual elite to adopt a rather sappy respect toward the culture—sort of an American version of Rousseau's 'noble savage.' Sentimental hogwash, if you ask me, but remunerative hogwash none the less."

Mr. Elliot cut in. "This could be a good opportunity for you, daughter. A chance to show your talent and reap the rewards of your hard work."

Laurel sighed and put down her pen. Then, she picked it up again and twirled it in her fingers, considering before she responded. "I have no problem with being paid for my work. People have to eat off of some kind of dish, so why shouldn't it be something beautiful that I made? I have no issues with that at all, but I'm not sure the kind of commerce-driven life you're talking about is right for me. I've never needed much money to live the way I want, and I've always gotten along fine. You have to understand that about me. I'm not really a businesswoman."

Cooper looked at her father with an indulgent grin, then leaned over and covered her hand with his. "I know you aren't," he said gently, "and that's why I'm being so insistent about this. I promise, I'll help you safely navigate the shark-infested waters of capitalism."

Laurel felt a mild stab of annoyance that neither man seemed to be listening to her. "It isn't enough for me just to throw pots for the sake of having something to sell. I create pottery because I'm an artist, and it's what I love to do. Of course, I need to make enough money to live on. But above that, any success I have is only a by-product of that creative drive, not a reason for it. To be honest, I'm content with whatever level of success I attain. My greatest happiness comes from meeting people who have real appreciation for my work because it appeals to them on some emotional level, not because they want to show the world how varied and eclectic their tastes are."

Cooper's self-assured smile widened with amusement. "Ah, the naïveté of youth—it's charming, isn't it, Walter?"

"I've always admired my daughter's talent and her unique charm."

"Dad…" She admonished him, blushing in spite of herself. Cooper looked at her with unnerving intensity.

"Yes," he muttered, so low she could hardly hear him, "very charming indeed." Louder, he turned again to Walter and said, "I agree your daughter is extremely talented. I would hope she would want to share that talent with as many people as she could." He turned back to Laurel with an earnest look. "Promise me you'll at least consider meeting with Neil to discuss this. I would be happy to arrange an introduction and even accompany you if that would make you feel more comfortable."

Laurel paused a long minute. *Really, what could it hurt?* And it would please her father. It might even please her mother a little too.

"Okay," she acquiesced. "If he really wants to meet with me, I'll go. And I'll gather a few pieces for him to see."

"Wonderful! I know you won't be sorry." He sat back in his chair, looking like the cat that ate the canary. "Make sure you bring some of that bright blue and gray group you had at Woodland. Those colors are very much in vogue right now. We want to show him not just how lovely and talented you are, but also that you're hip to the current trends."

Laurel mentally rolled her eyes at the outdated slang and changed the subject.

PART III

CHAPTER 22

EARLY FALL, 2000

*I*n the end, the meeting with Neil Crenshaw went better than Laurel expected. He was certain that people would admire her work and offered her a showing during the Craft Fair of the Southern Mountains in October. She would have space in his gallery to display her work, complete with professional brochures to hand out. It was quite a step up from the usual Crosby-made materials printed at Kinko's and a small booth at the Woodland Craft Fair. For his trouble, Mr. Crenshaw would receive a percentage of the gross sales.

Another bonus for Laurel was that the preparations gave her something to focus on besides James. The last few months hadn't been easy for her. To have had a glimpse of another chance with him, only for it to be yanked away, was painful. But she reminded herself she had endured the loss once before, and she was convinced she would endure it again simply because she had no other choice.

Her family was thrilled about what both Cooper and her father billed as her big break, and they talked about making the trip to Asheville with her.

At first, even her mother thought she might go, but at the last minute, she changed her mind. Of course, Laurel was disappointed. She had held out a secret hope that this might be the event that turned her mother around, but it was not unexpected, so she put that frustration out of her mind. It was a coping skill she had practiced for many years.

ON THE FIRST day of the fair, Laurel rose bright and early. She dressed carefully, choosing a flowing rayon skirt and a simple sleeveless blouse that left her arms free for pottery demonstrations. After twisting her long red hair into a large braid, she put on a dangly pair of silver and turquoise earrings and just a touch of makeup. She smiled at her reflection, realizing she looked every inch the part of the Bohemian artist.

Soon after she arrived at the gallery, Cooper came by to check whether she needed anything and to critique what he had seen so far of the festival.

She thanked him but said she had all she required, except maybe a cup of tea to ward off the morning chill. He gallantly offered to fetch "whatever the talented artiste requires." In truth, Laurel was interested in getting him out of her hair for a while. She appreciated his help, both in securing the interview with Crenshaw and his support at the fair itself, but his biting cynicism about the other artists, the fair, and the patrons threatened to interfere with her enjoyment of the event. It was a joyous occasion for her, and she wanted to feel...joyful.

Laurel was setting up for a ten o'clock demonstration when she heard a vaguely familiar voice behind her.

"Laurel Elliot, is that really you?"

She whirled around and gasped. A tall young woman with dark skin and expressive brown eyes stood there with a coffee in her hand.

"Adrienne? Adrienne Smith?" Laurel held her arms open wide and the two hugged and squealed like high school girls.

"Yes, it's me! How in the hell are you? It's been what…four years?"

"Since graduation. What have you been up to? Are you one of the artists here?"

"Oh no, not here, no. I'm working."

"Working?"

"I work for Neil Crenshaw. I'm making the rounds to double check that everything's set up and ready to go. I saw your name on the roster, and I just had to come over and see if it was my Laurel Elliot in the big fancy gallery. Is this your work?" She stopped to examine one of the pieces.

"Yes, it's mine."

Adrienne nodded appreciatively. "Simple and beautiful, but then I'm not a bit surprised."

"Thanks." Laurel checked the time. "Hey, listen, I've got to do this demonstration, but I should be finished by eleven thirty, and the gallery will be closed until one. You wanna go grab some lunch somewhere?"

"I'd love to! Can we make it eleven forty-five? That will give me time to finish up my morning and get back here."

"I can meet you somewhere."

They made arrangements, and Laurel hugged her old school friend one more time. "It's incredible to see you. I can't wait to have a nice leisurely lunch and catch up."

Adrienne cocked her head at Laurel, a question in her eyes, but then she gave her an enthusiastic nod. "I'll be there," she promised.

———

"WHAT DO you mean you're not coming to lunch? Cooper will be there." Mr. Elliot was unusually stern when Laurel told him about her plans.

"Just that—I'm not coming to lunch. I promised Adrienne, and I haven't seen her in ages. I've already seen Cooper this morning —twice."

Her father tried a patient voice instead. "Laurel, I know you'd like to see your friend, but this lunch is quite an honor. Cooper had to pull some strings to get us in, and I think you ought to go. It will give you a chance to see what these people are about and how to fit in with them."

"Dad, is this you talking or is it Cooper? Since when have you worried about any of us 'fitting in'?"

"This weekend is important, daughter. Finally, you have a chance to be successful at what you love to do. It's what you've always wanted, isn't it—recognition for your talent and your hard work?"

"No, it's what you've apparently decided you want for me, Dad, and I love you for it. But recognition wasn't ever my motivation for my art. It was never what I always wanted. I wanted—"

She paused.

"You wanted what?"

A life with James. She didn't utter that out loud, however, and just shook her head a little. "I just want to see my friend, and she's free for lunch. I won't break my plans with her because some better offer came along."

"Well, when you put it that way, it does sound rude, but if she works for Neil Crenshaw, I'm sure she'd understand."

"Perhaps she would, but that doesn't make it right."

Mr. Elliot sighed.

"You taught me to be like this"—she reminded him—"to follow my own path."

"I know," he said with some sadness. "What was I thinking, eh?"

"Go have a good time, Daddy. Make my apologies to Cooper and the rest of them. I'll meet them tonight at the party."

"All right, you win."

"I'll see you later, okay?"

Her time with Adrienne was enjoyable, and Laurel had no regrets over missing what would have been a stuffy and pretentious luncheon. She wished Cooper would ask before he made plans for her. That quirk of his was becoming an annoyance.

On her way back to the museum, she was again accosted by a familiar voice. For being two hundred fifty miles from home, she sure was running into a lot of people she knew! She turned and was thrilled to see Susan and Gary.

"Laurel!" they chorused, waving at her with frantic gestures.

"Hi, you two." She gave Susan a quick hug. "What brings you to this neck of the woods?"

"You." Gary put an arm around his wife. "Susan can't resist a craft fair."

"And when we heard you were going to be here, how could we not come to support our friend and neighbor?" Susan added.

"Thank you. I'm so glad you came! Have you seen my exhibit at the gallery yet? How did you know I was here?"

"No, we're on our way this afternoon to see your work. And, to answer your second question—your brother Crosby's been spreading the word all over town. So, I knew even before James told us you'd be here."

"Pardon?"

"James, my brother. He mentioned it to me on the phone."

"Oh, and how is he?" *And how did he know I would be here?*

"He's fine, but as to what he's doing, I'm not sure. It doesn't seem like he's very busy. We've told him he should come back out and stay with us at the lake."

"What about the cabin he rented? Can't he stay there? Or did he give it up?"

"He's pretty much turned that over to Benwick, I think. And given the circumstances, he might feel like a third wheel if he stayed there now."

"Circumstances? What circumstances?" Had Laurel been so out of touch while she prepared for this fair?

"Well, Benwick started seeing that Pendleton girl, the one who broke her ankle," Gary said. "What's her name again, Susan?"

"Heather. Like the plant—Heather." She looked at Laurel, amused. "He can never remember first names."

"Didn't need to know first names until I retired." He turned to Laurel and explained, "Aboard ship, all you need to remember are last names."

Any other time, Laurel might have kidded him about his memory, or remarked to herself what a sweet marriage they had, but she only had ears for this latest news. Heather and John were dating?

She had wondered about all the time John was spending up at Stu and Virginia's place, but this was very unexpected! Bubbly, shallow Heather and brooding, intellectual John? It didn't seem to fit, but then what did Laurel know? The state of her own love life certainly indicated that she was no expert.

"Serves James right for running off," Gary said.

"What do you mean?" Laurel asked tentatively.

"Why, just when he could have made his move on that girl and she couldn't run away, he took off like a shot. Benwick swooped right in and took his place before James could bat an eye."

"Was James upset?"

"You know, I don't think he was. That's why I feel I can joke about it, I suppose."

"You shouldn't provoke my poor brother like that." Susan pushed playfully on Gary's shoulder. "I think James was a little worried at first. After the accident, we really thought… He was so worried about Heather, talked about the accident constantly and, even after he left, he kept calling to check on her. Then there were all those flowers." She shook her head. "I started to think he had fallen for her."

Laurel felt a familiar bolt of hurt strike her heart.

Then Susan chuckled. "I wasn't the only one, either. I think Stuart even asked him what his intentions were toward his sister, half-joking, of course. But then James told me he had a long phone call with Heather, and he made his position on their friendship clear."

"Yes," said Gary, lips twitching, "the dreaded 'friend' speech."

"I see." But Laurel didn't see.

"He must not have cared about her that way," Susan broke in, eyeing Laurel in a careful, appraising kind of way.

Laurel's heart was pounding as if she had just run a marathon. *James didn't start something with Heather? And now she's with John?*

Maybe it meant nothing, but her heart surged when she realized the door of opportunity was not slammed shut as firmly as she had feared.

"Where are you off to, my dear?" Gary asked. "Can we tag along?"

With some difficulty, Laurel pulled her thoughts back to the present and managed a smile. "I'm on my way back to the gallery. Would you like to join me?"

"That sounds like a perfect way to start the afternoon," Susan said.

Laurel walked beside them, but her mind was far away. She sent her love out toward California. Wherever he was, she hoped that the call of her heart was strong enough to find him and bring him home.

CHAPTER 23

*A*lthough Laurel had no way of knowing at the time, her love didn't have to travel far to reach James Marshall. He was already in the air on the second leg of his flight from San Francisco, high above the Cumberland Plateau.

As if in response to her surge of hope, he awakened from a light doze and adjusted his long frame in the cramped coach seat. He preferred first class, and he'd gotten spoiled about having it, but the decision to travel had been somewhat last minute, so he settled for whatever seat he could get.

He rested his chin on his hand and stared out the window at the rolling terrain below. Odd how his life, after heading one way for so many years, had taken this sudden change in direction. Or maybe it wasn't so odd, given everything that had happened since last New Year's Eve, that night James broke his long silence and finally told Eric about Laurel. In January, Fiona was diagnosed with cancer. Her passing in April left John a broken man. In May, Susan met up with Stuart and Virginia in Kentucky in an incredible coincidence.

All those events pushed James to face his demons once and for all. He came to Kentucky to show Laurel what she had missed out on, and instead, he had the uncomfortable experience of watching her grow closer to John.

And then, there was the night of Heather's accident, when he had lost control of his emotions in Laurel's kitchen. At first, he was angry with himself, but then a strange acceptance settled over him.

He wasn't over Laurel. He would probably never be over her, and it was time to come to terms with that—even if it was too late.

Then he got a phone call a few days earlier from his old friend and new house sitter, John Benwick.

After a few minutes of stilted small talk, John said in his quiet, but resolute way: "James, I have something to tell you."

"Okay, buddy, shoot."

"I'm thinking about relocating to the East indefinitely."

"Oh." James paused, letting that sink in for a second before he went on. "Well, I can't say I'm surprised. You seem to really like it there. Are you going to pick up the lease on the cabin?"

"Perhaps, at least for a while, but it isn't the place that's keeping me here."

Every nerve in James's spine went on alert, and his carefully suppressed worries about John and Laurel rose immediately to the surface. Could she be the reason he wanted to stay? Strong and unacceptable emotions welled up inside him: anger, jealousy, despair, possessiveness, and most of all, deep sorrow at an opportunity lost.

"Okay…"

"I know this might surprise you, and I'm not sure how you're going to feel about it, but I'm seeing someone."

John's voice seemed far away as the sound of blood rushing in his ears drowned out everything but his own frantic thoughts.

"Who?" he said much harsher than he intended.

"Heather Pendleton."

The cacophony of emotions popped like a balloon stuck with a pin. After several seconds of shocked silence, James found his voice. "Heather?"

"Yes."

"Stuart's sister?"

"Yes, James. How many other Heather Pendletons do you know?" John sounded amused.

"Wow...um, I see. Well, uh, congratulations. Yeah"—his voice picked up strength—"congratulations. Heather's a great gal."

"She is, isn't she? I'm not sure yet, but I think I can see a future with Heather."

"Well, I'll be damned. When did this happen?"

"After you left. You know how it is around here—pretty isolated, especially for a woman like Heather who's used to being with people. Then she's stuck at Stuart's house right after everyone went home, so I started visiting her. She's very interesting—deeper than you'd think. I never saw that before because she was always talking with...well, with other people."

James cringed. He knew John was thinking how Heather was always talking with him. He hadn't considered how all that attention he had given her and Carrie would look to others. No, his mind was full of beautiful, serene Laurel sitting in the corner, ignoring him, engaged in deep conversation with John Benwick.

"Anyway, we had some great discussions about books. She has a minor in English literature. Did you know that?"

"No, I didn't." James felt a little embarrassed. He'd never bothered to ask those kinds of questions. He was more interested in making an impression on Laurel than finding out much about Heather; he'd been content just to talk about himself.

"She's looking for a job now that her cast is off and wants to be out of Stuart and Virginia's house so they can start getting ready for the baby. She doesn't want to wear out her welcome."

"Makes sense."

"She's interviewing several places around this area, so I offered for her to stay with me."

"Oh?" James was even more surprised. "It's pretty serious, then."

"Yeah." He heard John's smile over the phone. "It's pretty serious. When is the lease up on the cabin here?"

"It's up the end of September, but I bet you could pick it up after that. It's hard to rent those places in the off-season."

"Good idea. I'll talk to the guy tomorrow then. I just wanted to run it by you first. See what your plans are."

"I have to say, I'm a little shocked, John. I mean, I kind of thought maybe you and Laurel—"

"Oh no, not at all. It's not like that at all with Laurel. I mean, she is a terrific woman."

"Yes, I know," James said softly.

"Heather just loves her—for obvious reasons—but she loved her even before the accident. Everybody loves Laurel, but she and I are just good friends. I don't think she's real interested in men, because she never talks about anybody. Do you think maybe she's a lesbian?"

James gave a short laugh. "No, John, I'm pretty sure she's not a lesbian."

"Oh, well, you never know."

"Well, I know she isn't. She dated somebody—when we were younger."

"Ah."

"Have you seen her recently?"

"Who, Laurel? Nah, she's been really busy getting ready for that art show in Asheville."

"Art show?"

"Yeah, it's a pretty big deal—real prestigious gig—and a gallery is going to do a showing of her pottery. That friend of her father's— what's his name again? Heather says he started hanging around last summer."

"Edwards?"

"Yeah, that's it—Cooper Edwards. He set it up for her with some friend of his."

Once again, James heard warning bells go off in his head.

"It's all the Elliots can talk about these days. They're so proud of her. Crosby and her dad are going with her."

"My sister would probably be interested in something like that. She likes Laurel's work. I'll have to call and tell her."

"You should go too. You've got nothing better to do, right? No job yet?"

"Nope—nothing to do but sit around and waste my savings."

"Somehow I don't think you'll have to worry about running out of that anytime soon. But why don't you come back East?"

"I might. I don't know. I've been working on some music, but we'll see. I might fly back. I didn't get to spend as much time with Susan as I wanted when I was there before. I should. I probably will." James was suddenly in a hurry to get off the phone. "Well, I'd better go. Let me know about the house when you decide what to do, okay?"

"Sure. Wish me luck then—with Heather and all of it."

"Good luck."

"Hopefully we'll have some even better news to share in the near future."

Whoa, buddy! Slow down there! James thought that last bit, but he somehow managed to stop himself from saying it out loud. He couldn't believe how impulsive John sounded, especially so soon after Fiona's passing. But his friend was lonely, and James knew about loneliness. He wasn't going to question John about his choice of girl-friend, although a part of him did wonder how compatible they could actually be. They were so different, but then he'd always heard that opposites attract. Besides, what did he know about it? His own love life was a disaster.

James's next phone call was to his sister.

"Little brother!" Her happiness at hearing from him charged across the two thousand miles separating them, making him feel warm and loved—and a little guilty that he'd only called her once since he came back to San Francisco.

"Hi, big sis," he replied. "How are you?"

"We're good, James. How about you? You doing all right?"

"Um, fine."

After the obligatory small talk, James paused. Suddenly, the whole story—his confused feelings after meeting up with Laurel again last summer, the accident, the stolen kiss in her kitchen, his rapid departure followed by months of emptiness, and now, the phone conversation with John—tumbled out of him in a rush. He could almost imagine himself sitting in Susan's room at home, pouring out his middle school troubles while she put up her new U2 poster.

"Wow," she mused. "You don't do things the easy way, do you?"

He laughed without humor. "John told me he was seeing somebody, and I swear, Susan, at first I thought it was Laurel. It was like a gorilla was sitting on my chest." He rubbed his hand across his front as if he still felt it.

"So, I'm in love with her. I never stopped loving her, I guess. Stupid, huh? She cut me loose years ago, and there I was, all last summer, still panting after her like a twenty-year-old kid. And after I tipped my hand and let her know how I felt, what did I do? I ran away —like an idiot."

"Not one of your best moves, that's for sure, but it is your usual MO. Run off before it gets too scary, upsetting, provoking—and not just with women, I have to say. I mean, isn't that why you went to Nashville in the first place—to avoid dealing with Dad not paying for school? You could have stuck it out. There were ways you could have made it work."

"Now you sound just like Laurel did back then."

"I knew I liked her. Can't blame you though after the miserable excuse for a marriage we saw growing up, but James… Well, maybe I should stay out of it."

"No, tell me. I need advice. Hell, I'm begging for advice. You and Gary were the only truly happy couple I knew before I met Eric and Millie."

"Okay but remember—you asked for it. You're not happy now, right?"

"No."

"You did what you always do, and you're not happy."

"That's the long and short of it."

"So, do the opposite of what you usually do."

"Huh?"

"Come back, James. Find her and work it out. Come home."

"It might be too late." He shook his head. "I really blew it in July, and I panicked. I never even saw her after that—not to talk or apologize or anything. All I wanted was to get back home, back to my familiar life, but once I got here, it was—"

"What?"

"Empty, lonely. I've been alone a lot over the years, but since I left Nashville, I've never been really lonely. I thought I'd be better once I got home."

"San Francisco isn't your home. It's just the place you live. We grow up thinking of home as a place, and all a sudden, if we're lucky, we wake up and realize home is really a person.

"How do you think I could move all over the country, even all over the world, time and time again? It's because all those places don't mean much, James. What matters is Gary. He's my anchor, my port." She laughed. "Sorry—bad naval analogy."

"Gary's a lucky man."

"You're sweet. But you know as well as I do that, many times in life, you make your own luck. It wasn't easy being apart, but I went with him when I could and endured when I couldn't. We made it work."

Susan's choice of words made him stop and think. It sounded like something he might say himself. But now, there were decisions to be made. It was another big Crossroads of life—with a capital C.

"What do I do? How do I reach her? We have nothing in common anymore—maybe we never did. I live in the city—she lives on a mountain. I work with computers—she molds clay with her hands. I have this stupid shitload of money—she has barely enough to scrape by. She has this big family—I have you and Gary. She's cautious—I take risks."

"How long did it take to come up with that list of lame excuses, James?"

"Been reciting it daily since July," he said.

"So, try this list instead: you are both artists, you both love the Kentucky foothills and the lake, and you were each other's first love. In many ways that matter, you are very much alike. And the ways that you're different—that's what makes love exciting."

"Another man might suit her better—one who understands her more."

"You want my honest opinion?"

"Yeah, I'm floundering here."

"She doesn't need a male version of herself. We all seek the other to complete ourselves. It just may be that you're one of the only men who *would* suit her. You should at least give her the choice."

"You know, it's only a weird quirk of fate that John's not seeing her. They've been spending all this time together, getting to know each other. If Heather hadn't been right under his nose—and bored..." He squirmed, as if something vile was crawling up his back. "How long will it be before some other guy sees the amazing woman John saw? Except the next guy might be interested for real."

"Don't waste any more time. As to how to reach her—I don't know. The best advice I can give you is to say what's in your heart, James, in whatever way you can wrest it from your jaded soul."

He looked at his guitar, leaning against the bookshelf. His fingers itched to touch it, to play the melody that had been his constant companion for all these years.

Susan's voice called him back to their conversation. "I know one thing, though."

"What's that?"

"You can't win her if you're out there in California."

"Is this an attempt to get me closer to home?"

"It's an attempt to get you closer to happiness. Fight for what you want, James. You did it with Nashville, with college, the company—this is very much the same."

"Except she can say no—and that's the end of it."

"Yes, she has the final say over whether she loves you, but I'll bet you have more persuasive power in this than you think. Even though she's very private and tries to hide it, I've seen how she lights up when your name is mentioned. It stirs something deep inside her. I think you have an excellent shot."

"Honestly?"

"Don't you have to try?"

"I do. I know I do."

"Oh, baby bro." She sighed in empathy.

"I've decided. I'm going to Asheville."

"I'm glad, James. She's lovely. She's worth it all."

"Yes, she is." Now that he had a plan, he was full of energy. "I've got reservations to make. I'll talk to you soon." He paused. "Thanks, Susan."

"You're welcome. Safe travels."

"Love you."

"Love you too."

AFTER JAMES LANDED IN ASHEVILLE, rented a car, and dumped his things into a hotel room, he showered off the travel dirt and went in search of the gallery where Laurel had her show.

The craft fair was scattered throughout the downtown area, but he found a brochure with a listing of all the participants and saw her name. She was showing her work at the Phoenix Fire Art Gallery. According to the map, he was about two blocks away.

He wondered what she would say when he showed up unannounced.

He had a way of doing that to her, he realized: coming back in the summer, the time he had tried to talk her into going to Nashville despite her reservations, and then there was that Christmas. He had shown up unexpectedly at her cabin all those years ago, and it had been the best three weeks of his life. This time, he was hopeful, but he didn't know how she felt about him.

The last time he'd seen her, he was forcing his tongue down her throat while she clutched the door frame to keep from being knocked over. Not exactly welcoming on her part, but then, it wasn't the best of circumstances. Still, he wasn't sorry for it. That kiss reminded him what real desire was—not the fleeting feeling of physical lust, or the intellectual curiosity about a woman who interested him. What he felt for Laurel was a deep, abiding connection, even after all those years apart and everything that had happened between them. He was inexplicably drawn to her in a way he'd never been drawn to anyone else. Now that he was sure of what he wanted, he had to take this chance to make it happen.

He rounded the corner, and there was the gallery, a brilliant red, orange, and yellow phoenix emblazoned on its white stucco exterior. His lips twitched. Was it some weird quirk of fate that he was going to try to resurrect her love for him in a place called the Phoenix?

There was quite a crowd inside the little place, and he watched as people milled about, looking with admiration at the pottery on display. He felt a swell of pride as he wandered, overhearing patrons compliment the quality of Laurel's work and the beauty of her designs. A group of four people was examining a serving set, and he sidled up to them to eavesdrop on their conversation:

"Yes, it's marvelous work," said one of the women, "but I'm wondering how a relative unknown scored a venue like this. There are so many deserving artists around."

"I heard," said the other woman, "that she has connections through a friend of the owner."

"She knows Crenshaw?"

"Through a mutual friend—some professor at a little college in the mountains—fellow by the name of Edwards. Fancies himself a bigwig in the art world."

"Are she and this big-wig a couple?"

"What do you think?" was the knowing reply.

"He's crazy if they aren't," one of the men said. "Have you seen her? Pretty hot stuff in that granola kind of way."

"She's giving a demonstration at three thirty. I guess we'll get to judge for ourselves in about five minutes."

James resented the implication that Laurel had to sleep with someone to get this opportunity, even as he considered whether or not there was something to the gossip, but he seethed inwardly and kept his opinions to himself. He followed the crowd upstairs to the loft and stood over to the side to wait. His breath caught in his throat when she appeared through a side door.

The gray apron she wore gave her a serious artist look, but her hair shone like the setting sun under the recessed lighting above, and the blues, violets, and greens of her flowing skirt peeked out in defiance of her attempts to subdue them. An older man with silver streaks in his dark hair came up beside her and whispered into her ear, putting a gentle hand on her lower back. When he turned around, James recognized him as Cooper Edwards, Mr. Elliot's professor friend—and the apparent player in the overheard conversation.

Laurel chuckled at whatever Edwards said to her and made her way to the platform. James ducked behind a group of onlookers. He didn't want her to notice him just yet. He wanted to watch her in her element, working and interacting with people. She had this incredible gift, a way of relating to everyone she met in a gentle, nonthreatening manner.

"Hello!" Laurel stood behind the potter's wheel and addressed the crowd with a brilliant and disarming smile. "I'm Laurel Elliot, and I'm so pleased you all chose to come today. Pottery is an ancient art, and there are some estimates that the use of the potter's wheel dates back to anywhere between 8000 and 1400 BCE. I love pottery because it's beautiful and expressive, but useful too. It's art with a purpose. But I think you'll find as you wander around the fair that a lot of the art from the Appalachians is art with a purpose. Quilting is one example —making baskets is another.

"Today, I'm going to start with a lump of clay and take you through the process of forming a vase. I'll be describing what I'm doing as I go. Feel free to shout out a question or two, but if I don't respond right away, don't be offended. I'm just concentrating too hard to formulate an answer. And don't be shy about repeating your question later, okay?"

Amid nods and murmurs of assent, she sat down at the wheel and turned it on. James watched in fascination as she opened the clay using slow and methodical movements to coax beauty from an unformed lump of nothingness. He was mesmerized by the way she bit her lip while forming the rim with expert fingers and by the gentle, rhythmic movement of her hands up and down the vase. To a man who treasured the long-ago memory of her hands on his skin, the way she pulled and shaped the clay was almost erotic, and he had to look away for a second, worried that his admiration would be obvious to anyone who looked at him. Sure enough, he almost immediately drew the attention of Cooper Edwards. The two men made eye contact, and to James's alarm, Cooper made his way over to him.

"Fascinating, isn't it?" Cooper murmured to him.

"Yes, interesting," James answered curtly, hoping the man would go away. He didn't want this man anywhere near when Laurel saw him for the first time.

"Have you ever seen pottery being made before?"

"No, can't say that I have."

"Most people are surprised their first time. It seems so simple, but it requires a great deal of skill."

James didn't care for the patronizing tone, but he decided to feign ignorance for a while longer. "So, she made all of these?" He gestured around the room.

"Yes, she is an incredible talent—a real artisan."

James gave the man a pointed look. "I know. I've known that for quite a while."

Cooper looked triumphant. "I thought I recognized you. You're a friend of hers, aren't you? I haven't had a chance to meet many of Laurel's friends yet." He held out his hand, which James reluctantly shook. "Cooper, Cooper Edwards. And who are you again? I know I've seen your face somewhere."

"James Marshall," he replied, his voice cold. "We met at Elliot's Marina last summer."

"Ah, yes! James Marshall, the software gazillionaire. I've heard of you." He wore an expression of mild amusement. "How do you know Laurel?"

"I've known her most of my life. Her brother-in-law, Stuart, is a childhood friend of mine."

"That's right, that's right. I remember now. Walter told me about you. You're the boy from Ohio who made it big in computers or some such thing. He told me you went out to California and struck it rich in Silicon Valley—a real modern day 'Miner, Forty-Niner.'"

"It was a little more involved than discovering gold nuggets lying in a river. A lot of people are surprised. It seems so simple, but it does require a great deal of skill."

"Of course, it does, of course, it does," he said, missing the irony in James's reply and dismissing the conversation with a wave of his hand. "Well, James, it was good to see you again."

James nodded, and Cooper made his way to another little group standing in the room. Laurel was winding up her talk, answering the questions of a woman with a little girl about eight years old standing beside her. Suddenly, the mother exclaimed, "No, Sarah! Don't touch, honey!" The girl had her hand out, reaching toward the wheel.

"Here," Laurel replied, covering the little hand with her own. "It's okay to touch—just ask me first so I can make sure you don't get hurt."

James watched, completely charmed, as Laurel placed a scoop of clay on the wheel and turned it on low. She took the girl's hand and gently guided her fingers over the clay, making a little depression in the top of it. "See? That's how you start to make a bowl. Can you feel the bowl under your hand?"

The girl gave a nervous little nod, and Laurel's lips curved into a smile. "I think maybe you just got a little more than you bargained for here, didn't you?"

The girl nodded again, and Laurel let her fingers go. She pulled her hand away and Laurel gave her a towel. "I was about your age the first time I saw someone make pottery. It was at a craft fair like this one."

"Thank you for your tolerance. Sometimes she's a little impulsive. She has autism, you see. I'm surprised she let you take her hand."

"Oh, I hope I didn't frighten her." Laurel looked surprised, too, but aimed her kind smile down at the little face, still staring intently at the wheel. "Maybe you can learn to make pottery someday." The girl looked at her but said nothing.

"Say thank you to Ms. Elliot, Sarah."

"Thank you," she whispered.

"It was good to meet you, Sarah." The mother and daughter moved off.

Behind him, James heard a whispered voice. "She's marvelous, Cooper. She has a real gift with people, and her work is very appealing."

"Yes, I know."

James rolled his eyes.

"She's very pretty, too."

"I know that as well."

James could just picture his smug expression.

"Are you two…? You know."

"A gentleman never tells, Richard. All I will say is that I'm helping her out with her little project."

"I think she might be *your* little project."

"No comment."

James was insulted on Laurel's behalf. She was no one's project. He knew, now that he had sold his company, what it was like to be valued for what you did rather than for who you were—and Laurel was so much more than a "project" to feed an arrogant man's ego. He moved off before he said something angry. He would be keeping an eye on Cooper Edwards, though.

Cooper went up and spoke to Laurel again. She answered him with a weary expression, and he reached up and brushed a smear of clay off her forehead where she had wiped her brow earlier in the demonstration. James seethed at the intimate and possessive gesture, and, of course, she chose that very moment to make eye contact with him.

She startled in recognition, her eyes opening wide, arrowing into a place deeper than his groin or his heart. It had to be his soul. He gave her a small, secret smile, and she returned it, adding a beguiling spark that propelled his feet toward her.

"Well, hello, Mountain Laurel."

"Hi," she said, breathless. "I didn't know you were here."

"Just arrived today."

"Oh."

"Congratulations on the show. It seems to be going very well."

"Yes." Cooper cut in. "Very well, Jake."

"It's James," he said, not taking his eyes from Laurel's.

"Thank you," she said quietly.

"Well, I'm sure you're busy." James looked around at the crowd. "Maybe we can catch up later?"

"Yes—there's a reception for the artisans later tonight at the hotel, but anyone can come. You'll stop by, won't you? I think Susan and Gary are coming, and, of course, my father and Crosby will be there."

"Yeah, that would be nice."

"Great."

"See you then."

"Okay."

He moved off, keenly aware of two pairs of eyes on his back as he went.

He heard her tell Cooper, "That's Stu's friend, James. We've known each other a long time."

"Yes, he introduced himself to me."

"He's a software engineer now."

"So I've heard. Wildly successful, new money—they always think they can invite themselves anywhere."

James paused, ready to go back and say something, but before he could, Laurel spoke up. "He didn't invite himself. I invited him, and I'll be thrilled if he shows up."

James grinned and kept walking. He would be at that reception with bells on.

CHAPTER 24

*J*ames approached the hotel ballroom with a spring in his step but some trepidation as well. Once inside, he got a beer and wandered the room. He saw Mr. Elliot in the middle of a group of people, and they exchanged curt nods. They had managed to avoid each other for most of last summer except for the most basic civilities, and it seemed that was going to continue for the short term. Rebuilding any kind of rapport with Laurel's father would take time and effort, but James wasn't ready to start down that road tonight. His relationship with the daughter was his first priority.

A flash of red hair drew his attention, but it was only Laurel's brother Crosby. He waved, and James walked over to speak to him. The younger Mr. Elliot had a small crowd gathered around him.

"James, my man!"

"Crosby." They shook hands.

"I'd like you to meet some people. This is Luke Hatton, Robert Jennings, Marian Ivers, and Scott Barrows. Everyone, this is James Marshall, lake area resident and software genius."

"The James Marshall? EMP software James Marshall?" Luke asked, eyebrows raised.

"The very one," Crosby said smugly. "He occupies a little lakeside hideaway on occasion, similar to the ones I was telling you about earlier. He loves it there."

There was a muted chorus of "nice to meet you" and a once-over from Marian.

Crosby clapped him on the shoulder. "You clean up nice, James."

"Thanks."

"Has my sister seen you yet?" he said as he steered James from the group, adding, "Excuse us, just a minute."

"No, I just arrived."

"Well, I'm glad you're here now." He leaned toward James and lowered his voice. "Maybe you can keep old Cooper from sniffing around her all evening."

James almost snorted beer up his nose. "What's the matter, Crosby? Don't you like the professor?"

"In the immortal words of our little sister, Spring Violet, 'he skeeves me out.'" He shrugged. "He's fine, I guess. I'm not too keen on the idea of him spending so much time with my sister though. Dad, on the other hand, seems to think he's a great guy."

"What does Laurel think?"

Crosby rolled his eyes. "Who knows what Laurel thinks? She's too polite to say anything regardless of whether she likes him or not."

Crosby gestured across the room with his beer. "There she is. You can ask her yourself."

He turned, and for the second time that day, James was thunderstruck by the woman he saw. Laurel stood with a group of other artisans, smiling and nodding in conversation. She wore a simple yet stunning blue silk dress that emphasized her willowy figure. Black stilettos accentuated her height and her long legs. She had pinned her hair back on one side, but flaming red waves cascaded down her back in hedonistic bursts of color. James's mouth went dry, and he felt a nudge at his back.

"Get up there. And close your jaw before you trip over it," Crosby said with a mischievous look.

James barely heard him. He approached Laurel and stood a few feet away, willing her to look in his direction. She stilled as if she sensed him, and then turned so they caught each other's gaze. She stepped away from the crowd and held out her hand. He took it—not in the shaking hands motion of friends, but in the almost possessive, holding hands motion of lovers—and enfolded it in his, caressing her fingers with his thumb.

"You're here." Her words tumbled out in mild surprise.

"Of course I am."

"I'm glad to see you."

"I'm glad you're glad."

"How have you been?"

"Fine. Better now."

Their conversation lagged, making him feel awkward. "I don't think I've talked to you since the day of Heather's accident."

"No, I guess not."

"That was an awful day."

"Yes." Her face was neutral. How he wished he could read her expressions as easily as he did when they were younger!

He hurried on, worried that she might think he meant the kiss in her kitchen was the awful part. "I can imagine how wiped out you must have been after Heather fell and then all that waiting and worrying by yourself at the hospital."

She cocked her head and looked at him, a multitude of questions in her eyes.

He forged ahead. "It was an awful day that has apparently resulted in some good, however."

Her brow furrowed. "What—?"

"The thing between Heather and John."

"Oh yes. Who'd have thunk it?"

"Not me, that's for sure."

"Not me either, and I thought I knew John pretty well."

"Well, I know I knew him pretty well, and I was still surprised. I mean, nothing against Heather. At all. I know she's a great gal, but it surprised me because—" He stopped, not knowing whether it was the right venue for this comment.

"Because?"

"I don't know—it's just that he loved Fiona so much. He was devastated when she died. I don't know how much he told you about her."

"Quite a bit, actually."

"Then I'm sure you know. She was a special girl—beautiful, good, extremely bright. John's a smart guy and Heather"—he paused—"well, he and Heather just seem different in some pretty important ways."

"I see."

"John found his soul mate in Fiona, and then he lost her. I didn't expect him to get over that in a matter of a few months."

Laurel didn't comment.

"But maybe Heather and John's differences were what drew them together. I hope it works out for them," he said.

"Me too."

"If anyone deserves happiness, it's John."

She smiled again, and James realized he didn't want to be talking about John and Heather; he wanted to be talking about Laurel and James. He was interrupted by the dry, slightly nasal voice of Cooper Edwards.

"Laurel, dear— Oh, hello again." He paused, expecting another introduction.

"James," they chorused, before sharing a look.

Cooper looked back and forth between the two of them. "Right. Laurel, the Dearingers had a question about ceramic glazes, and I told them you were the person to ask."

"Excuse me," she said, laying her hand on his arm.

"Of course. Gotta take care of business," James replied, trying to disguise his annoyance.

"Thanks for being a good sport, Jay. I knew you'd understand," Cooper said to James, "being an entrepreneur yourself."

Cooper took Laurel's arm in a protective gesture and led her away. She stepped aside to shake him off. "I can walk, Cooper."

"I wasn't sure if you could in those shoes," he said in a silky voice. "They do marvelous things for your legs, but they can't be very good for standing on your feet all evening."

She rolled her eyes, and he laughed as if he were teasing a child who couldn't take a joke.

Laurel spent the next several minutes talking with the Dearingers, and then Cooper led her to someone else—and someone else and someone else. James stood, unsmiling, watching her. When she caught him looking, he turned away and joined Crosby in conversation with a group of art patrons, and Cooper continued to monopolize her attention for the next half hour.

James took another swig of his beer as he watched Edwards parade Laurel about the room as if she were a prize poodle. She looked miserable, and James couldn't figure out why she wouldn't just tell the guy to get lost, but then, she never would say anything like that to anyone—and that had always been the problem. She wouldn't stand up for herself, not then and, evidently, not now. Unless...

He put the empty bottle down and sighed. Was she miserable because of Edwards, or was she merely uncomfortable at the necessity of promoting herself? Perhaps she was grateful for Cooper's guiding presence at her side.

He needed to regroup—to think this through. After his conversation with John Benwick, James hadn't expected any competition for her. That was a stupid assumption on his part. Then, his heart stopped for a moment. If Cooper Edwards is a family friend, could her parents persuade her to...? No, this couldn't be happening to them all over again. If that was the case—well, he wasn't going down without a fight. A twenty-year-old James Marshall might have been young and stupid enough to walk away from her; but at twenty-eight, he was made of sterner stuff and had become used to getting what he wanted.

She was right all those years ago when she told him the mountain laurel was poisonous. This Mountain Laurel had certainly poisoned him: spoiled him for life and ruined him for any other woman.

So, Marshall, what are you going to do about it?

One thing was certain, he needed to leave before he lost his temper. That night was too important to her, and he wouldn't embarrass her with a confrontation. He said an abrupt good night to Crosby, who looked confused but didn't stop him from leaving. As James approached the door, Laurel caught up to him at last.

"Hey," she said, her hand on his elbow, "are you all right? You're not leaving already, are you?"

"Yeah, I'm pretty tired. It was a long flight, and anyway, you're busy. I don't want to get in the way."

"You should stay, James. There's going to be music later—local talent. You'll like that—that's worth staying for."

"I don't think so. Thanks." He cast a surreptitious glance around the room, frowning when his gaze landed on Cooper. A mirthless chuckle escaped him. "Your warden is looking for you again."

She turned to see who he meant, and when she turned back, James was gone.

CHAPTER 25

The following day, Laurel found herself trying to shake off a foul mood—a rarity for her. Part of it was exhaustion from late hours the night before, but a big reason for her irritability was her so-called mentor. Cooper was beginning to annoy her beyond her limits, and Laurel had pretty high limits. He had a proprietary air when he was around her as if he owned her. Yes, he played a key role in securing her the art show, but he acted like that entitled him to micromanage her life and her time. For a woman who had spent the past four years in frequent solitude, having someone always in her business was becoming unbearable.

There had been two bright spots the previous evening: one was meeting Jack and Delores Dearinger. Delores's interest in Laurel's pottery was genuine and gratifying. She had bought some pieces at the Benton craft fair three years earlier and was impressed with their durability and functionality. Pleased to discover Laurel at a larger, regional fair, Delores had a list of questions for her: Was she interested in expanding her business? Was she wedded to producing single pieces or had she ever considered selling designs for mass distribution? Would Laurel be interested in talking to her husband, Jack, a manufacturer, about a collaboration? And by the way, who was that nice looking young man she was talking to earlier, and why did he keep staring at them? The last question she asked with amusement, and it made Laurel whirl around and then blush profusely when she saw whom Delores meant.

And that was the second bright spot in the evening: James.

James, striding in and talking to Crosby. James, monitoring her every move from the sides of the room. James, telling her how happy he was for John and Heather.

But the highlight of the evening—and the lowlight—had been James's departure. It was the lowlight because he left, but it was the highlight, because after thinking a little, she realized that he possibly left because he was jealous of Cooper.

Cooper, of all people! Oh, she would admit that when she first met the man, he seemed mildly appealing. However, the reality of Cooper was far less intriguing than the initial impression. Laurel had been flattered by his interest in her. After all, how much male attention had she ever garnered living on a mountain in southeastern Kentucky? Since college, she hadn't dated anyone, but then no one could ever live up to…

James passed in front of her mind's eye once again: tall, broad-shouldered, self-assured, and handsome. And brooding—maybe because of her. She was more than flattered by that possibility; she was just plain thrilled. *But how am I supposed to let him know that if he keeps running off?*

Laurel slipped on jeans and a t-shirt and went to meet Adrienne Smith for breakfast before the last day of the fair.

A bell rang as she opened the door of the coffee shop. Adrienne looked up from a corner booth and gave Laurel an excited wave. Laurel slid into the seat across from her.

"Morning there, Miss Famous," Adrienne said.

"'Miss Famous?' What do you mean?"

"You were quite the charmer last night. Now don't deny it, and you're proud of yourself, too. It's written all over your face that you had fun at the reception."

Laurel looked down at the menu, trying to hide her sheepish expression. "Yeah, I guess I did, a little bit."

"Uh-huh. I saw you talking to the Dearingers. Do you have any idea who that man is?"

"Delores's husband? The manufacturer?" She thanked the waitress who had just brought her hot tea.

"Yes, the manufacturer! He's only one of the wealthiest men in the Southeast. Has clothing factories all over North Carolina and Virginia and looking to expand into housewares. That's why he's here—to look at dishware, woodworking, glassware—trying to decide what to move into next. Meeting him was a big coup, Laurel, if you want to sell some of your designs."

"Wow, I didn't know it was that big a deal. I wonder why Cooper didn't give me a heads-up."

"Cooper Edwards?"

"Mm-hmm."

Adrienne shifted in her seat and ran her finger around the rim of her coffee mug. "Maybe because he doesn't want you to achieve any real success on your own."

Laurel looked at her friend, eyebrows raised.

Adrienne cleared her throat. "So, tell me again: How well do you know Cooper?"

"I told you, he's an old friend of my dad's. I saw him last summer at a craft fair in Lexington. He helped me get into this event by introducing me to Neil Crenshaw."

Adrienne looked at her with a forthright, unwavering gaze. "Are you sleeping with him?"

Laurel almost choked on her tea. "What!"

"You heard me—are you sleeping with him?"

"Do you mean Cooper or Crenshaw? Not that the answer would be any different."

Adrienne snickered. "I meant Cooper."

"Absolutely not! I mean, not that he's repulsive or anything, but no. I'm most definitely not sleeping with him."

Adrienne gave Laurel a piercing look. "You do know that's what people are saying, don't you?"

"Huh?" Laurel was floored. "Who? What people?"

"The organizers of the fair, the other artisans, some of the business people."

"I can't believe this! Don't these people have anything better to do than gossip?"

Adrienne shrugged. "Not really, no."

"Why would they think that about me?"

"It's not you they're thinking that about. It's him."

"I don't understand."

"It's his trademark, his standard operating procedure."

Laurel opened her mouth, horrified, and then shut it again.

Adrienne went on. "He is kind of infamous for having affairs with young women just starting out in their careers: artists, writers, models, musicians, whatever. He likes to mentor them along, play the big shot, introduce them to his influential friends, and then he gets tired of the girl and moves on to someone else. This can't be news to you. I thought you said he was a friend of your dad."

"They hadn't seen each other in a long time, not until last summer. I wondered why Cooper didn't mention any family."

"Cooper's wife finally had enough of his games and left him about three years ago."

"Good for her."

"Yeah, I agree, good for her. Honestly, I was hoping you weren't seeing Cooper, but I didn't want to say anything."

"Why ever not? You could have warned me."

"It's not that simple. When I found out he was being seen around with you—I mean, he knows your dad. It's possible that he was trying to settle down—and with someone levelheaded like you, I thought maybe he was serious about it this time. If that were the case and you were in a relationship with him, how could I say anything?"

"So, what made you decide to tell me? What changed your mind?"

"Three things: one, I overheard him talking last night to one of his friends about how being 'settled' couldn't hurt his standing with his colleagues. Two, he told Neil all about how he was 'helping you with your little project.' Then I knew it was just the same old, sleazy Cooper talking."

"And three?"

"Three, you just told me you weren't sleeping with him, which shows pretty good judgment on your part, I think." She took a sip of coffee. "Oh wait, there's another reason."

"Yes?"

"I saw you talking to James Marshall"—her voice boomed like an emcee's—"Most Eligible Bachelor of Silicon Valley." She fanned herself. "Oh my, he's a much better deal than Cooper Edwards on all counts: young, rich, smart, single, and good-looking too. That strong jaw and those stormy green eyes. So serious—mm-mm, sexy!" Adrienne was teasing her, obviously enjoying the embarrassed reaction she was getting. "I bet he's a firecracker in bed."

"He is," Laurel said in a dreamy voice before she caught herself.

Now, Adrienne sputtered her drink. "He is? He is!" She lowered her voice to an excited whisper, "Girl, are you getting some of that hunky millionaire on the side?"

"No!" She looked around, mortified. "I'm not sleeping with him either."

"But you said—"

Laurel just looked at her and rolled her eyes. Adrienne's eyes and mouth opened into big round O's.

"You have a history? With James Marshall? Wait—Ohmigod! He's 'Jim Dandy,' isn't he? That guy you were so sprung on freshman year? The guy who called you every Tuesday night at 8 p.m. without fail? Laurel! Holy shit! And now he's back here making goo-goo eyes at you across crowded rooms. Why on God's green earth are you sitting here having breakfast with me instead of him? What are you waiting for?"

Laurel sighed, exasperated. "I'm waiting for him to quit running off all the time, so I can tell him how I feel about him."

"Ooohhh." Adrienne leaned back and sipped her coffee. "Okay, girl, spill. I think you need some advice, or at the very least, you need to think this one out loud. Come on, tell Auntie Adrienne your troubles"—she gave Laurel a genuine, helpful smile and patted her hand —"so we can figure out how to fix them."

LATER THAT AFTERNOON, Laurel was in the Phoenix Fire packing the remainder of her pottery and equipment. Her family had offered to help, but she liked doing this part on her own, making sure everything was secure. The gallery was quiet except for the occasional passerby. The bustle of the craft fair was over, and it was time to return to real life.

Talking with Adrienne had been a godsend. Strange how people moved in and out of her life, leaving an imprint on her that could shift her thoughts in a completely new direction. That morning it had happened again. Adrienne had made her face the truth and, more importantly, had helped her see her options. She now had a choice to make: She could passively wait for whatever life might hand her or she could make plans to shape her own destiny. The more she thought about it, the more she was inclined to choose the latter option. As Adrienne had said so eloquently earlier, "There is a time to wait on Fate and a time to seize the day." So that night when Laurel got home, she would think and plan, and the next day she would begin the journey that would lead her to happiness.

She heard the door open and the bell chime. Footsteps on the stairs announced that she had a visitor, but he spoke before she could turn around.

"Laurel dear, I'm sure we can find someone to do this for you."

She huffed in a burst of irritability and disappointment before she turned around. "Hello, Cooper. How are you today? Me, I'm fine. Thank you for asking. And there's no need to take anyone else away from their work to do mine. I can manage by myself."

His eyes widened, taken aback by the unusual display of sarcasm, but then a distracted smile crossed his face. "Are we a bit tired after all the excitement?"

She turned back to her crate and continued packing. "I *am* ready to go home, I suppose."

"My little homebody—so domestic."

She wriggled her shoulders to shake the unpleasant feeling his words elicited in her. She had Cooper to thank for this opportunity, and she tried to force herself to remember that and not overreact to his condescending remarks.

"You've done well this weekend. I spoke with Neil earlier, and he's very pleased."

"It's more than I've ever sold at one event. And that *is* pretty exciting."

"You're well on your way to great success."

"We'll see."

"You're going to the top. I'll make sure of it."

"Cooper—"

He crossed the room and held out his hands to her. "Come over here and sit for a minute. I have something to tell you." He led her to a bench and sat down beside her. She pulled her hands away, and he laid his own awkwardly in his lap before finally settling them on his knees.

"When you get back to Uppercross, I think we should give some serious thought to your moving a little closer to civilization—up toward Lexington, perhaps."

"What?" she asked, incredulous. "I can't leave Uppercross. For one thing, I don't have the money. For another, Mom and Dad need me. You know I do Dad's books for the marina."

"I've already spoken with your father about it, and he approves the idea. I can help you with your finances while you settle into an apartment of your own."

Laurel sat speechless.

Cooper smiled. On the surface, it was his familiar, oily smile, but underneath she could sense something else, something real—almost like nervousness?

"I have an ulterior motive for moving you closer to the college. I intend to get to know you better because I think there's a future for us, Laurel Elliot."

"But Cooper," she blurted out, "I don't feel like that…about you."

He looked a little shaken, but he went on anyway. "Perhaps— No. You're far too sensible to jump into a commitment right away. I understand that."

Commitment? Where did that come from? No wonder people think we're sleeping together!

Laurel closed her eyes, searching for the right words. "Dr. Edwards, I don't know what I've done to lead you into believing we have that kind of relationship, and I'm truly sorry if you thought we did, but I'm not interested in being the latest in your long line of women friends." That was the most polite way she could think to say it.

His face clouded. "I can imagine what you must have heard. I know how people talk about me, and unfortunately, there was some truth to those stories at one time. I've certainly made mistakes, but I've changed, Laurel."

She shot him a skeptical look.

"No, really. Things are different with you, and you could make me different too. I'm ready for this."

"For what exactly?"

"If we were together, you'd never have to worry financially. I'd take good care of you. We have interesting conversations, a lot in common, really—in spite of the difference in our ages. You're so lovely, so unspoiled…" He reached out to touch her cheek, and she instinctively drew back. He dropped his hand.

"You're an intriguing woman with so much depth and talent and such a kind heart. Are you really surprised that a man with some maturity would appreciate those qualities and find you attractive?"

"I don't think I could ever…love you, Cooper." The words love and Cooper in the same sentence sounded bizarre rolling off her tongue.

"Do your reservations have anything to do with that tech wizard who came to see you last night? Your father did tell me you two had an adolescent tryst of some kind."

Laurel felt the sting of her father's betrayal—to tell such a private thing about his own daughter to someone like Cooper Edwards! What could he have been thinking?

"I guess I can't blame you for taking a second look. I mean, he does have plenty of cash these days."

"That's not why—"

"And he's a good-looking kid. I suppose there's some appeal in that." Cooper's patronizing expression appeared, but then he grew more serious. "However, you need to be realistic. The past is gone. You can't rewrite it, and you can't resurrect it. No one knows that better than I. Look ten years into the future. James Marshall is so different from you—different interests, different lifestyles. He lives in a world of machines and commerce. Didn't you once tell me you were no businesswoman?"

"Yes, but—"

"Young men like him are shallow and impulsive. He'll tire of you. As the years go by, you'll have to fight off progressively younger and younger women who'll be after his money. I've seen that kind of thing happen time and again."

Laurel's eyebrows rose in shock. Cooper was certainly pulling out all the stops to convince her. And then he said the thing that made everything click into place.

"In time, you would learn to love me. Think about how pleased your parents would be to know you're cared for—to know you're safe and sound."

A sad smile crossed her face, born from the seasons of going through heartbreak and back more often than she could count with the people she loved.

"If there's anything I've learned in life, it's that there's no such thing as safe and sound—for any of us." She stood up and took a step back. "Cooper, I am grateful for the help you've given me with my career and for your friendship to my dad and me, but gratitude isn't love, and love is what I'm holding out for."

He sat back, eyes wide with disbelief, and then bitterness crept across his features. "Well, I guess I have my answer." He stood and walked toward the staircase. Pausing at the top, he turned back and said, "But I think you're making a mistake, Laurel, and I'm afraid you might live to regret it."

A brief flash of panic raced through her, but she had lived the last eight years with regrets, and she had made it through somehow. A life without Cooper could never be more difficult than the years of loneliness and the roller coaster of emotions she had experienced since James Marshall roared back into her life. Regardless of what happened to her next, she knew she would be intact at the end of it.

"Even if I end up alone, I have to try for the life I want and the love I deserve. Anything else is living a lie, and I won't do that. I can't."

He looked at her a long minute. Then he shrugged and continued down the stairs. His voice floated up to her from below. "Goodbye, Laurel."

WHILE THEY LOADED THE TRAILER, Laurel told Crosby the gist of her conversation with Cooper.

"Stick close, if you don't mind, Crosby. I'm mad as hell at Dad right now and miffed at Cooper, and I don't want any kind of confrontation with either of them while I'm feeling like this."

"I understand. Dad shouldn't have shared your personal business—that's for damn sure. And Cooper must have fed the gossip about the two of you."

"At the very least, he didn't say anything to quell the rumors."

"If James heard that tripe, maybe that was why he made such a hasty exit last night. One more reason to put Cooper on my bad list," she said, frowning.

There had been many times in her life when Laurel felt naïve about how the world really worked. This was one of them. What a sheltered life she'd led at Uppercross Hollow! How could she lead a man like Cooper Edwards on and not even know it? Or was he just so sure of himself that he never considered she'd say no?

Crosby was indignant when she told him what Cooper had said about James, his money, and her. "He doesn't know the first thing about you, Sis, if he believed any of that crap he was spouting off. What a jackass! I knew there was something wrong with that guy and so did Spring, remember? She was right when she said he skeeved her out."

"Yep, she sure was right—out of the mouths of babes."

"What are you going to say to Dad? Do you think he'll ask you about any of this?"

Laurel sighed and rubbed her temples. "That's a tough one. I still can't believe Dad would interfere in my life like that. Our Dad—the 'find yourself, do what you love, explore the world' free spirit who named his sons after singers and his daughters after flowers. It doesn't make any sense."

"Dad's been different lately—like he's starting to realize all that freedom he told us to find costs too much, and he's trying to back-track and do things over."

"But there are no do-overs in life. Not really."

Her brother studied her for a second. "I want your word, pinky-swear, that you'll stand up for yourself if he tries to run your life again or if Creeper Edwards doesn't leave you alone and keep his mouth shut. I got your back, sister—and so do Dylan and Spring and Ginny and Stuart— and I bet underneath all that meddling, Dad does too if it came right down to it."

She hugged him and held out her hand, her little finger crooked in a C.

"Thank you. I will stand up for myself, pinky-swear."

Crosby hooked his pinky with hers. "Although maybe Cooper was on the level. Maybe he really was trying to mend his ways like he said. I mean, it's not like you were all alone in the world and susceptible to his bullshit."

"It's possible he was serious, and in that case, I guess I'm a little sorry for him, but I'm just not interested. I hope this doesn't hurt his friendship with Dad. He seems to enjoy talking with Cooper, and I would hate to deprive him of that."

"Have you considered that it might be Cooper who deprives Dad of his friendship since you didn't fall in line?"

She frowned. "Well now, I have no control over that."

"I know. I wasn't trying to suggest that you put up with him. I'm just glad he didn't get his hooks into you."

"Me too, although there was never too much danger of it anyway."

Crosby grinned. "Not after hot-stud Marshall started prowling around the place again."

She gave him a playful slap on the arm. "Stop it, you!"

He put his arm around her shoulders and drew her close for a one-armed bear hug. Then he kissed her temple. "I hope—"

"Yes?"

Crosby shrugged. "I just hope. That's all."

CHAPTER 26

*L*aurel peered into the dim bedroom that was her mother's sanctuary. The sun was shining outside, but the shades were drawn, and any light inside came from the television. Cross-stitch, yarn, and sewing projects were lined up around the walls, perched on top of each other.

"Can I come in?"

"Of course." Mrs. Elliot cleared off a chair and put the pattern pieces in a stack after a few seconds of careful consideration. "I've got some more things ready to go to that craft fair down in Gatlinburg next month. Some Christmas items: aprons and sweaters and such. Didn't you say there was a big market for Christmas things down there at this time of year?"

"I did say that, but I'm not sure I'm still going to Gatlinburg next month."

"Not going? But don't you do a lot of business down there?"

"Yes, as a rule, but I may have something else in the works that I'll need to concentrate on." Laurel pulled out a piece of paper and handed it to her mother.

Mrs. Elliot turned on a lamp and read through it, lips moving with the words. She looked up at Laurel with wide eyes, dark crescents underneath them. "This is good news, isn't it?"

"Yes, Mama, very good news. Mr. Dearinger is an expert in manufacturing. He has a lot of people working for him who know about making dishes, and he wants to talk to me about designing some patterns for his company. He'll help me mass-produce the ones his marketing team thinks would be most popular. And the best part is, if this works out like I think it will, I'll still be able to design my own pottery too. It's the best of both worlds. I can make a good living as an artist now."

"Has your daddy seen this?"

"Yes, he's very happy for me. I thought you would be too, so I came over to show you the proposal."

"I am, I am happy." Her mother's face was without emotion; her eyes were without sparkle. "I'm sorry I can't show it more. I'm afraid I'm not feeling too well today."

"It's okay. I understand." Laurel felt a mild stab of disappointment, but it was about what she had expected and probably as much as her mother was capable of giving her. Laurel had other news that she wasn't as sure her mother would be happy about.

"Mama, I have something else to tell you too."

"Okay."

"Do you remember James Marshall, the guy who wanted me to move away with him to Nashville when I was in college?"

"Yes, I remember." Her mother's expression was guarded.

"Well, I caught up with him again last summer. I saw a lot of him, and he came to Asheville this weekend."

"Oh."

"I want to get back together with him, and I think he might want the same thing."

"I see."

"I still love him, Mama, and I have to find out if he loves me too."

There was a silence.

Finally, her mother spoke. "So, if he wants you to, you will leave Uppercross?"

"Yes. But even if I go with him, I'll still have to come back East sometimes to meet with Mr. Dearinger's people and, hopefully, get the pottery thing going. And I'll still come see you and Dad as often as I can. Spring will be off at college in a few months, so you won't need me to help take care of her anymore. I might not move right away, but given the opportunity with my pottery, I'll probably have to eventually anyway. And I think moving might be a good thing for me, regardless of what happens with James."

She covered her mother's hand with her own and pressed it gently.

"I know you're upset, but I'm a grown woman now, and I want to make a life for myself. And if I can have it, I want a life with James—more than anything."

Her mother shook her head. "No, Mountain Laurel, you misunderstand me. I know I was adamant about you not going with that boy and moving far from home, but that was then, and this is now.

"You see, when I said those things all those years ago, I wanted to keep you from being trapped in a life you didn't want, like I was."

"I know, but—"

"It's a cruel irony that because you followed my advice, you ended up trapped anyway, except, instead of being up on a mountain with a husband and a bunch of children to love, because of me, you were up there all alone."

"Oh, Mama," Laurel said in dismay.

Mrs. Elliot's eyes filled. "I never thought you'd be alone. You were so pretty. You had so much spunk and life. I thought some nice, steady man would see that and love you for it. I thought I was telling you right. I really did. I was afraid you would end up like me if you left, but I realized too late that it wasn't my circumstances that trapped me. I was the one who trapped myself. It's too late to change anything now, but I think—I've thought for a few years now—that maybe I made a mistake persuading you to stay. But it was too late. Too late…"

Mrs. Elliot was slipping back into herself, but Laurel had to try and make her understand. There were so many things about her mother that she couldn't control, so forgiveness was the best Laurel could offer to the woman who gave her life. She reached out and grasped her mother's hand.

"Mama, listen. I've thought a lot about this over the years—about whether I made a mistake all those years ago. And do you know what I've determined?"

"What?"

"I've determined that I'll never know the answer to that question, and I have to accept that. If I had gone with James the first time he asked me, there's no guarantee that things would have turned out well. Maybe they would have. I'd like to think that we were meant for each other and would have found a way to make a good life together no matter the circumstances, but I know in my heart of hearts that timing might have played a much bigger role in this than I could ever have imagined, for both of us."

Her mother looked at her and waited for her to continue.

"Ideally, people meet someone they can love all their lives at a time when they're ready to make that commitment—like James's sister Susan and her husband did. Sometimes that someone has been there all along, and then one day both people wake up and realize that they want to be together—like Stuart and Virginia. But sometimes, I think there must be a mismatch between finding the person you love and the time in your life when you find him, and I think that's what happened with James and me. We both made mistakes. If he had been more patient, or if I had been less scared, we might have been able to work around that mismatch all those years ago. But then, he wouldn't be who he is now, and I wouldn't be who I am. And now I think we can be really happy together, so how can I argue with that?"

Mrs. Elliot gave her daughter a thin, watery smile. Laurel kissed her cheek.

"You know Daddy's favorite saying? 'Find wonder in all things, no matter how pedestrian'? I used to think that meant we should notice and celebrate even the smallest details of our lives, but now I see it another way. Now, I believe it means that all those ordinary things are wonderful—even the sad ones and the mistakes—because, no matter how we perceive them at the time, they all come together and serve a purpose in the end. Life is an intricate, magnificent orchestra, and each event—big and small—has a part in it. We have to listen for opportunities to be happy. But it isn't enough just to listen, we also have to seize them when they present themselves, and it's time for me to do that now.

"I don't blame you, Mama, for these years that I was without James. I don't blame him, and I don't blame myself. I know I had to learn to reach for happiness. At eighteen, I wasn't wise enough to discern that, but now I am wiser, and now I choose out of strength and love—not out of fear of the unknown. Now I have a chance at the life I might never have had otherwise. Do you understand at all?"

"I think so, but mostly, I'm just grateful that you forgive me. Perhaps my life wasn't a complete failure after all if I have a wise, strong daughter like you."

Laurel reached over and hugged her mother. "I don't pretend to understand what it is you go through day after day, but Mama, I really do believe that no life is a failure."

Her mother drew back, a flat look descending like a curtain over her face.

"I'm so discombobulated today. Maybe I'm just tired. I guess I should rest a little more." And in the span of a moment, her mother's spirit was gone, buried beneath the years of chronic depression from which Laurel wasn't sure she would ever emerge.

CHAPTER 27

*L*aurel drove into town to see Virginia and Stuart the next evening. She had thought long and hard about it all the way home from Asheville and decided it was time to approach James herself. He had come to her twice now, once to the lake and once to her art show, and that had to mean something. Besides, it was getting annoying—the way he appeared out of the blue and then ran off just as suddenly, leaving her confused and without an easy way to find him again. This time, it should be fairly simple: Stuart, as James's old friend, might know how to reach him. If not, Susan and Gary, or John Benwick would know his whereabouts, and she had resolved to go against her reticent nature and hunt him down. What she would do when she found him, she had no idea. The thought made her quake in her boots, but she pushed her anxieties down deep. This time, she would reach for happiness with both hands and hold on tight. This was her moment of truth, and she must somehow gather her courage and her faith and navigate her way through.

That newfound determination faltered, however, when she saw a minivan rental in Stuart and Virginia's driveway. How could she quiz Ginny and Stu about James if they had company? And who could it be?

Unwilling to give up once she had set her mind to it, Laurel squared her shoulders and knocked. She opened the door part way and called out, "Hello?"

Virginia's voice came from the other room. "Come in, Sis. Guess who's here?"

Laurel walked into the living area, and enthusiastic greetings assaulted her from all sides. Millie rushed her and gave her an exuberant hug.

"Laurel! Surprised to see us?" She giggled. "We're just passing through for a couple of days—wanted to see some fall color and check in on John, of course. So, I sent Ginny an email, and here we are! Looks like we're all descending on you again, 'cause John said James is here too—visiting his sister."

Laurel's heart fluttered in her chest. Her task of finding James had just gotten that much easier. He was already close by.

"Stuart and I were getting ready to head out to The Loft for local talent night. Stuart says it's the best gig around these parts," Eric replied as he picked up his jacket. "You wanna go with us?"

"I called Dylan and Crosby," Stuart added. "They're going to meet us there."

Ginny was already showing Millie into the guest room where she could set up Trevor's port-a-crib, so she wouldn't be available for a chat that evening.

"Um, sure, I guess."

"You can leave your car here," Stu said, "and make us look good when we escort you into The Loft." He held open the door.

When Laurel walked into The Loft a few minutes later, her heart stopped.

James—her James—was sitting at a bar table, smiling while he conversed with Susan and her husband. He looked up when he saw Stuart and Eric enter and lifted a hand in greeting but stopped stone cold when Laurel walked in behind them. He quickly rearranged his face into an expression of careful neutrality.

Gary waved them over to join the group, barstools were pulled up all around, and Stu ordered some drinks for the three newcomers.

Eric slid his stool close to Susan's, and Laurel boldly hopped into the seat next to James, greeting him with a warm smile despite her inner jitters.

How on earth am I supposed to talk to him with all these people around? What do I say to him?

Eric handed her a soda bottle. "Well, here we all are again—out in the boondocks."

"Yes, here we are."

"It's good to see you all again. Millie loves this place—and the people in it. I think we all do." He leaned forward and looked across her at his friend.

"Don't we, James?"

"Hmm?" James looked startled, pulled his bottle away from his lips and swallowed. "Oh...yeah."

Eric's smile faded a little bit. "John does too apparently. It looks like he'll be staying around these parts for a while. Did you hear that Heather's moving in with him?"

"I did," she answered.

"I was surprised, weren't you?"

"Yes, it's surprising I suppose, but I hope they can make it work." Laurel was trying to be diplomatic.

"Oh, I do too." He looked down at his hand holding the soda bottle. "Yeah, I do. It's just kinda sad, you know? Fiona was devoted to John—absolutely nuts about him."

Laurel considered how to answer that for a second. She knew Fiona was Eric's cousin, and he didn't exactly sound happy about John and Heather.

"It may seem sudden, but don't be too hard on him. As a rule, I think men find it harder to hold on to a lost love, not as long as a woman might anyway."

"Do you think so? Me, I've always considered women to be the fickle ones. Millie, of course, is a rare exception. Fiona was too."

"You say that women are fickle," Laurel said with a gentle firmness, "yet the first two women you call to mind are exceptions?" She shook her head. "Perhaps your opinion of a woman's loyalty is biased because you typically only hear the man's version of things."

"So, you think a man is quicker to forget a woman than vice versa?"

"Oh, I don't know, maybe not forget, although I think women are more prone to make relationships—all kinds of relationships—a bigger part of our identities. We can't seem to help it. It's not that men don't love deeply, but—"

"I'm sure Millie would agree with you. She is always touting the superiority of the female sex. But I wonder about the wisdom of stubbornly hanging on to a true lost cause."

"And I think you just made my point for me." Laurel tried to keep her attention on Eric, but a prickle on the back of her neck made her turn toward James. She felt a jolt of emotion roll off him, as he stared—no, almost glared—at her. She turned back to Eric and boldly pressed on.

"A man is much quicker to call the cause a lost one, pack up his life and start over. A woman will continue to love, even when all hope of her love being returned is gone."

Just then, Eddie, the owner of The Loft, stepped up to introduce the next singer on the open mike list. Laurel wasn't sure whether she was disappointed or relieved at the distraction, but his next words surprised her so much that she never got the chance to figure it out.

"Hey you all, we've got some talent here tonight all the way from California, and word is that he can play a mean guitar and sing a little, too. We've heard him here at The Loft before, but it was a loooong time ago, so let's give a warm welcome back to—James Marshall."

A couple of hoots and polite applause rose from the audience, and James stood, looking like he was at a loss. A little urging from his friends and a nudge from Gary sent him up to the stage. He picked up the guitar sitting there, played a few chords, and noodled up and down the scale, deep in thought. Then he looked up. "I was going to suggest a little Motown—"

Somebody let out a "woo-hoo!" from the back, and James chuckled.

"But instead of an oldie but a goodie, how about one I wrote instead?"

Several people nodded, and someone hollered out, "Go for it!"

"I wrote the music a long time ago. It took a while, but over the last couple of weeks I finally found the lyrics in my head." James's low voice rumbled into the mike. "This is for Laurel."

Laurel's heart stopped and then began to pound so loudly she thought everyone could hear it, even over the *woo-woo*'s and *hubba-hubba*'s of the crowd.

The guitar hummed out the rhythm of an introduction, and her mouth ran dry when she recognized the melody from a far-off winter's evening spent in a dilapidated, old cabin up the road.

James pinned Laurel with a look, took a deep breath, and sang:

> Tell me it's not too late.
> I can't perceive my fate.
> Here I stand, agony, hope intertwined.
> Will I be yours till the end of all time?

He closed his eyes then, and the longing and pain spilled out into the room, as if he was trying to purge it from his own soul.

> I must speak, knowing that I've been unfair to you.
> You pierced my soul with yours long, long ago.

Laurel realized the entire table was staring at her. Susan and Gary exchanged one of those looks that couples use to communicate without talking. Eric's eyebrows shot almost up to his hairline, but she couldn't say anything to him. She couldn't even give them all her reassuring smile.

> You brought me here to your side,
> Right where I belong.
> You kept my heart safe with you all these years.

Tell me that you still care.
Answer my ardent prayer.
We had a love so rare,
A life we meant to share.
Give me a look, a word.
Can't you see? Don't you know?
I've found real wonder in you.

At last, mercifully, the song was over, and as the final chord still hung in the air, James looked up. Their eyes met, he put down the guitar and, amid clapping and hoots, walked straight past the next performer and out the door. She watched him leave, walking away from her—one more time—and it was one time too many. Something inside her snapped.

"Oh no you don't! Not again you don't! Don't you dare throw down a gauntlet like that and walk away from me!" she said under her breath. Her stool scraped against the floor as she bolted to her feet and followed him outside into the dark.

"James!" she shouted, more harshly than she meant. He halted and turned around, and she sped up to catch him.

"What the hell was that about?"

He said nothing, just shook his head in a daze, green eyes staring into hers.

"Where are you going?" she demanded.

"I hardly know."

"How dare you!"

"Huh?"

"I said, how dare you! How dare you…blindside me like that?"

"I don't—"

"James Marshall, every time I see you these days, the blasted event ends with you giving me one of those heated looks and storming off into the night."

"I don't—"

"What am I supposed to think? That night after Heather's accident, you kiss me like there's no tomorrow, and then you apologize for it like it was some monumental mistake!"

"I thought you didn't—"

"I don't see or hear from you for three months"—she held up her fingers for emphasis—"and then you show up out of the blue at my art show. You stand around the reception and stare at me all evening—and don't say you didn't. People noticed." She pointed her finger accusingly at him.

"You have no idea…" Her voice grew quiet. "It was so incredible to see you, but once again you left even though I encouraged you to stay."

"That Edwards guy—"

She pierced him with a glare. "That Edwards guy is nothing to me! He's my dad's friend—that's all."

"Oh."

"So, I work up the courage to try and find you. You don't make that very easy by the way. Finally—finally, I'm going to tell you how I feel about you—"

"How you feel about me?" he asked in a low voice, a slow smile warming his expression.

But Laurel was on a roll, and eight years' worth of emotions spilled from her mouth, a torrent of words held too close for too long. "And I have this little speech all set for when I go up to Susan's tomorrow, but no, you're not there, you're here! At The Loft! Of course!" She was pacing back and forth, gesticulating in wild motions with both hands. "It's just my luck. I only see you when I'm completely unprepared!"

"You were coming to find me?"

"And before I know it, you're standing up in front of people and saying, 'This is for Laurel' in that deep, sexy voice of yours."

"You think my voice is sexy?"

"And then you sing that song in front of everybody—you make that big, dramatic gesture—and now you're just going to walk out the door? Nuh-uh, buster—not this time." She stopped directly in front of him. "This time you face me like a man and tell me what's in that thick head of yours, 'cause I can't figure it out, and I can't stand it anymore. Tell me!"

He narrowed his eyes, considering, and then in a flash, he yanked her to him. Before she could react, he kissed her on the mouth, hard— a kiss infused with a hint of possession. Setting her back at arm's length, he watched her breath come in short, agitated pants, hands on her hips, red hair shining, glorious and garish under the streetlight.

"I promise to answer every question you ask, but give me a minute, okay?"

She lifted trembling fingers to her lips. "Why should I?"

"'Cause right now I'm so damned turned on I could take you against this pickup truck here and not blink an eye."

Laurel's eyes widened, but then James closed the distance between them and took her hands in his. He placed a kiss on her palm and looked into her eyes.

"And that's not what we need right now, Mountain Laurel." He straightened up, keeping hold of her hand, giving her a lopsided smile. "Mountain Laurel. You'd never know by looking at its delicate blooms that a tough and hardy shrub is hiding underneath. Of course, *you* would know that, wouldn't you?"

She nodded.

"You're like your name, darling. Maybe most people don't see, or can't appreciate it, but I've seen it—your quiet strength. I've never met another woman who could compare to you, ever—so beautiful, but with such inner grace, such…endurance."

She stood, speechless, as he shook his head in that charming, self-deprecating way of his and went on.

"You're an amazing woman. It's true, but even you aren't omniscient. You didn't know what was in my head when I first came back here, but then I didn't know it myself. I tried to convince myself that what we had all those years ago couldn't have been real, that I had built it into some impossible fantasy. But it wasn't a fantasy"—he paused—"it was a dream. A dream I persuaded myself I could never have, and not having it made me kind of an asshole, I have to admit. I was angry, jealous, resentful, and I acted poorly, but every time I searched my heart, you were there. Once I saw you again, I couldn't think about anyone else, and I felt a hopeful, little flicker of love I thought was long forgotten.

"I told myself I came because I needed closure, needed to get rid of the illusion, but my resentment was no match for the reality of you. I realized I've never loved anyone else, and I couldn't stay away any longer. I've come here to the lake to find you, Laurel. That's what's in this thick head of mine, sweetheart. I'm desperately planning how I can make a life with you."

He paused, waiting to see what she would say, but since she was incapable of speaking, he continued.

"Years ago, I wanted to drag you into the limelight with me." He shook his head. "But I guess Mountain Laurels don't do well under the harsh light of the sun. They need the shelter and safety of the forest in order to thrive, but I didn't realize that. Somehow, you found a way to bloom there in the quiet woods of Uppercross. It's been your refuge, hasn't it? But now, could you consider letting me have the honor of being your safe haven? That's what I wanted all those years ago, but maybe I wasn't up to it then. I was too bull-headed, too stubborn to give you what you needed from me—too young and stupid to even know what that need was—but now, I believe I could do a better job, and I'd sure as hell like to try. I'd offer to give my heart and soul to you, but they've always been yours. I belong to you, Laurel. Please tell me it's not too late—that, like you told Eric, you haven't given up on a love you thought was hopeless."

She stared at him, completely bewildered. "You're forgiven," she whispered.

He grinned and pulled her into his arms.

"Not entirely, but for the most part," she murmured into his chest.

"It's more than I deserve." He kissed her temple.

"Just don't run from me anymore. It hurts so much when you run." Her voice wobbled with emotion, and she blinked back tears in a frantic attempt not to cry.

He smoothed his hands over her back. "I won't. I promise. Sorry I blindsided you. I wasn't thinking straight, I guess. I wanted to ask Susan and Gary for advice before coming back to convince you that we should be together. We were talking out my strategy when I looked around and there you were. You sat right next to me—so close." His voice dropped to a whisper. "So close." He cleared his throat and went on. "I could feel your warmth and breathe in the scent of your hair. Then I heard all that stuff you said to Eric about loving when all hope was gone, and it just hit me wrong. I couldn't bear to think how unhappy I might have made you, and I wanted to tell you how sorry I was. I just needed a minute— or maybe a lifetime—to figure out what to say." He stepped back and hung his head. "And then Eddie called me up there, and my head was full of you and your song, but then I panicked, like I usually do where you're concerned—so I bumbled ahead anyway and blew it."

She reached her arms around his neck. "Well, we can't go back in there now. I'm sure we just shocked the hell out of Stu and Eric and anyone else who pays attention to song lyrics."

"Eric won't be surprised. I told him about you."

"You did?"

"Mm-hmm."

They stood in silence a minute, just clinging to each other.

"Crosby knew some about you too."

"You told big-mouth Crosby?"

She chuckled.

"Speak of the devil—I mean—devils." James released her, and she turned around to see both her brothers at The Loft's entrance. Crosby was leaning against a post, and Dylan stood scowling with his arms crossed over his chest.

"Just checking you're okay," Crosby called.

"I'm okay," she called back.

"Then we're going back inside." He paused. "Mess her over, Marshall, and Dylan and I will put your ass in a sling. You got that?"

"Got it."

Crosby held up his hand and disappeared into the building. Dylan followed after giving James an "I'm watching you" gesture, a la Robert De Niro.

James ran his hands up and down her arms. "Let's go somewhere—somewhere quiet where we can talk."

"It's too cold to sit by the lake. What about my house?"

"Perfect."

CHAPTER 28

*W*hen James slid into the driver's seat, he turned to her with a big smile.

Laurel raised her eyebrows and pursed her lips.

"This is a lot different than the first time we went somewhere together."

"It's a nicer set of wheels—that's for sure." She ran her hand over the leather seats of the BMW.

James turned the key and the engine roared to life. "Oh, I don't know. I kind of liked the old pickup truck you used to drive. I could slide over and sit right next to you. This one has a gear shift in the way."

"Well, sorry to disappoint you, but that truck is long gone now."

"Oh?"

"Now I've got"—she paused for effect—"an '86 Jeep Cherokee."

He smirked.

"I can see you're impressed."

A heavy silence settled over them, an almost unbearable emotional tension. James turned on the radio and fiddled with the tuner but found only static as he went up and down the dial.

"How soon he forgets. You won't get any reception here, Buckeye, not until we get a little higher up the hill," she reminded him.

"I can't believe it's almost the twenty first century, and there's still no radio or decent cell service here."

He stopped at the sound of an electric guitar zooming through the speakers. Then, he recognized the song, a suggestive number about love in the afternoon. Awkwardness settled over the car. James realized he was humming and groaned inwardly. He stared straight ahead, knowing that turning off the stupid song would just draw more attention to the lyrics. He hoped she didn't think he only wanted to get into her pants. Well, to be honest, he did want that eventually, but it could wait if waiting meant they would be headed down the right path together at long last.

Laurel tried unsuccessfully to stifle a chuckle. He turned to look at her and saw she was amused at his obvious discomfort. Her eyes sparkled in the glow of the dashboard lights. He waggled his eyebrows at her in invitation, and she started singing along with the radio. He joined her at the chorus, laughing, and he almost missed the turn off to the cabin. They were both singing at the top of their lungs by the time they reached her place. She zoomed her hand up into the air with the final chord.

As they got out, James leaned on the car's roof, gazing at Laurel with a stupid grin on his face.

"What?" she asked.

"I'm just marveling at my good fortune. I can't stop looking at you."

She looked down, embarrassed, but then she took a deep breath and resolutely raised her head to face him. "I don't understand."

"Don't understand what, darling?"

"How this all could have happened so fast."

They met in front of the car and began walking up to the cabin.

"Fast? Laurel, we could have been together for years by now."

"That's not what I mean. I feel like I know you, but I don't know you. Eight years is a long time. So many things have happened to you and for you—life changing events." She slowed her pace. "Things I'll never understand or be a part of."

He started to pull her along by the hand, but then he turned back, coming to meet her and taking her other hand. "And you haven't changed at all?"

"I haven't—not down deep."

He looked at her thoughtfully for a second. "No, I don't believe you have. You are who you are: constant, steady, unwavering—"

"Boring."

He shook his head. "Deep, unending. The inner part of you simply exists, Laurel. You don't realize how unusual that is. Throughout any storm in life, you are…you. Do you know how precious I find that quality in you?"

She raised her eyebrows, questioning, not understanding. "I'm not fishing for compliments here. I'm honestly confused."

He smiled at her. "No, you would never fish for compliments. You don't need them."

"I do like them though."

His low chuckle rumbled through the night air. "And you deserve them. No, what I mean is nothing in your life can tear down that inner self—not your father's weaknesses, not the lack of material comforts, not the trials of prematurely taking care of your family, not your mother's troubles, not my leaving."

"You make me sound cold and unfeeling."

"There was a time when I thought you were, but…" He leaned over and kissed her gently on the mouth. "Mmm, not cold at all. Sweet and warm." He sighed. "I never told you why I came back here last summer."

"To see Stuart. Susan and Gary met Stuart and Virginia, and they told you, and you called Stuart and they invited you for a visit."

"Maybe that was my reason on the surface, but mostly, I came back to see you." He backed up against the hood of the car, keeping hold of her hands.

"You know, I'd never told anyone the whole story about how we broke up, not even Susan, although she knew we dated that summer.

But last New Year's, I told Eric. I'd tried to forget you, but it was pointless. You're unforgettable.

"Eric's a true friend, one of the few I've ever had, and he isn't just smart, he's wise too. I'm very fortunate to know him. He was watching me—he and Millie—and they knew I wasn't happy down deep as you would say. Don't get weirded out or anything, but after our conversation at New Year's, he looked you up—found out you were still free and where you were—and he told me. Said I needed to either face you or let you go."

"And that's when you decided to come back?"

"No." His lips twisted in the lopsided grin she loved. "I blew him off."

"Oh."

"A couple of weeks after New Year's, we found out Fiona had cancer. That took over all our lives for a while. It happened so fast, and by the end of April, she was gone. It was my first encounter with the death of someone my age. Talk about a life-altering experience—not only to accept that young people can die but to watch what happens to everyone around them when it occurs." His voice broke, and he cleared his throat.

"Oh, James." Laurel's eyes welled up, and a tear rolled down her cheek. He brushed it away with his thumb.

"How could I ever have thought you were cold, my only love?" he whispered. "There's so much compassion in you.

"So, there we were," he went on, "dazed and muddling through, and it's the end of May. I get this call from Susan, and she tells me about looking for a house here, about seeing Stuart and Virginia, and I get this—this longing in my gut to come back to a place where I was untainted by the harsh realities of life—and death. To see my friend who was so much a part of my growing up. To see my parents for the first time in a long time. To see the only girl I'd ever said 'I love you' to.

"The first couple of times I saw you were a shock. Like you said, my life had changed, and I thought for sure you had changed too."

"But I was the same old me?"

"Yes and no. You were still you, but you were more somehow. Stronger, sweeter, more beautiful. A full-grown Mountain Laurel. When we were young and in love"—he pulled her into his arms to give her a squeeze—"I just lived in the moment. God, it was a wonderful time, wasn't it?"

She nodded.

"But when I came back, I took some time and watched you, to see what you were really about so I could finally let you go and move on with my life. But you baffled me at every turn. I thought you would be angry with me, but instead, you were kind. I thought, maybe even hoped, I would find you bitter and alone, but I saw how everyone loves you and that other men wanted you." He scowled. "Like Cooper Edwards."

She started to reply, but he cut her off. "We'll come back to him later. I thought your family would have manipulated you into being at their beck and call, but although you still helped them out, you lived your own life too. I thought you were unfeeling, but then I saw how compassionate you were with John. And you were so tolerant of Heather and Carrie's silliness, even though I tried to irritate you by flirting with them."

"We'll come back to them later," she returned.

He looked away in embarrassment, but then he faced her once more. "The more I watched, the more you fascinated me, and then I kissed you that night. I was so scared, realizing how much I still wanted you and thinking there was no way you could still want me. So, I ran. But that kiss sealed my fate. A couple weeks ago, John and I were talking about things, discussing our plans. When I hung up, I thought, 'What the hell am I doing?' Hadn't I just spent the last six months telling myself that life was too short to live with regrets? I had to know if I still had a chance, so I came to your art show to see you. And there was Edwards always at your side, whispering in your ear, touching you like he had the right. God, I wanted to punch him."

"Thank you for not doing that. I don't know what I'd have done if you and Cooper started brawling at the biggest event of my career."

"You're welcome. I showed admirable restraint, I thought." He stroked her hair. "But now, perhaps our timing is finally right. It's a miracle that I found you again and at a time when you were free."

She laughed, a wry little chuckle, and shook her head. "No worries there. I've been available since you left."

He stared at her as if she were an alien. "Laurel?"

She looked away and drew her arms up to hug herself. "You must think I'm so provincial—never to have seriously dated anyone after all this time."

"Are you telling me there's been no one else? In eight years?"

She shrugged. "Who am I going to meet here at Uppercross Hollow?"

"But you went to college… You travel places sometimes. You must have…with someone."

Her eyes sought his and held them—a steady blue flame lit her from within. "You don't understand. Maybe I thought about it every once in a while. God knows I was lonely—but I never could make myself act on it even if the opportunity arose. You see, I've never loved anyone else either."

"I don't believe this."

She stepped back, shock and pain spreading across her face.

He shook his head suddenly, realizing how that sounded. "No, no. I believe *you*. I just don't believe… How is it possible for me to feel so ecstatic about this and so much like a heel at the same time? I don't know what I did to deserve you."

"You loved me."

"Past, present, and future," he said as he held out his arms and drew her close. "I will always love you, Laurel Elliot. Always."

There was a long pause while she seemed to struggle to keep her composure. She looked away, took a deep breath of the cold night air, as if trying to control the emotions building up inside her, and then she gave up and burst into tears. "I'm so sorry I hurt you all those years ago."

"No, darling. I'm the one who's sorry. Ssh, don't cry. It's okay." He tried to keep her close, but she resisted, pushing against his chest with her forearms, shaking her head violently.

"And I'm sorry I hurt me when I let you go. I didn't want to, but everything was happening so fast, and I didn't know what to do. After you left, I mourned for you, but I thought you wouldn't want me after I sent you away, and then later, Stuart told me you moved to California. I thought you were gone forever."

He managed to keep her in his arms, petting, comforting—unsure what to do with tears from this woman he loved so much but had never seen cry.

"I needed to take a leap of faith to go with you or ask you to wait, and I just…I couldn't do it, James. And I'm sorry."

He drew her head to his shoulder and murmured to her. "You did the best you knew how at the time, and who knows? Maybe you were right. I thought I knew everything back then, so I pushed too hard. Maybe you were too much woman for the man I was."

A quick laugh escaped through her tears, but then she grew serious. "I don't know what would have happened if we had made different choices, but I know the pain and emptiness of living without you. I know that I still love you. And without a second thought or knowing what comes next, I know I can take that leap now—without even looking first—if it means I'll be with you."

There was a long pause. "Laurel, would you have come with me to California if I'd asked?"

She met his gaze straight on, her heart in her eyes, and nodded.

"Good god, you would have. I can't believe I was so stupid." He shook his head in disbelief. "It's been one ill-timed event after another for us, hasn't it? But no more. If anything good came out of being away from you all these years, it's that I'm absolutely sure about this. You are what I love. You are what I want. Everything else is secondary to that truth."

He kissed her then like he was trying to make up for all the time they lost, and when he finally released her, Laurel lifted her face to the sky.

"What a beautiful night."

"I first made love to you under the stars. Do you remember?"

"I could never forget it, but that was a warm summer's night. It's chilly out here in October. Let's go in, okay?"

He nodded, and they continued hand in hand up the steps and across the porch. She took her key out of the flowerpot beside the door. "You'll have to take me down to Stuart and Ginny's tomorrow morning to get my Jeep."

He stepped in behind her and whispered seductively against her ear. "So, I can stay the night?"

She turned and looked him straight in the eye. "You can stay forever."

Pulling him by the hand, she backed into the house. "Please, stay." She flipped a switch by the door, and a lamp cast a warm glow over the room. He nodded, and without a word, she started down the hallway that led to her bedroom. He watched her, his pulse pounding in his head when he realized where she was going.

Looking over her shoulder, she halted for a second, one hand on the door frame. "Are you coming?"

He nodded and followed her into the hallway before he found his voice. "Laurel?"

She faced him again. "Yes?"

"Have we said what we needed to?"

"Yes, I think so."

"We start from here, right now—no more *sorry's*, no more regrets?"

"No more."

He approached her, reached up to touch her face, and put his hand back down.

"James?"

"I'm almost afraid to touch you. Once I do, I think I'll lose control of myself." He paused, and his voice dropped to almost a whisper. "It's been a very long time since I've let that happen."

She took his hand and brought it up to her cheek. "I've dreamed about this, especially since you came back last summer—what it would feel like for you to touch me again." She drew his hand down her neck, over her breast, along the curve of her waist, over her hip.

"Holy hell," he growled in a ragged voice.

"No, I think it would be just like heaven." She moved his hand over her abdomen, up to the left center of her chest. Her heart was under his hand, beating wildly against his palm.

"This is yours—yours to own, to keep—yours to break."

"Oh god, Laurel. I don't think I can stop."

"Then don't."

He pushed her against the wall, his lips devouring hers, tongue in her mouth, hands unbuttoning, unzipping, tugging on clothing, and casting it aside. She pulled his shirt off, and her hands fumbled at the zipper of his pants. He drew back a little and looked at her—her eyes closed, naked as the day she was born, the rise and fall of her chest as she took little gasping breaths. He grabbed her hands and trapped them above her head, pinning her body with his. "Need you... Need to be inside you, be part of you." He dove back in to possess her mouth. "Please, sweetheart."

She nodded.

He lifted her, and long arms and legs wound around him as he walked her toward the bed, grinning like a kid at Christmas. He gently tossed her on the covers and fell on top of her, holding himself off her with his arms while she squealed with delighted surprise.

The playful roughhousing gave him a much-needed respite from his driving need to take her right then and damn the consequences. He didn't want to rush her, and a part of him felt insecure about loving her again after all that time. He slid down her body, kissing, touching each part as he went—shoulders, arms, hands. He drew her fingers into his mouth one at a time and felt his blood go up in flames at the erotic noises she made. His mouth traveled over her middle, and he nibbled on her hipbones, less sharp and angled than he remembered—rounder and more womanly than those of an eighteen-year-old. Somehow that made her exciting in a completely different way, better than any fantasy he could concoct from long ago memories. He raised his head to see her face, breathed in, and moaned with fierce longing as his mouth descended to her inner thigh.

"I remember this." Her voice was plaintive and raw. "Oh god, I remember..."

He was speechless, unable to answer, except by enflaming her more. He touched her with his fingers, pushing into her, and then he took her with his mouth. She shattered against him, calling his name. When he stood to finish undressing, he saw tears in her eyes and her lips were trembling.

"Sweetheart?" he asked, concerned, anxious.

She wiped the tears away with her hand and smiled up at him. "They're happy tears. How I've missed you. How I've wanted you." She sighed and held out her arms. "James."

He fell into them, sliding into her and closing his eyes against the surge of his own emotions. "So good," he muttered in a thick, hoarse voice. "It's still so damn good."

His world stopped as he filled her, and in the bliss of a union born of love and loss, he buried his soul in hers.

CHAPTER 29

FIFTEEN YEARS LATER

ASHEVILLE, NC

*J*ames sat on the couch noodling his Mountain Laurel melody. It always helped him think when he ran across a particularly thorny programming glitch. He had spent the last four months working on an interactive software program with funds from the Elliot-Marshall Foundation—the organization he and Laurel founded the year after they married. The software he was currently developing was a pet project of his: using computers to teach music to children. The Foundation funded some of Laurel's favorite causes too: reclaiming strip-mined land, art classes for children and adults, and education and treatment for people with depression.

For years, James had watched in admiration as Laurel's confidence and poise rose to meet each new challenge. Never comfortable putting herself on display, she learned early in their marriage that speaking and mingling would be a necessary part of her life. She worked hard to develop those skills, but her inner grace was the root of all her inter- and intrapersonal strength. He had seen ample evidence of it over the years: demonstrating her work, accompanying him to social gatherings for the various software companies he contracted with, and handling the devastating news that she was unlikely to conceive a child.

That was a blow, but after many tears and long discussions, they reached a decision—no fertility treatments. As she told the doctor, "We're going to let Fate decide this one. After all, Fate has been very kind to James and me."

James had to agree. Fate had been kind in ways he never expected and knew he didn't deserve. And their lives were full of their families, including Laurel's nieces and nephews, and their friends—like John and his wife Marissa, Eric and Millie and their kids.

So, the Marshalls had both poured their energies into parenting the world in a variety of ways, and life had gone on as it had since the day they'd found each other again until one morning about four weeks after their ninth anniversary. Laurel met him at the door of their bedroom with a tearful smile on her face and an EPT in her hand.

He, of course, panicked—as he usually did where she was concerned—but she quietly carried out every special medical instruction for moms over thirty-five. He worried how a new little person would fit into their well-ordered life, but she calmly reassured him that everything would turn out fine.

A BLUR of black cape and blue pajamas whizzed behind him and leapt over the back of the couch, summoning him out of his memories.

"Whoa there, buddy! You almost impaled yourself on my guitar."

"What's 'impaled'?"

"Fell and stabbed yourself with it. You need to look before you jump, Elliot."

"Not Elliot! I'm Batman!"

James chuckled. "Riiight." He thought for a second. "Did you know that Batman plays the guitar?"

"Like you?"

"Yep."

"I never seen that."

"He keeps it secret, but Alfred knows."

"Nuh-uh."

James shrugged and said, "I could show you how, but I guess you're too little anyway. It's for big kids."

"I'm a big kid!" Elliot was indignant as only a four-year-old could be. "Show me!"

And that was how Laurel found them when she ventured up from her studio twenty minutes later: James fingering chords and Elliot strumming and singing in an angelic voice. The boy could carry a tune—even at four.

She leaned against the doorway, and James's eyes met hers for a long, silent moment, during which they said a multitude of sweet nothings to each other.

"Hey, big guys, whatcha up to?" she asked, coming in to sit beside them on the couch and putting her chin on her husband's shoulder.

"Playing music," James answered.

"Like Batman," Elliot piped in, wriggling into his mother's lap.

"Batman plays guitar?" Laurel gave him a little squeeze. "I like it. I always knew Batman had a sensitive, artistic side."

James rolled his eyes, and she smiled at him before addressing their son.

"Elliot," she began, "how would you like to go to Uppercross and see your cousins for a couple of months?"

"Yippee! See Aunt Susan and Uncle Gary too?"

"Yep, them too."

"I wanna go. Daddy says Uppercross is the best place, 'cause it's where there's Mommy's broom."

Laurel looked at James, confused.

He squelched a laugh. "No, Elliot, not quite. Uppercross is the best place"—he leaned over to kiss his wife on her clay-spattered cheek —"because it's where the Mountain Laurels bloom."

Finis

DEAREST READER

Thank you for letting me tell you a story! If you enjoyed *Find Wonder in All Things*, please consider leaving a review on your blog, an ebook distributor, social media, or your favorite reader site. Reviews help other readers decide if they, too, would like a book.

So reach out :)

Website: www.karenmcox.com

If you would like to read some more of my stories and get tidbits of authorly goodness in your inbox from time to time (updates, sales, book recommendations, etc.), I want to invite you to receive my **News & Muse Letter**. It comes with 3 free short stories you can download. (You can access the News & Muse Letter from my website.)

I love to hear from readers, so don't be shy. You can contact me through social media, my website, or on-line stores.

Happy Reading!

BOOK GROUP QUESTIONS

1. *Find Wonder in All Things* is a modern variation on Jane Austen's last novel, *Persuasion*. The theme of the novel might be termed "It's never too late for second chances."

Do you agree that this is *Persuasion*'s main theme? Does *Find Wonder in All Things* convey the same theme as the Austen story that inspired it?

2. Sometimes it's a challenge to bring an Austen character into modern times. If you have read *Persuasion*, do you think Laurel Elliot is a good representation of Anne Elliot in *Persuasion*? What difficulties do you see in writing a modern Anne? How successful was the author in translating her to modern times?

If you have not read *Persuasion*, try to describe Anne Elliot based on your knowledge of Laurel. How do you think they would be different?

3. *Find Wonder in All Things* discusses regret in several of its scenes. Do you think Laurel and James end up regretting their past decisions? Why or why not?

4. Do you think Cooper Edwards was ready to change his life when he met Laurel? What do you think will happen to him after the story ends?

5. What do you see as James Marshall's best and worst character traits?

6. The novel is structured so that Part 1 is in James's point of view, Part 2 is in Laurel's, and Part 3 roughly alternates between the two. Does this structure make sense to you? How else could it have been done?

7. Part 1 reflects the part of the story before Austen's *Persuasion* starts, the time when James and Laurel first fall in love. Did you enjoy reading about the beginning of their relationship? Why or why not?

8. Who would you cast in a movie of *Find Wonder in All Things*?

9. Who—or what—is the antagonist/villain of *Find Wonder in All Things*?

10. What did you like best about the book? Who is your favorite character? Which character did you not like? Why?

Mountain Laurel Theme

KM Cox

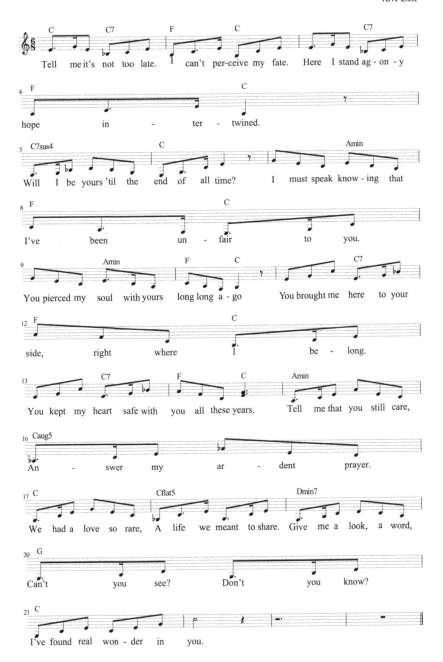

2011

ACKNOWLEDGMENTS

I first thank Jane Austen—for her wit, her humor, her incredible gift to the world. How I wish she'd had more time here to share her stories with us!

While writing this story, I received valuable advice from some special people, so special thanks are due to Karen Adams for honest and hilarious feedback, to Terry Jakober, for encouragement and reality checks, and to Jane Vivash for wanting more from the characters in just the right places. Chelsea Fortenberry Quillen provided her expertise on emergency response teams and procedures.

I'm eternally grateful for my editors on this story: Gail McEwen, who edited the first edition, taught me much about the craft of writing at a time when I needed and was ready for the guidance. Christina Boyd, who edited this second edition, put the extra polish on a story I loved and took it to the next level. The pride and joy she takes in her work is a continual inspiration to me.

I also wish to thank the staff at Meryton Press for publishing the first edition of *Find Wonder in All Things*. In addition, the great readers at *A Happy Assembly* generously shared their interest, offered support, and made thoughtful comments on an earlier version of the story. 100Covers did marvelous work on the cover for this second edition.

Finally, I thank my family: My husband—a conversation we shared one summer morning started this story percolating in my mind. My son—his casual bravery first lent me the courage to share my writing. And my daughter—she brings me joy every day just by being her indomitable self.

ABOUT THE AUTHOR

Karen M Cox is an award-winning author of five novels accented with history and romance: *1932, Find Wonder in All Things, Undeceived, I Could Write a Book*, and *Son of a Preacher Man*, and a novella, *The Journey Home*, a companion piece to *1932*. She also loves writing short stories and has contributed to four Austen-inspired anthologies: "Northanger Revisited 2015" appears in *Sun-Kissed: Effusions of Summer*, "I, Darcy" in *The Darcy Monologues*, "An Honest Man" in *Dangerous to Know: Jane Austen's Rakes and Gentleman Rogues*, "A Nominal Mistress" in *Rational Creatures*, and "Resistive Currents" in *Elizabeth: Obstinate, Headstrong Girl*.

Karen was born in Everett WA, which was the result of coming into the world as the daughter of a United States Air Force officer. She had a nomadic childhood, with stints in North Dakota, Tennessee, and New York State before settling in her family's home state of Kentucky at the age of eleven. She lives in a quiet little town with her husband, where she works as a pediatric speech pathologist, encourages her children, and spoils her granddaughter.

Channeling Jane Austen's Emma, Karen has let a plethora of interests lead her to begin many hobbies and projects she doesn't quite finish, but she aspires to be a great reader and an excellent walker—like Elizabeth Bennet.